BORN TO BE MY BABY

JACKIE PAXSON

ALSO BY JACKIE PAXSON

Other Works

Dirty Laundry Series

Tabloid

Scandal

Rumors

Secrets

Standalone

The Ugly Christmas Sweater

A Work in Progress

Unexpected

Novellas

A Bark in the Park

This one is dedicated to all of my newsletter folks. Without you Chord and Rhapsody's story would never have been told.

1

RHAPSODY

I looked at the card in my hand. Table 13. The table was placed the furthest from the bride and groom's table, but it was closest to the kitchen and the exit. I wove through the people mingling and reminiscing. As I approached the table, I noticed only two seats remaining. Seated on one side was a very stern looking woman with a severe bun, sitting ramrod straight and holding onto her purse with a white knuckled grip as if she'd get mugged at a wedding. On the other side of the open pair of seats was a man with a plaid suit. His hair was shiny and slicked back. The collar of his shirt was open, showing a thick gold chain nestled in a nest of dark chest hair. If I had to guess, he was definitely a used car salesman. He spied her approaching and jumped from his seat.

"Welcome to the table of misfit guests." He smiled showing a pair of gold front teeth.

I smiled and circled the table away from him. All the guests seated at this table appeared to be miserable. This was definitely a punishment. I don't know what I did to my best friend to deserve this, but he was going to get payback after his honeymoon.

Sitting down next to the librarian I grabbed for the champagne. The used car salesman moved seats, sliding his chair close enough for me to smell the Greek food he'd had earlier in the day, which he tried to cover with a heavy layer of cologne. A migraine began to pound behind my left eye.

"You are so sexy," Captain Skeevy hissed.

I imagined the smile I tried to paste on my face came across as a grimace when he blanched. Recovering quickly, he smiled and ran his tongue across his teeth. It highlighted the gold teeth. My inner bitch, aka Queen B, shrieked, *"Run! Run! Run!"* She needed to shut up! I was here for my best friend and if I had to suffer through an uncomfortable evening fighting off a weirdo, then I would do that. He would pay in the future but there would be time for that.

"Hey, baby." A deep voice caught my attention then the feel of warm soft lips on my cheek had me paralyzed. "I believe you are sitting in my seat." His large hand landed on Captain Skeevy's shoulder.

"Oh. I thought you were available." Skeevy stared at me.

"You thought wrong but thanks for keeping my girl company." A warm hand slid onto my exposed shoulder. Tingles caused my toes to curl inside my uncomfortable pumps.

"Sorry," Skeevy mumbled and moved over toward the seat he'd vacated earlier.

My brain finally kicked into gear as he sat in the seat. I took in the beautiful sight in front of me. His light brown hair was short but long enough to style. The dark blue suit he wore was tailored to fit his muscular body. He clearly worked out and the way he wore the suit would make panties melt. Navy eyes glittered as they met mine. Kissable lips lifted to one side showing a dimple in his cheek.

Mr. Perfect leaned toward me. "I'm sorry if I was too forward but it looked like you needed saving."

"You aren't wearing armor," I said.

A confused look had him furrowing his brow. "Armor?"

"Yeah. If you are going to be a knight in shining armor you need the whole get up. Plus, how did you know I needed rescuing? I am perfectly capable of saving myself."

"I can tell you are a very capable woman. However, I am a very insecure man who needs to rescue a woman once in a while. Would you let me finish rescuing you from the dragon?" He motioned toward the weirdo who was now preying on another woman who clearly wanted nothing to do with him.

"Hmmm…I suppose so." I gave him a smirk.

He grasped his hands over his heart and bent forward in a small bow. "Thank you, m'lady. I will forever be in debt to a beauty such as you allowing this poor knight to save face."

A giggle escaped my lips. Warmth filled my veins. It was either the champagne that I downed or the sex symbol come to life sitting next to me. I hid my smile behind the quickly emptying champagne flute.

Sticking one hand out to me, he said, "Chord Reedy."

"I know."

"What?"

I pointed toward the card he'd placed on the table when he sat down. "Your name card."

"Oh. Well, I'm Chord Reedy. I am good friends with the bride."

I stared at him. His lips mesmerized me.

He cleared his throat. "And you are?"

My face flamed. I was such a spazz. I'd been paying such attention to his lips that I wasn't paying attention to the words escaping those lips. Queen B was banging her head on the table. *"Answer him! Don't be an idiot."*

"Oh…uh…sorry. I'm Rhapsody Bell. My best friend is the groom." I took his hand like a normal person and shook it. I didn't expect him to cover our linked hands with his other one.

"Are you here alone tonight?"

"Yes." Ugh! Was that my voice? I sounded like a phone sex operator.

"Not anymore."

"Okay." I squeaked.

"Tell me about yourself."

Before I could say a word, the DJ called for everyone's attention. It was time for the toasts. The maid of honor made a very sweet speech featuring the bride and her times in their sorority. The guests did the appropriate oohs and ahhhs.

Sexy leaned over and said, "Jane hated that girl and being in a sorority. The only reason she did it was because her mother had been in the same one. It was expected. For them to say it was the best time in her life is bullshit."

I snorted and the people at our table looked at us. Pretending to be enthralled by the airhead's speech, a warm hand landed on my hand. My mouth was very dry all of a sudden. Just in time, the maid of honor said cheers, and we raised our glasses to toast the happy couple.

When the best man grabbed the microphone, I knew it was going to be a train wreck. The best man was also the younger brother of the groom. He had no filter and even less ability to hold his alcohol if that was even possible. He tapped the mic then blew into it, causing serious feedback.

"This should be good," Sexy said with a smile.

"I doubt it," I mumbled.

"Welcome, family, friends, co-workers of Rufus and Jane, not so close family and friends, and all the freaks out at table thirteen. I see you back there, Rhapsy. Looks like Mother had her way and separated Rufus from his true love." The groom's brother walked toward their table.

My eyes bugged out of my head. "Dear God! This isn't happening."

"Yeah, it's happening and will be one hell of a story."

"You know, Mother never liked you. She hated how close the two of you were. So much so that she convinced his now wife to put you in wedding guest purgatory." He paused and looked at the bride. "Hi, Jane." He waved with the microphone in his hand.

Would it be obvious if I sprinted out the closest exit? That was a no-go in these heels. Maybe if I focused really hard I could become invisible or teleport out of the reception. At a time when I needed Queen B, she was passed out from too much champagne. Damn lush.

"I've always loved you, Rhapsy. This should be our wedding. It should be our forever. Why can't you love me like I love you?" He was crying while sitting in the middle of the dance floor.

The father of the groom stormed up to his inebriated son and snatched the mic out of his hand. The best man curled into a fetal position and continued to cry. I glanced over to my best friend who had his head in his hands while his new bride rubbed his back.

"Let's toast to Jane and Rufus." Guests lifted their champagne and quietly toasted to them.

"I love her!" The best man wailed as the other groomsmen dragged him out of the reception.

"That was the best speech ever," Mr. Sexy said, squeezing my hand.

"Are you serious?"

"Oh definitely. It had action, adventure, romance, and even a little suspense. Ten out of ten." He looked at me and must have gotten concerned. "Let me get you a drink. I will be right back."

I watched as he stood and removed his jacket, placing it on the back of his chair. He definitely worked out. As he moved past the other guests, women were pulled from their conversations just to watch him walk by.

"How dare you?" The shrill voice felt like ice water over her skin.

"Hello, Mrs. Brown." The groom's mother looked like a thunderstorm aimed directly at her.

"Why are you here, Rhapsody? To ruin my Rufus's day?

What did you do to Toby? You always were a spiteful girl who needed attention all the time."

"Rufus invited me. I am here to celebrate Jane and Rufus's marriage." Queen B picked up her head and scowled at my best friend's mother then said, *"Shank the bitch."*

"Marianne, what are you doing?" Rufus's father joined them.

"Robert, she showed up. I told Rufus not to invite her." She stomped her foot like a child not getting a piece of candy.

"Hello, sweetheart. How is my love?" Robert pulled me into a bear hug.

"Hello, Papa Rob. I'm doing well. It has been a beautiful wedding. "

Marianne huffed and stormed off.

I grimaced. "You may be in trouble."

"Don't worry about me, Rhapsody. It's not the first time I've been in trouble nor will it be my last." His face grew serious. "I'm sorry about Toby. I don't know what has gotten into that boy."

"Probably a few Long Island iced teas if I had to guess."

His deep laugh felt like a warm blanket. Rufus's father was a constant during my tumultuous childhood. He was as close to a real dad as I'd ever had.

"Well, sweetheart, I need to go mingle. Enjoy your time and don't be a stranger. You got it?" He pulled me into another hug.

"I will do my best." I smiled then sat back down, waiting for my drink to arrive.

Watching Papa Rob walk away, I felt eyes on me. The people at my table sat in silence, glaring at me. An overwhelming feeling to flee descended upon me. Judgment and hate filled their gazes. Even the skeezy car salesman seemed turned off. Finally, a good thing had come out of the train wreck of a reception. Maybe it was time for me to go. Inner bitch stood on wobbly legs. *"Fuck 'em. Don't let these losers intimidate you. Get a shot and dance on the table."*

"Shut up," I said under my breath.

"Talking to Queen B again?" Rufus's voice had her spinning around.

"I have no idea what you're talking about."

"Please. You don't have to hide your crazy from me. I already know you're crazy. I've met your mother. Remember?"

"How could I forget?" I pulled Rufus into a hug. "Congratulations! I'm so very happy for you."

"Thank you, Rhapsody. I can't believe my mom conned Jane into putting you at this table. It really pisses me off."

"No worries. I'm all good. You need to focus on your new wife and the rest of your guests but mostly focus on your new wife and knocking her up."

Throwing his head back he laughed loudly, pulling the attention of those around us.

2

CHORD

I took the two wedding themed drinks from the bartender. They were pink and smelled like fruit. Normally, I'd go for a whiskey or a dark beer, but since it was Jane's wedding, I felt I had to at least try the concoction she'd told my sister about. Weaving through the increasingly intoxicated mob of people felt like an obstacle course that would end with me spilling these frilly ass drinks on my overpriced shirt.

When Jane had initially invited me to the wedding I bulked. We were friends, but I wasn't sure we were "go to each other's wedding" kind of friends. After discussing it with my overbearing sister, I was gently persuaded to attend. What I didn't count on was being placed at the misfit table. Who the hell knew those really existed?

As I initially approached the table, I almost turned right around and left. It was a very sad table. Each person sitting there knew it was the sad table. However, when I saw that gorgeous curvy blonde attempting to get the sleazy guy wearing a plaid suit away from her, I knew my night had improved. She became my goal. I needed to see what was under that bombshell dress she wore. Just the thought of seeing it for the first time was giving me a semi. It made carrying our drinks back to the table even more difficult.

"Hey!" A soft hand landed on my arm.

I looked over to ward off another handsy woman but stopped. Jane smiled at me. "Hey there, Mrs. Brown."

She rolled her eyes at me. "You're going to say that all the time, aren't you?"

"Damn right."

"You're an asshole," she said, punching my arm and sloshing some of the drink onto my hand.

"What? For calling you by your new name. How can I be an asshole for doing that?"

"Because I know you aren't being sincere. You're being a dick."

I just smiled my innocent school boy smile that I knew worked on everyone.

Jane just shook her head but then sobered when she looked over at her new husband chatting it up with my cute blonde. A weird feeling roiled in my stomach. What the hell was that? Was that sketchy shrimp thing tainted? When the hell did I consider her mine? I needed a drink. Stronger than the one I had in my hand.

"Sorry for seating you at the loser table," she whispered.

I looked back over at the table. Oh yeah it was the loser table, but Rhapsody definitely wasn't that. She was so much more. Damn, I was going to need a cold shower if those sexy images continued to play through my head.

"No big deal. I'm having fun."

"With Rhapsody?" she asked flatly.

"Yep. Not to mention that epic best man speech. I hope someone loaded that on YouTube."

She tried to swat me again, but I dodged out of her reach.

"That was horrible. He made such a laughingstock out of himself," she said.

"It wasn't that bad. It made for one hell of a memorable wedding speech."

Her annoyed demeanor cracked, and she smiled again. "It really was."

"It was. Now, let me get back to delivering these drinks." I nodded my head toward the table.

"What do you think of Rhapsody?" she said quickly.

I blinked. What did I think? She really didn't want to know what I thought about her. I would make her more than a blushing bride with the scenarios and positions I've already run through my mind. The touch and taste of her skin. Her sitting on my face riding my tongue. Red tinged lips and tongue wrapped around my cock.

"Well?" Jane prodded.

Shit. How long had I been standing there thinking about Rhapsody? I needed to say something. "She's okay."

Jane squinted her eyes at me. "Just okay? Okay enough to get her a drink?"

"Yep. We are wedding buddies. I protected her from the skeezy guy. She feels a bit indebted to me now." I shrugged.

"Oh God! That's Uncle Marcus, my dad's half-brother. He really is a sleazeball. He works at a used car lot. Who knew they even made plaid suits?" she said.

"Well, I better get her this drink. Enjoy the rest of your reception and make sure you get lots of sweaty sex during that honeymoon." I wiggled my eyebrows at her.

She laughed but sobered quickly. "Just be careful okay. You don't know her."

"And you do?"

"Let's just say I know who her family is."

Jane walked away and into another crowd of screaming ex-sorority girls. I wondered what she had meant by that, but the drinks in my hand were becoming warm, and my hands felt sticky. Making my way over to the table, I avoided roving hands from both men and women. When I approached, Rufus stood from my chair.

"Here he is. We were beginning to wonder if you'd gotten lost." He smiled.

"Shouldn't you be with your new wife?" My voice came out more irritated than I'd meant for it to.

Rhapsody and Rufus looked at me with the same confused look.

"He just stopped by to chat," Rhapsody said.

"Well, I'll be going. I see you are in good hands." Rufus stuck his hand out for me to shake. I took it with my sticky hand.

His gaze narrowed then he quickly smiled. He took a few steps away then stopped abruptly. Turning back to Rhapsody, he said, "Remember what I said. You don't know."

Rhapsody nodded then looked at me. "What was that all about?"

I sat in my seat then shrugged. "Nothing. I just think he should be spending time with his new wife not the woman his brother just professed his love to." Dammit! I hadn't meant the last part to come out.

Her eyes narrowed with fury. Damn, she was sexy when she was pissed off. "Excuse me? I know I didn't hear what you just said."

"I'm sorry. I didn't mean that. Sometimes my mouth just runs away from my brain."

"And turns you into an asshole."

"Yes. It does that," I admitted.

She fought a small smile that tried to break free. I slid the drink to her. "I brought fruity very unmanly drinks."

Taking the drink in her hand, she said, "Thank you."

I raised my glass to toast with her, but before I could say anything she chugged the drink as if she'd just escaped the Sahara. When she placed the empty glass back on the table, she looked at me with flushed cheeks.

I took a sip of the fruit punch drink then said, "Thirsty?"

"These events do that to me."

"Make you thirsty?" I asked.

"Something like that."

The DJ began playing a popular line dancing song. With a smile that lit up her face, she turned to me. I couldn't help but smile back.

"Let's dance." Rhapsody grabbed my hand as she stood.

"I...uh...don't dance."

She lifted one eyebrow. "Scared?"

"No. I just don't."

Rhapsody took my drink and finished it while looking me in the eye. "I dare you."

Warmth and arousal shot through my body. I stood and tightened my hold on her hand. "Game on."

3

RHAPSODY

My head felt light with the two drinks I had just guzzled down. Not to mention the champagne I'd had earlier. Chord's warm hand in mine sent shivers down my spine. As he walked me out to the dance floor, his smile caused a warmth in my belly that made my thong damp.

"Are you gonna show me how to do this ridiculous dance?" he shouted to be heard over the music.

I looked around and we were standing in the middle of the line dancing. If we didn't move soon, we'd get trampled by the other dancers.

Grabbing his hand in mine, I pulled him to the end of the line. "All right, follow me."

I began the simple steps. Three to the right. Three to the left. Kick twice. Shuffle turn to the right. Start all over again. Music, alcohol, and lust controlled my body through the automatic steps in the dance. Losing myself within the dance blurred the world around me. That was until someone crashed into me, knocking us to the ground. My legs were tangled with the culprit. That culprit had the dazzling smile that I'd be remembering in my dreams.

"I told you I didn't dance," Chord said, extracting himself from our heap.

Jumping to his feet he reached down and helped me up. "Well, you weren't wrong," I said breathlessly.

"Move it or lose it." Rufus's grandmother pushed me into Chord's arms.

As she moved with the other dancers she winked and gave me a thumbs up. I felt a blush creep up my neck. I looked into Chord's fathomless blue eyes. The popular line dancing song was fading, and a slow song began to play.

"Let's get the couples out on the dance floor," the DJ announced.

The sweating line dancers wandered off in search of drinks while couples began to surround us. Couples of varying ages drew close together as the opening notes of a classic love song played. Butterflies fluttered in my stomach. I wasn't sure if we should stay and dance or head back to the table.

Chord made the decision for me. "This is more my speed. Will you dance with me?"

His hands gripped my waist. *"Say yes to the man, you idiot."* The Queen was back to being bossy. I noticed fear quickly cross his features. My heart stuttered then said, "Absolutely."

Chord smiled then took my right hand into his and pulled me closer with his other hand on my lower back. We swayed to the soft rhythm of the music. He flexed his hand on my lower back as he inched me closer. When our pelvises met, I felt something hard press into my stomach.

He leaned down to my ear where his lips ghosted my earlobe causing me to shudder. "I could get used to his kind of dancing."

"This is nice." My voice was back to being squeaky.

"Tell me more about you, Rhapsody."

I laughed a little. "There isn't much to tell. I'm an accountant by day and by night I'm a phone sex operator."

Chord froze. An elderly couple buzzed us as we stood still. "Did I hear you correctly?"

"What? I'm an accountant."

He continued to stand frozen. When another couple almost collided with us again, I said, "Are we still dancing?"

"Yes." Taking back control, he pulled me tight against him, avoiding another near collision.

"Why are you looking at me like that?"

Shaking his head as if to clear his thoughts, he said, "I'm just wondering if I've talked to you before."

I furrowed my brow at him. "You did. Just a few minutes ago."

"Not here but on the phone."

He was being incredibly confusing. Then it occurred to me that he didn't realize I was joking about being a phone sex operator. A giggle burst out. The mixture of booze and nerves made it hard to stop laughing. Then it happened. A giant snort escaped. I clamped my hands over my mouth. He was now laughing like an idiot too. The dancing couples around us gave us dirty looks because we'd stopped dancing again.

"Did you just snort?" he said while laughing.

With both hands still covering my mouth, I just nodded my head. Thankfully, the song ended, and Chord put his arm around my shoulders, helping me back to the table. The table was empty when we returned so I sat down, still holding back my giggles.

"You're still holding back a laugh aren't you."

I nodded again. Queen B shook her head and said, *"This is the most ridiculous thing ever. This hottie will not get in our panties if you keep up the snorting. Pull it together."* She stomped her little foot in my mind's eye.

"Sorry. While we were dancing it finally occurred to me that you didn't realize that I was joking."

Now, it was his turn to look confused. "What do you mean by joking?"

"I'm not a phone sex operator. I was joking about that. I only added it because I know accountant isn't very exciting for people to hear."

"Oh," he said.

"Yeah. Like I said it isn't very exciting."

"Well, my job isn't very exciting either."

"Really? What do you do?"

"I'm a stripper," he said flatly.

Queen B popped up. *"Do not have a reaction! This could be the best thing to ever happen to you. Now, you know why he works out. Keep it cool and maybe you will get yourself a professional tonight."* She ended with two thumbs up.

"Okay."

"Okay," he said but only seconds later his face had a huge smile lighting it up. "I'm just fucking with you. I couldn't help it."

I punched his arm. "Jerk."

He rubbed the spot I'd just hit. "Ouch! Be careful that's one of my money makers."

"You're an ass." I crossed my arms and flopped back in my seat.

"Yes. Yes I am."

"Don't think I haven't put together that you also call phone sex hotlines. I caught that," I said with a smug smile.

"Dammit. I was hoping you'd not connected those dots." He sighed.

"Oh, I connected them all right. You better tell me what you really do for a living to distract me from the fact that you have a sex hotline saved on your phone."

"It is not saved on my phone, and it's only when I'm lonely."

"Sure, it is. Come on, stripper boy…what do you really do?"

A blush painted his face. "I'm a children's librarian."

I studied his face, not sure if this was for real. If it was, it added a whole new level of sexy to him. If it wasn't, I may just punch him in the balls.

"Are you fucking with me?"

"Nope. I work at the Chicago Public Library. I head up the children's area."

It may have been the alcohol I drank but I swore I heard angels singing and saw a halo around his incredibly sexy head. My ovaries joined Queen B for a dance. I blame her and my ovaries for what I did next. With no control over my body, my hands shot out, latching onto his neck. I crashed my lips against his and could still taste a bit of the fruity drink from earlier. I pulled back and his eyes were glazed over.

"What was that for?"

"You work with children and you read. That is sexy as hell." I crashed my lips against his again.

4

CHORD

Who the hell would have figured that being a children's librarian would have been a turn on? Why was I working so hard at the gym to get ripped? Rhapsody continued to kiss me. The little noises that kept escaping her were making my pants tighter and tighter.

I pulled away, taking a deep breath. "Whoa! Maybe we should slow down. We have an audience."

Rhapsody gazed around, noticing the woman who looked like a librarian back at the table was staring daggers at us. Rhapsody waved her fingers at her then turned back to me. "Let's go get a drink."

She jumped up but our legs were tangled together, causing her to land in my lap. I let out a groan as the bulge in my pants jammed into her as she landed. Pulling her down onto my getting painful erection made her giggle. My restraint was shit. Wrapping my hand around her neck, I pressed my lips to her smiling ones. Urging her mouth to open, I slid my tongue inside her warm mouth.

"Eh-hm." A voice broke through my clouded sexed up brain. I looked up to see a familiar older man.

With her own glazed look, she gazed up at the man and immediately straightened. "Papa Rob?"

He glanced over at her but refocused on me. "Son, do you think you should treat a woman like this?"

A feeling I hadn't felt since I got caught making out on my high school girlfriend's couch came rushing over me. My cheeks heated with embarrassment as I tried to figure out what to say. I did have a grown woman in my lap after all.

"Papa Rob. We are just having a little fun," Rhapsody said.

"Uh-huh. I think you two should find separate seats and cool down." His gaze continued to bore into me.

"Yes, sir," I sputtered.

"We are going to get drinks. Papa Rob, stop being so protective." Rhapsody stood, straightened her skirt, then pulled me to stand. "We are going to get drinks."

A shiver of fear slid down my spine as Papa Rob continued to stare at me.

Rhapsody pulled on my hand and said, "Come on. I'm thirsty."

I shrugged but just as I was about to turn around, he pointed two fingers at his eyes then at me. The universal sign that he would be watching me. I swallowed and let Rhapsody drag me to the bar.

"Finally," she said as we approached the bar. Leaning forward, she flagged down the bartender. "I want a merlot."

Turning to me to order, I said, "Whiskey on the rocks."

The bartender quickly handed us our drinks. We wandered quietly over to a more secluded area and an awkward silence descended over us. Talking seemed irrelevant when I just had my tongue in her mouth.

"So, I think we got a little carried away over there," she said to her drink.

"I don't regret tasting your lips." I watched as my words caused a blush to rise up her neck. Leaning close, I said, "I do, however, regret that we aren't in a room alone so I can taste all of you."

She sucked in a gasp. I smirked taking a sip of my whiskey. When I looked at her again, her eyes were as big as saucers, and she was turning purple.

"Oh shit! Are you okay?"

She furrowed her brow, shaking her head. I put my whiskey on a nearby high table and began slapping her back. After a few more slaps, Rhapsody began coughing. I breathed in a relieved breath. Walking in front of her, I give her a look. The color was coming back into her face.

I framed her face with my hands. "Are you okay?"

Just as she was about to answer I was sprayed with liquid. Instead of saying anything, she coughed, spraying her wine in my face.

"Oh my God!" she said between deep breaths. "I am so sorry." Rhapsody stepped away from me and swiped a napkin off the nearby table I'd set my drink on.

She dabbed my face and shirt. I looked down to see the red from the merlot staining my white shirt. Damn. I didn't have many and this was the nicest I owned.

"Shit," she said, moving away from me.

"It's okay." My voice came out flat.

"Come with me."

The napkin fluttered on the floor. She grabbed my hand and dragged me down the hallway to the winding staircase in the hotel lobby. Quickly, I grabbed my drink, downing it in one gulp. I forced myself not to start coughing from the burn.

"Where are we going?" I asked.

"My room."

"What?" I tried to stop but she was stronger than I'd thought, and she pulled me along.

"I have some stain remover. I can save this shirt if you stop dragging your feet. Come on."

Up the winding the stairs we went. The hallways were quiet

with just the echo of the party downstairs. A paisley red and gold carpet lined the hallways. Floral wallpaper plastered the walls between numbered doorways. Stopping in front of room 215, Rhapsody pulled a key from a bag I hadn't realized she was holding.

"Get in and take your shirt off," she ordered.

I blinked at her. This girl was serious. She went into the bathroom while I wandered into the small bedroom area. I began unbuttoning my shirt while listening to her rummage around the little bathroom. I had finished unbuttoning my shirt and cufflinks when I heard a whoop. Rhapsody came out of the bathroom holding what looked like a pen in her hand.

"I found—" She stopped in her tracks and stared at me.

"What?" I asked.

She bit her lip and reached for my shirt. "It's nothing. Let me take that."

Biting her lip like that sent a thrill through me. I was back to that moment she was in my lap. With my brain short circuiting, I tossed my shirt on the bed and pulled her to me.

"The shirt can wait. I need another taste."

Wrapping one arm around her waist, I used a finger and tipped up her chin. Her eyes closed with her pouty lips calling to me. I softly met her lips with mine. Lightning went through me and straight to my cock. The soft kiss soon became intense.

In one swift move, I picked her up and walked her over to the wall. Her legs wrapped around my waist. Nails dug into my scalp as I cupped her plump ass. When she bit my lip and pulled my hair, I knew I wasn't going to be able to leave this room without being inside her. This was too good. She was too good. If this was going to stop it needed to now.

Pulling back, I looked at her. "Rhapsody, I want you. Tell me you want me too."

She nodded and tried to capture my lips again, but I pulled away from her.

"How drunk are you?" I knew I was feeling some effects of

the whiskey but it sure as hell wasn't going to stop me. However, if she was the least bit drunk, I was hitting the breaks.

"Will you shut up and fuck me already, Chord?"

I smirked. "If the lady insists then her knight must comply."

We kissed with an eagerness that I'd never felt before. Unzipping her dress, I set her back on down. When her feet hit the ground so did the dress. She was a vision in a red bra and matching thong. I had to step back for a minute and think about my grandmother so I didn't embarrass myself right there. This girl sent my lust into overdrive. I hadn't felt like this since the first time I'd seen a naked girl.

"Everything okay?" Her voice wavered.

"Everything is perfect. Get on the bed on all fours." I put a little heat in my voice.

With a raised eyebrow, she sashayed over to the bed, giving me a perfect view of her round ass. She crawled on the bed, and I pushed my stained shirt on the floor. On all fours, she glanced over her shoulder with a look that made me pray I could last for longer than one pump.

"Are you coming?"

Her innuendo wasn't lost on me, and I cocked an eyebrow at her. "Oh, I definitely will be doing that. Preferably inside you."

My belt was already unbuckled, so it only took a moment to unzip my pants, showing that the only thing between us were those pants. When they dropped and she saw my straining cock, her eyes widened, and she licked her lips.

I stepped out of my pants and shoes then joined her on the bed. I knelt behind her gorgeous ass. It begged for me to massage, smack, and kiss it. Dragging my hands over her soft mounds, I took the thong and slid it over each inch. Kissing the path of where the thong went made her squirm. With a moan, she leaned back into me. Running a finger over her wet lips and clit dragged out another moan. I couldn't help the smile on my face.

"You are such a tease," she panted.

"It's only fair. You've been teasing me all night with that sexy as fuck dress you were wearing."

Her light blue eyes met mine and in that instant, I felt a connection I'd never felt before. She was special. This moment was special.

"Christ, Chord, what are you waiting for? An invitation?"

I smacked her ass. She yelped then relaxed as I rubbed the sting away.

"Gonna use that smart mouth again?"

"Only if you promise to smack my ass again."

Damn! This woman was perfect. I couldn't handle much more foreplay. I needed inside this vixen.

"I'm going to take a raincheck. My cock needs your pussy."

She moaned and pushed her ass toward me.

Sliding into her tight sheath, I felt my orgasm coming on quick. Oh shit! I refused to be a one pump chump. I hadn't felt like this since my first time. Stopping the minute I was in her, she pushed against me, and I moaned. Baseball stats floated through my mind. Music lyrics were next but when "Let's Get It On" floated through my brain, my cock had a mind of its own and the orgasm I'd been avoiding exploded through me.

Son of a bitch!

My groan echoed through the room. Rhapsody froze underneath me. When I finished coming inside her, she pulled away from me and lay on the bed. I couldn't read the look on her face. Damn if it didn't look like a mixture of shock and disappointment.

"I'm going to get a washcloth to clean up."

"Okay," she said softly.

Escaping into the bathroom, I grabbed a washcloth and turned on the faucet. The mirror that took up the entire wall with fluorescent lights illuminated exactly what a one pump chump looked like. I looked down at my semi-hard cock.

"You couldn't cooperate this one time could you, Stan." I

stared at my cock like it was going to answer. Yes, my cock's name was Stan. Stan the man to be exact.

"All right, I'm going to make a deal with you. If you stand at attention again without going off, then I promise you will get to be inside her again. I know you liked that Stan but you gotta cooperate. No more blowing your lid before I tell you. Got it?" Stan began to grow again.

Feeling confident again, I marched out of the bathroom with my hardening cock. It slapped against my leg as I approached the bed. Rhapsody had been busy while I was giving Stan a pep talk. She was now completely naked, and she'd raided the mini fridge. It looked like she was on her second bottle of some alcohol.

"I'm ready to go again," I said weakly.

"Me too. Let's do body shots now." She waved around a small bottle with an amber liquid inside.

"All right." I looked down at Stan. He looked back as if to say 'but you promised.' "Just a detour, buddy," I mumbled under my breath.

"What? Who were you just talking to?"

"No one. Now, did you say something about body shots?"

She handed me the bottle. I chugged it then pounced.

5

———————

RHAPSODY

Two Months Later

"Rhapsody, are you ready for the presentation on the Webster account?" Mr. Boswacker asked.

"Yes, sir. Just putting the finishing touches on the PowerPoint."

"Good. This needs to be perfect. I can't stress that enough. We need this account."

"Understood, sir." I watched my boss march out of my office.

Being a junior accountant looking to move into the senior accountant position put me a half a step above slave. I was probably more of an indentured servant. I'd been working for Anderson Accounting since I graduated college eight years ago. I was lucky at the time to get an internship with them. When I proved myself, they offered me a junior accountant position. I thought at the time that this would be my chance to make it. Here it was eight years later and promotions blew past me as if I didn't exist. I'd heard from more than one source that my boss, Mr. Boswacker, felt I was too valuable to get promoted. Who the hell heard of such a thing?

The Webster account was one of the biggest the firm had

ever had a chance to acquire. I'd been on the account from the moment it was mentioned. Most of the presentation was solely my work. I was hoping the bigwigs who would be present would see my hard work and the open senior accountant position would be a shoe in.

"You ready, Rhapsody?" Sophie, my partner for the project and office neighbor, popped her head in.

"Yep." A wave of nausea swirled through me. I braced myself on my desk.

"You okay? You look a little green around the gills."

I took a sip of my tea hoping it would settle my stomach. "Yeah. I hope I'm not getting that stomach bug that's been floating around her."

Sophie looked at me and nodded. "Those things are nasty."

With a deep breath, I picked up my laptop. "Let's go nail this thing."

"You bet." She bounced out of my office with a way too excited bounce in her step.

The large conference room sat empty as we approached. With every step I took my stomach roiled. It was the worst possible time for the stomach bug to hit. I stopped outside of the bathrooms near the conference room.

"Sophie, can you start setting up? I will be in in a moment."

She furrowed her brows at me but took the laptop and strode off to the conference room. I ran into the bathroom and slammed the stall door behind me. My stomach revolted just as I'd made it into the stall. Every possible thing I'd put in my body that morning made a reappearance. Queen B sat powdering her nose then said, *"Told you not to eat sushi from that sketchy place last night."*

"Shut up," I murmured between heaves.

When I was finally done, I flushed the toilet and stepped from the stall. I quickly fixed my makeup and hair to hide any evidence of getting sick. A glance in the mirror showed I couldn't hide it that well. Oh well, I had to suck it up. Time to get that promotion. Marching out of the bathroom and into the conference room, I saw that Sophie hadn't done anything other than lay the laptop on the table. She was sitting on the table near a good-looking guy I'd never seen before. As he leaned back in the chair, I was sure he could look up her skirt from where he was sitting.

"Sophie. I thought you were going to set up everything."

She jumped down off the table, shot a smile at the guy she'd been talking to, and walked over to me. "I did. I put the laptop on the table. Was I supposed to do anything else?"

I blinked at her. With a sigh, I said, "Yes. I will take care of it."

"Okay. Great." She bounced back to the guy she'd been flirting with.

"Ready to get that promotion?" A familiar voice drew my attention as I plugged wires into the laptop and projector.

Daniel Evans stood next to me. At six-foot-five, he was an imposing force. He looked like a linebacker posing as an accountant. With his gorgeous dark skin and hair, he could have just walked off a runway in Paris. His eyes, however, hid an intelligence that few got to see. Daniel had been my first friend at Anderson. We started our internships together. In only two years of being there, he got promoted. I didn't mind at the time because we were dating. After only three months, we realized we were better as friends than lovers. Now, he has a beautiful wife and a daughter I love to cuddle whenever they force me to come over for dinners.

"I'm going to nail this."

He held up his fist. I bumped it with my own then went back to setting up the presentation.

"Ms. Bell, are you ready for us?" Mr. Boswacker asked as he led in the client and the board of directors for Anderson.

"Yes, sir."

Sophie finally detached herself from flirting and stood next to me. We stood to the side waiting for John Anderson our CEO to address the large crowd. He did a spiel about the prestige associated with Anderson and how competent all the employees were. Daniel caught my eye and rolled his eyes. I covered my mouth when a giggle threatened to escape.

When Mr. Anderson finished and introduced Mr. Boswacker, he stood to address the crowded conference room. It was painful to watch. Sweat pooled on his head, wetting his substantial combover. As he stumbled over all the information on the cards I'd made for him, I smelled a sickeningly sweet smell. One of the board members was wearing a cologne that made my stomach twist.

"Let me hand this over to our experts, Ms. Rhapsody Bell and Ms. Sophie Fletcher."

I grabbed a cup of water and took a swallow. Forcing my shoulders back, I walked over to the laptop, turning on the presentation. After a few deep breaths, I began my portion of the presentation. My responsibility was to illustrate the needs of the client and how we could tackle them. Sophie's part was a projection of how being part of Anderson accounting would benefit them in the future.

Through my part, I was able to hold back the nausea that continued to threaten to break free each time I inhaled that sweet smell. I moved a bit faster through the presentation than I'd have preferred, but I made it nonetheless. A few times I made eye contact with Daniel. He kept giving me a questioning look that I ignored.

"Now, on to the future. Sophie?" I looked to where she'd been standing but saw she had disappeared. I had been so focused on the presentation and not getting sick I hadn't even noticed she'd left. Fuck me. I was screwed.

"Rhapsody, it looks like Sophie had to leave unexpectedly. Please continue the presentation without her," Mr. Boswacker said.

I swallowed when a wave of nausea swept over me again. "I

will continue…" I began but before I could get another word out, I ran over to the trashcan and threw up.

"Oh my God! Rhapsody, are you okay?" With my head in the wastebasket, Daniel's voice penetrated the noise of my heaves.

Soon after my nausea receded. I stood slowly and took a napkin from Daniel. Wiping my face, I pushed back the tears that were threatening to break free. Any chance I'd had at getting the promotion just went in the trash.

"I apologize, everyone. I fear I may be coming down with a stomach bug. However, I would like to finish the presentation."

Daniel whispered next to me, "Rhapsody, I think you should probably go home. You don't look so good."

I turned back around to the group and to Daniel. "I have to look better than I did a moment ago with my head in the wastebasket. If all of you are okay with me continuing, I promise I will make this fast."

Mr. Boswacker looked utterly disgusted. He was about to chime in when Mr. Anderson nodded with a smile. No one dared to contradict him, so I finished the presentation. When the final slide was shown and I answered all follow-up questions, everyone left with satisfied looks on their faces. The only person upset was Mr. Boswacker.

"Ms. Bell, I will need to have a talk with you once you clean up in here." He marched out the door, leaving me with Daniel.

"Well, you do know how to liven up a party." He sat in the chair next to me.

"I don't know what is wrong with me. I'm exhausted, nauseous, ill-tempered, and all around just miserable."

Daniel bit his lip.

"What?"

"Okay. Don't take this the wrong way but could you be pregnant?" he asked.

A loud, long laugh escaped me.

"Me? Pregnant? By who?"

"I don't know, Rhapsody. You don't tell me everything but

what you described is exactly how Izzy felt when she was pregnant with Olivia."

"That's ridiculous. I haven't had sex in ages." The moment those words left my mouth, fear iced my veins. The last time I'd had sex floated through my mind. Granted, I could barely remember it thanks to the alcohol, but I was sure we used protection.

Daniel raised his hands in surrender. "Okay. Okay. If it is a stomach bug, then you should get your butt home.

———

"Rhapsody darling, is that you?" My grandmother's voice floated in from the living room.

"Yes, Grams. It's just me." I shoved the bag from the pharmacy into my purse.

"Come in here. Look who's here for a visit."

I knew who was visiting. I'd seen the rental car in the driveway. My cousin Cassie was sitting in the chair next to Grams. She was dressed in tight leather pants, biker boots, and a tank top that barely held in her size double D boobs. Normally, she and I could pass as sisters but with her hair teased and the makeup that was caked on her face, we couldn't even pass for being related.

"Hi, Cassie. How long are you here for?"

"Hey, cuz. What kind of welcome is that?" She moved her legs to hang over the arm of the chair she sat in. Grams reached over and rapped her legs with her cane.

"You know how to sit in a chair, Cassandra. Sit properly or sit on the floor."

"Sorry, Grams. As for your question, I'm here between gigs."

I looked around a bit frantically. "She isn't here is she?"

Cassie giggled. "No. Though she did say she was going to call you or something. I don't remember. I'm here until she calls me back."

My stomach flopped again. This time it had nothing to do with nausea.

"Okay. Well, I've had a rough day. I'm going to go to bed."

"You aren't going to eat?" Grams asked.

"I had a late lunch." I turned to Cassie. "It's good seeing you, Cassie. Night, Grams."

"Night, sweetheart."

I climbed the stairs one at a time. My body was so exhausted it felt like there were lead weights on my ankles. When I finally made it to the top, I went into the bathroom and locked the door. With shaking hands, I pulled out the bag I'd shoved in my purse. In an attempt to cover the sounds of the bag, I quickly turned on the shower. I didn't need a suspicious Cassie or Grams knocking on the locked door.

The three boxes sat ominously on the counter. When I'd purchased them at the pharmacy, I tried to be inconspicuous. However, the cashier decided to tell me about how wonderful babies were and how she knew she was pregnant with each of her five kids. I couldn't help but think about the story I'd tell my child about finding out about him or her. Shaking those thoughts from my head, I opened each box and laid each stick next to its corresponding box. I must have been standing and staring at those little sticks longer than I'd thought because the mirror began fogging up from the steam of the shower. I needed to get this done now. No more wasting time. I quickly sat on the toilet and peed on all three sticks. How I had enough pee for three pregnancy tests was beyond my comprehension.

After setting down each stick, I stripped and jumped in the shower. Taking a shower would kill the three minutes I needed to wait to see what fate held. While I showered my mind began to wander. How had my life gone down this road? In the past year, work had been my life. Dating just didn't fit into my schedule. I'm not one for casual flings so I bought stock in batteries and enjoyed my plastic pleasurer. I'd named him Fred. However, Fred couldn't get me pregnant. I'd only been with one man in the past year. Chord Reedy. Sexy as sin and unfortunately, a one pump chump. We'd both been drinking that night, and it definitely wasn't the best performance for either one of us but was it possible we hadn't used protection?

Soap dripped through my fingers as I thought about the idea of having a baby. Fear gripped me in icy fingers. I had no idea what to do with a baby. I was good with numbers not people. Babies were little people. I would royally screw up a child. My own childhood was fucked up.

A banging broke me from my daydreaming. "Are you almost done, Rhapsody? I'd like to shower before bed," Cassie said.

"I'll be out in a few."

Rinsing off the soap, I shut off the water and stepped onto the bathmat, taking one of the soft towels and wrapping it around me. For a split second a vision of not being able to wrap the towel around me thanks to a big belly flashed through my mind. I froze. With a deep breath, I looked down at the three sticks. All three had the same result. Two lines.

"Holy fuck," Queen B said then fainted.

"You can say that again," I mumbled.

6

____

CHORD

Bang.

Bang.

Bang.

My sleepy eyes refused to open.

Bang.

Bang.

Bang.

Dammit. Benny had brought one of the bar bunnies home, and they were testing how many times his headboard could hit the wall before breaking through into my room. I looked over at my alarm. 6:59. One minute until my alarm went off. I reached over and shut it off before the annoying voice of Darth Vader ordered me to rise.

I stared at the ceiling. I hadn't slept well again. In the past two months, I've had one dream after another featuring one person. The one person I ghosted and regretted it. I didn't really ghost her, but she clearly didn't want to talk to me. So, I will continue to boost my bruised male ego by saying I ghosted her and not the fact she was disappointed with our one night and refused to talk to me again.

All of a sudden, the door to my bedroom slammed open and Oscar strolled in with a giant bowl of cereal. He plopped down on the end of my bed and stared at my fish tank. I wish I could say this was a surprising occurrence, but I'd be lying. My roommate who does just a bit too much weed comes in every morning with his bowl of sugar o's and stares at my colorful fish.

"Morning, Oscar," I said through a yawn.

"Murenin, Card," he mumbled with a giant spoonful of cereal in his mouth.

Shuffling over to my attached bathroom, I stripped down to shower. Stan had been having a hell of a time. Every morning he woke up hard and wanted to be back in his happy place. I stroked down my hard shaft. I'm always so close to coming after a dream about her.

"Don't worry, buddy. I'm going to take care of you."

"Stop talking to your cock and get a shower. We need to leave soon." Alec, who was my third roommate, cousin, and best friend, banged on my bathroom door.

"Fuck off, Alec. I wasn't talking to my cock," I yelled as I stepped into the shower.

"He was definitely talking to his dick, again," Oscar said to Alec.

"You two shitheads can get the hell out of my room."

I could hear Alec laughing.

I really needed to get my own place. If I wanted, I could have my own place today. However, getting my own place meant I'd have to deal with someone I'd rather not deal with. So, I am stuck with these three fuckers.

Taking a bit more time than normal, just to piss off Alec, I took care of Stan. Hell, I needed to do that just to fit him in my pants. He could get pretty sizable when he wanted. After my shower, I dressed in a pair of blue jeans, a red and white striped shirt, a matching beany cap, and large framed glasses. It was Where's Waldo day at the library. When my look was perfect, I strode out to the kitchen for my daily dose of the nectar of the Gods, also known as coffee.

Alec sat at the kitchen counter completely engulfed in his phone. He was dressed in his normal three-piece suit. I grabbed my travel mug that said 'Librarians do it by the book.' Alec hated that mug, so I made sure to use it every time he drove me to work. Usually, I rode my bike but on special days at the library, I made sure to get a ride so I didn't ruin the look.

"What in the fuck are you wearing?" Alec asked.

"It's Where's Waldo day."

"No one is going to miss you that is for sure. If anything, you kind of look like the picture of a child perv."

"Alec! That is not cool or funny."

"I know. That is why I was telling you."

"All of the librarians will be wearing this today. Plus, the kids love when we have these theme days."

Alec got off the stool he was sitting on then grabbed his briefcase. "Ready, weirdo? I'm contemplating making you sit in the back, so I can just pretend I'm an Uber driver and can disavow all knowledge of who you are."

Before I could reply, Oscar walked into the kitchen. He looked at me and blinked. "Holy shit! I need to stop smoking weed." He turned back around, walking back to his room.

I looked at Alec, and he looked at me. We burst out laughing. "Let's get the hell out of here."

We walked out of our apartment to the elevator. It opened a few minutes later. The woman who had been on her phone when the elevator arrived had a startled look when she saw me. I smiled at her, but she slid closer to the corner.

Alec laughed and said, "Told you."

"Shut up," I whispered.

The elevator ride took an eternity. With each stop, people stepped onto the elevator and gave me questioning looks. I made a mental note to change into any costume at the library next time. It was starting to feel more like Where's the Weirdo instead of Where's Waldo.

Finally, we made it to the garage where Alec's car was parked. Everyone exited and went their separate ways. I got a few more strange looks but most ignored me and rushed to their vehicles. We walked over to where Alec's cars were parked. He had two. One was a gold 98 Honda Civic that he'd had since high school and the other was a restored 1970 Dodge Charger in candy apple red. We ignored the covered classic and got into the Civic.

"You're dressed up today. Big day?" I asked.

"Not really. Just meeting with the bigwigs to discuss which accounting firm we will be using."

"Oh."

Alec got excited all of a sudden. "I totally forgot to tell you what happened yesterday."

"It must be good because you are twitching in your seat like a puppy that's about to piss on the rug."

"It is so good. So, we've been taking proposals from some different accounting firms ever since ours went under thanks to the CEO and his pyramid scheme." I nodded only halfway paying attention. "Well, the chick that was doing the presentation was pretty boring. That was until in the middle of everything she puked."

I nodded absently when his words penetrated my unfocused brain. "What?"

"Yep. Puked right there in the middle of the PowerPoint. It's a shame too because she was pretty hot. Not as hot as her partner, who I banged later. But the most badass thing was she kept going."

"She continued after throwing up in front of everyone?"

"Yep. She asked to keep going. When she got the go ahead from their CEO, she straightened her shoulders then went on like there wasn't puke in the trashcan."

"Wow. That poor girl must have been humiliated."

"I wouldn't know. After she sped through the rest of the boring presentation all I could think about was banging that other girl."

"Of course."

My cousin really was a manwhore.

"She was a hot piece of ass. Wanted it so bad she left before it was her turn to do her part in the PowerPoint. She just waited for me in the bathroom."

"Uh-huh."

Thank God we'd finally arrived at the library. It was the longest ten-minute ride I'd ever had. Alec was still babbling on about the girl he'd notched when I practically threw myself out of the car.

"Whoa. Be careful, Chord."

"Remember to pick me up by four," I said.

"I know. I know."

"Okay. Thanks for the ride." I slammed the door then strode up the steps leading up to the large entry of the library.

Entering the library, I passed the security guard with a wave and a good morning. The overnight staff had been busy with setting up for the themed day. Banners, posters, and tables were set up leading people toward the children's wing of the library. Every employee I saw was dressed the same. I smiled as I passed Mr. Jenkins, the custodian, dressed like Waldo too.

"Morning, Mr. Jenkins."

"Keep moving, pretty boy," he mumbled as he swept the floor.

I smiled. When I came to work at the Chicago Public Library, I was very ambitious. I soon realized that ideas were great but having the funding to do what you wanted was something entirely different. So, I decided that I'd make a list and slowly check off those goals as funding and attendance increased. One of my non-library centered goals was to get a nice word out of Mr. Jenkins. It's been close to eight years, and I still haven't penetrated that wall.

Approaching the children's section, the Where's Waldo decorations exploded. There were books and activity stations everywhere. Sylvia, the head librarian, stood at the desk in the children's section. She wasn't participating. If you looked up librarian in the dictionary, you'd see a picture of her.

"Good morning, Sylvia." I pushed up my fake glasses.

"Mr. Reedy." She sniffed and took in my appearance. "Another one of your ideas I see."

I shrugged. "Well, it was a group effort."

"It sure was." A high pitched giggle followed.

I forced myself not to roll my eyes. Britnee, with two Es, Smith was an intern. She flounced around the library talking too loudly and annoying the regulars. Whenever asked about recommendations she would say she preferred movies over books. I had no idea why she wanted to be a librarian, but she'd gotten it into her head that she and I would be a couple someday. Alec tried to get in her pants a few times but apparently, she only had eyes for me. Lucky me.

When I looked over at Britnee, I choked on air. She'd dressed like Waldo if Waldo was a hooker. She had a barely there mini skirt, a striped shirt cut dangerously low, and the beanie rested gently on her head. After taking in the sight before me, I chanced a glance over at Sylvia. She was turning a shade of purple I didn't know a human could turn.

"Ms. Smith." Her voice whipped out. "That is an appalling and unprofessional outfit you are wearing today. I'm afraid you will need to go home."

"What? I look just like Chord."

Bullshit. I may look like a perv but I sure as shit didn't look like I earned my money on my back.

"I mean it, Ms. Smith. Go."

Britnee's bottom lip quivered, and she looked at me. Just as she was about to ask me for help, my phone chimed. To say a relieved sigh hadn't escaped would be a lie.

"Excuse me, I need to take this."

Sylvia nodded and continued to stare daggers at Britnee.

I walked down one of the many aisles. Swiping across my screen showed the one person I didn't want any messages from. I closed my eyes. If I didn't answer him, he'd just get Alec to call me. I couldn't take that since we were about to open for the day.

Jimmy Ray: Need to meet for lunch.

Me: Can't it's Where's Waldo day.

Jimmy Ray: What the fuck are you talking about? Meet me for lunch. It's urgent.

Me: What is it?

Jimmy Ray: Can't talk now. Just meet me at the place at 1.

I took a deep breath.

Me: Fine.

Jimmy Ray: That's my boy. See you then.

With his last words, I felt like I had leeches all over my body. That last thing I wanted to be was that man's son. However, if I didn't go, he'd sic Alec then Grandpa on me. I needed to focus on work then I'd worry about meeting with my father.

7

RHAPSODY

"You wanted to see me, Mr. Boswacker?" I walked into his office like I was going in front of a firing squad.

He wrinkled his nose at me, remembering my embarrassing episode the day before. "Yes, Ms. Bell, I need to talk to you about what happened yesterday."

"I'm sorry, sir."

He waved his hand. "Mr. Anderson wants to meet with you today. You don't need to apologize to me. I feel he will express to you everything that I would like to say to you."

My stomach dropped. "I understand. When does he want to meet with me?"

"How am I supposed to know? I'm not a secretary. You will be called up sometime today. I wanted to be the one to tell you." His words came with a sneer.

What a dick!

"Thank you, sir."

"Please shut the door behind you, Ms. Bell." He dismissed me.

With a nod, I left Mr. Boswacker's office. I felt numb and for the first time in the last twenty-four hours, it wasn't because of the three tests I'd passed. Lost in thought, I walked back to my office on autopilot. A strong hand stopped me.

"What did Ballslapper want?" Daniel asked.

I let out a laugh at his nickname for my boss. "Just to tell or warn me I was going to be summoned to Anderson's office." I looked at Daniel. "I'm fucked."

"You don't know that. Mr. Anderson is way more chill than you think." He stepped back and stared at me. "Are you feeling better?"

I blushed then whispered. "Come into my office. I have to tell you something."

Daniel furrowed his brow but followed me into my office anyway. I motioned for him to close the door then sat behind my desk.

After shutting the door, he asked, "What's with all the cloak and dagger stuff?"

"I'm pregnant," I whisper-yelled.

Daniel blinked then fell into one of the chairs in front of my desk. "Are you sure?"

"Yes. I took three tests. The one time I wanted to fail a test and I passed with flying colors on all three counts."

"Holy shit," he breathed.

"Yeah."

"Do you know who the father is?"

I blanched. "Of course I do. What do you think I do? Go out and sleep with so many people I wouldn't know whose baby it is?"

Daniel held up his hands in front of him. "I'm sorry. So, who is it?"

"It was a guy I met at Rufus's wedding."

"I didn't know you hooked up with anyone at the wedding. Does Rufus know?"

"First, I didn't tell anyone because honestly it wasn't the best night of my life. He was a bit overly excited and things ended quickly. Then we got pretty drunk, and I can't even remember if we did it more than that one time. Second, no Rufus doesn't know. I can barely wrap my own mind around it let alone share the news with him."

"Wait a minute, are you telling me the baby daddy was a one pump chump?"

"Yep. Also, I think he talks to his penis. That could have been my imagination, but I could have sworn it at the time."

"Geez, Rhapsody. You know how to pick 'em."

I let out a laugh with no humor. "Yeah."

"Are you going to tell him?"

"I don't even know how to get ahold of the guy. I woke up the next day to an empty bed."

"He ghosted you?"

"I guess. Seems he was as impressed with me as I was with him."

"Well, I'm sure you could ask Rufus for his info."

"I can see how that conversation would go. 'Hey, Rufus. Do you remember that hot guy that you sat at the loser table with me? Oh yeah that guy. Well, he sorta knocked me up. Do you have his digits so I can tell him?' Yeah. That would go over great."

"You have to figure out something. Maybe you can find him on Facebook."

"Another great idea. I will just tag the guy under life event of baby daddy."

"Come on, Rhapsody. I'm trying to help."

I put my now pounding head on my desk. "I know, Daniel. I'm sorry. I will figure out something."

Daniel rubbed my head with his big hand. "I am here for you. If you need anything, even if it is beating the crap out of the baby daddy, just give me a call."

Before I could answer, my office phone rang. I put one finger over my lips signaling him to be quiet.

"Rhapsody Bell."

"Hello, Ms. Bell. This is Sandra in Mr. Anderson's office.

He'd like to meet with you today at 3:00 p.m. Are you available?"

I took a quick look at my planner. "Yes."

"Fantastic. He will see you then. Have a good day, Ms. Bell."

"Thank you."

Daniel looked at me while I still held the phone. "That didn't sound bad."

"I don't think it is. Maybe I'm wrong, and I will get upset then throw up in Mr. Anderson's office this time. "

Daniel laughed. "If only. Well, I see your cell is going crazy too so I will let you handle that and freak yourself out over your upcoming meeting with the bigwig."

I threw a stuffed beaver I had on my desk at him as he left. It hit the door then fell to the floor. Picking up my phone, nausea built up in my stomach.

Mom: Hello, little beaver.

Dear Jesus give me the strength to deal with this woman.

Me: Mom I've asked you not to call me that.

Mom: What? It's cute.

Me: What do you want, mom? I'm kinda dealing with things here.

Mom: I need you. Can we meet for dinner?

Me: I don't know what time I will be done work today.

Mom: Come on, little beaver. I have something important I need to talk to you about.

Me: Fine.

Mom: Great. I will see you at my favorite place.

Me: Ok.

I threw my phone into my purse. The last thing I wanted to do was have dinner with my mother. Cassie warned me she'd be in contact, but I thought I'd have a few days to come up with fake plans. I thudded my head against my desk. The only good thing about my mother was she was so self-centered she'd never realize I have things going on in my life.

8

———————

CHORD

"Uncle Chord!" A sweet little voice forced me to look up.

"Uncle Chord? I don't know who that is. My name is Waldo," I said, teasing my niece.

"You're just playing pretend, Uncle Chord. Right, Mommy?" she asked.

"Yes, Alice. I think Uncle Chord was just joking," my sister, Miranda, said.

Alice ran at me like a charging rhino. I caught her and swung her onto my hip. I kissed my sister on the cheek then asked Alice, "Do you know who I am supposed to be today?"

She nodded her head. Her curly pigtails bounced. Her cuteness was almost too much sometimes. My sister was currently a single mom. Her deadbeat ex ran away to find himself. The last time he'd been heard from was when a hired PI found him to get him to sign custody and divorce papers.

"Wow! You really go all out on these days," she said, looking me up and down.

"It's fun. Plus, the kids get a kick out of it."

"So do the moms apparently." She nodded toward a group of moms who frequented the library on our specialty days.

"They like to bring their kids."

"Yeah. I'm sure it's the kids they are thinking about and not the hot librarian dressed like an idiot."

"Hey!" I looked at Alice whose gaze bounced between me and her mother. "Your mommy is being mean." I stuck my lip out like I was going to cry.

Alice hugged me and tapped my shoulder in comfort. "Don't cry, Uncle Chord. It will be okay. Mommy still loves you."

Cuteness overload was imminent.

Miranda rolled her eyes. "I heard the old man has requested your presence."

I grimaced then put Alice on the ground. "Alice, why don't you go over there with Ms. Mary. She's doing a really fun activity." Alice nodded then ran over with a few other children her own age.

"I have lunch with him in about..." I looked at the giant clock above the doorway. "Half an hour."

"What does he want?" Miranda asked while watching Alice glue pieces of paper to construction paper.

"No clue. He said "My Boy" in his text. So, who knows what the hell is going on?"

"You think he's dying?"

"We both would have been summoned for that."

She snorted. "Pity."

"Miranda! He's still our father."

She really did roll her eyes at that. "He was the sperm donor. You know Grandpa has been more of a father to us than him. We see him what? Every six months if he feels like gracing us with his presence. He hasn't seen Alice since she was born."

"I know." There wasn't much more I could say to that. She was right. Our father knocked up our mother and then went AWOL. The only reason he knew about us was because when our mother found out she had cancer she wanted to make sure we had another parent. It didn't matter in the long run.

"All I can say is better you than me." She smirked. "Are you changing before seeing him?"

"Nope." I smirked back.

Miranda lifted her fist, and I met it with mine and tapped it. She looked at the mothers staring at me then got a devilish look in her eye.

In an overly loud and dramatic voice, she said, "Did you finally get that ointment? I heard if you don't use it regularly the rash can spread from your balls to your penis. You better get that taken care of. Who would have thought that you could get poison ivy there just from taking a dump in the woods?"

A disgusted look crossed the mothers' faces then they went right back to whispering. Only seconds passed when the three women retrieved their children and huffed out of the library. They made sure to keep a wide berth from me and Miranda.

"Why the hell did you do that?"

"Now you don't have to fight off your hordes of adoring fans before you leave. You're welcome."

"I didn't thank you." I crossed my arms looking at her.

"Once you realize I saved you, you'll be thanking me profusely."

She was probably right. However, I couldn't tell her that. She'd go around thinking she was smart or something. Definitely couldn't tell my sister that.

"Come on, Alice. We need to go pick up Grandpa."

Alice ran over, holding the piece of construction paper that had a completed paper puzzle glued to it. "Look what I made, Mommy. Can we put it on the fridge when we get home?"

"You bet. Give Uncle Chord a hug."

"See you, princess."

"Love you, Uncle Chord."

There it went. My heart exploded with happiness from her cuteness.

Miranda hugged me again. "Call me to tell me what the

douche wanted. Love you, Chord. Remember he has no power over you."

A smirk tilted my lips to one side. "He isn't the goblin king." She loved the movie *Labyrinth* and took any chance she got to quote it.

"Isn't he?" She smirked back and grabbed Alice's hand then left the library.

I glanced at the clock again. Fifteen minutes until showtime. If only I could just tape this show instead of having a front row seat.

"Mary? I need to head out to lunch. Are you good here?"

She was in the middle of helping a toddler put glue on the paper instead of in his mouth. "I'm good. See you in an hour." She shooed me away.

"Damn," I said under my breath. Now, I didn't have an excuse. Wiping my damp hands on my jeans, I straightened my fake glasses and walked toward the exit. If I were lucky an asteroid would fall from the sky and hit me.

I wasn't lucky.

9

RHAPSODY

"Rhapsody Bell to see Mr. Anderson," I said to the receptionist at the desk outside of an opaque glass office.

"One second, Ms. Bell."

The receptionist picked up the phone to call Mr. Anderson. She talked quietly into the handset. I looked around the hallway trying to ignore that the woman was talking about me to the man who held my future in the palm of his hand. The click of the phone brought my gaze back to her.

"He will see you now, Ms. Bell."

"Thank you," I said as I walked toward the closed door.

Wiping my clammy hands on my skirt, I pushed on the door, and it silently opened. I was shocked at my first glance of our CEO's office. The office was surprisingly sparse. A large desk with two leather chairs in front of it sat in the center. A couple large glass bookcases sat against the walls facing the desk. Books were neatly lined with a few picture frames placed in front. The pictures were of a woman and two little boys smiling on a beach.

"Come on in, Ms. Bell." Mr. Anderson spun around in his

chair. He'd been watching me approach in the reflection of the window.

I bit my lip a bit too hard and a coppery taste of blood coated my tongue. Dammit. Now, I was going to bleed all over the place. First, vomit. Now, blood. A vision of my career going up in smoke fluttered through my mind.

Sitting in one of the large chairs, I said the obvious, "You wanted to see me?"

Mr. Anderson stood and walked around the desk. He sat in the chair next to me. "I did. I wanted to talk to you about what happened at the presentation."

My face felt hot and if I didn't pinch myself, I'd start crying. "I'm sorry, sir. I know I embarrassed the company, but I guarantee that won't ever happen again."

A strange look crossed his face. "What are you talking about?"

Dear Lord he was going to make me say it. Where was a convenient alien abduction when you needed it?

"Put on your big girl panties and answer the man that could make or break your career!" Queen B yelled at me.

I took in a deep breath then said, "I'm talking about the vomit incident, sir."

"Oh goodness. That wasn't anything, Ms. Bell. It has happened to the best of us." He furrowed his brow. "Did you think you were getting fired because you got sick?"

I shrugged.

"Yet another great answer, Rhapsody. I'm outta here." Queen B threw her hands up and disappeared.

"You would never get fired for something like that. I wanted to talk to you because I admire the perseverance it took for you to keep going with that presentation." He paused and stared at me. "I had Sandra look into your tenure here. Why have you been passed by on so many positions? Are you happy where you are, Ms. Bell?"

I stared down at my hands. "From my understanding, Mr.

Boswaker said that I am invaluable to him. That he couldn't bear to part with me."

"Hmm...do you want to move up in this company?" Mr. Anderson asked.

"Yes. I was hoping with that project and presentation I'd just given I might be considered for the next open position. But Mr. Boswaker pointed out that I'd be lucky to keep my job."

"Did he now? Let me set something straight. I am a very involved boss. I know all the standout stars in this company. How you haven't been brought to my attention astounds me. I have talked with your friend Daniel and I understand what Boswaker has been using you for."

I started to panic a bit. It felt like I was getting my boss in trouble. He was a dick, but I didn't want anyone getting fired. "I don't know if he meant to use me."

Mr. Anderson smiled. I finally really looked at him. He was clearly in his early forties. Definitely worked out with the way his suit hung on him. Salt and pepper gray feathered his temples. But it was the dimple in his smile that had to have had the women screaming his name when he was younger.

Queen B was back and fanned herself. *"These damn pregger hormones are making that boss look hot."*

I swallowed. The damn Queen B was a horny bitch sometimes.

"Ms. Bell? Are you okay?"

I blinked a few times. "Yes, sir. I'm sorry. You were saying?"

He smiled at her again. "I said, I want to make things right. Can you promise me that you won't be going anywhere until I do that?"

What the hell was he talking about? I didn't have plans to leave but maybe that was me being dumb. With a smile, I said, "I promise. No abandoning ship for me."

What the hell was coming out of my mouth? Nautical terms now? Now was not the time for my filter to bust.

"Good. Let's keep this conversation between us right now, okay?"

I nodded.

"All right then." Mr. Anderson stood. "I can't wait for us to work together on more projects. You are an asset here, and I bet you haven't been given the opportunities you deserve. You will soon though."

I stood and put my hand out. "Thank you, sir."

Mr. Anderson shook my hand. "I'll be seeing you soon."

Nodding, I turned to leave with my head in a daze. My heel caught on the plush carpet causing me to stumble. "Damn," I mumbled.

A soft laugh came from Mr. Anderson. "Are you okay, Ms. Bell?"

"Yes, sir." I detached my heel with a yank, knocking my knee into the chair and causing pain to shoot up my leg. I gritted my cry and walked with a slight limp to the door.

Leaving the office, I closed the door behind me, stopping to rub my aching knee.

"Are you okay, Ms. Bell?" Sandra asked.

"Yep. Just a bit of bruised pride and clumsiness coming out at the wrong time."

Sandra smiled. "I completely understand." She looked at the door then leaned toward me. "My damn heel gets caught on that stupid rug all the time. I've warned Mr. Anderson that if I hurt myself because of that ghastly thing, he will be ponying up major money."

I let out a laugh. "Glad I'm not the only one."

Sandra shook her head. "Not even close. I've even seen Mr. Anderson trip on that rug then curse it out like it jumped up and caused him to trip."

I grinned. "Thank you, Sandra."

"Anytime, Ms. Bell." Sandra's phone rang, and she waved to me as I walked away.

Maybe today was going to be my day after all.

10

———

CHORD

"What in the bloody hell are you wearing?" My father's angry whisper carried over to me before I could even sit.

"What? I was at work. It's Where's Waldo day." I smirked at him.

Pulling out the chair, I sat across from him. People at nearby tables stared at us. For once I knew it was me they were staring at and not my father. It was close though. He looked ridiculous. He wore a baseball cap with a long wig underneath. A shadow of stubble covered his face. His customary leather jacket was replaced with an old concert tee. To top off his whole ridiculous ensemble, a pair of aviator sunglasses were perched on his nose.

"You could have changed before meeting me." He crossed his arms.

"Didn't have time. Plus, I have to go back to work in…" I looked at my phone then said, "Forty-five minutes."

"Fine. Let's order then we can talk."

Dear old dad waved a waitress over and placed his order of a kale salad with water. I raised an eyebrow. He was either getting ready for a tour, which I knew he wasn't even close to a tour yet, or he was hungover and couldn't stomach anything with flavor.

When the waitress turned to me, I ordered a cheeseburger, a side of onion rings, and a chocolate shake. All the things I knew he'd want but couldn't order for one reason or another. The waitress nodded then strode away.

I pursed my lips. "So...you wanted to see me. What's going on?"

My father finally took off the stupid sunglasses and placed them on the table. "I have some exciting news."

"Okay. If it's so exciting, why didn't you ask Miranda to be here too?"

He grimaced at my sister's name. "Your sister hates me. I need someone who is going to be supportive not a Debbie Downer."

Anger filled my veins. I hated when he bashed Miranda. She wasn't perfect, but he had no right to talk shit about her.

"Are you dying?" I asked spitefully.

He blanched. "What? No. Why would you ask such a thing?"

I just shrugged and crossed my arms in front of my chest. "What do you want then?"

"I'm being inducted," he whispered.

"Inducted to what? Father of the year?" I spat at him.

He glared at me. "Do you have to act like a dick right now, Chord?"

"No, but I want to."

Rolling his eyes, he chose not to take my bait. "I'm being inducted into the Rock & Roll Hall of Fame on Saturday."

"Don't you mean the band is being inducted?" I corrected.

With a wave of his hand, he dismissed my comment. "There wouldn't be a Furious Storm without me."

Now it was my turn to roll my eyes. My father was the lead guitarist of a pretty big rock band. Pretty big was probably a bit of an understatement. They have been wildly successful since the 70s. That's how he met my mother. She was a groupie when she was eighteen. Toured with Furious Storm for one wild summer. When most people find out I'm the son of *the* Jimmy Ray of

Furious Storm their first assumption is that I must be a huge fan of their music. I'm not. Don't get me wrong I love rock 'n roll but Furious Storm is not my favorite band. In fact, if my father ever realized that Blue Vengeance was my go to he'd have a coronary.

I thought about that for a moment. If I dropped that bombshell, I wouldn't have to have any more of these painful lunches. But then I'd probably be charged with murder, and I am way too pretty for prison. I sighed giving up on that dream.

"That's exciting. What's it got to do with me?" I asked.

"I want you there with me." He beamed.

I let out a bit too loud of a laugh. The couple sitting at a nearby table shot me a dirty look. "Why do you want me to be there with you?"

His eyes looked everywhere but at me. "They said it would look good to have family there."

I cocked my head looking at him. "So, you only want one of your children there to represent your family?"

"No, your cousin will be there too."

This man was unbelievable. I shook my head disgusted for even being related to him. Then an idea struck. If he wanted me there, there were going to be conditions.

I smirked. "All right, I will go."

He sat up straight and clapped his hands. "Fantastic."

Raising my hand, I stopped him. "You want me to come. You invite Miranda and Alice too."

I watched as my sperm donor father blinked at me. He looked like an owl that I'd seen at the zoo when I took Alice. Watching my father squirm was one of my favorite hobbies when I was forced to be around him. Mr. Rock star could play in front of thousands of people but when it comes to having a normal interaction with his children, he looked like he'd rather go through Chinese water torture.

"Uhm...I don't think she would come."

"No Miranda. No me," I said with a smirk.

Before he could answer, the waitress delivered our food. I dug into my burger while my father pushed his salad around on his plate. He was formulating a plan. I could see the wheels turning. He was trying to figure out how he could get what he wanted without bending to my demands. It was fun watching him try but then give up.

"What happens if I ask and she says no?" He grinned.

"I'll go then, but you need to call her in front of me before we leave today. I don't trust that you won't say something douchey just to get out of having her come."

He bit his lip then said, "Fine. I will call right now."

"Go ahead."

He retrieved his phone from his pocket. I watched as he scrolled through his extensive contact list. When he finally landed on her name, he pushed the call button. The ringing of the phone was loud enough for anyone to hear. Thanks to those years playing next to an amp his hearing sucked.

"What do you want? Did you make Chord cry? If you did anything I will find you and kill you," Miranda screeched into the phone.

Our father glared at me. "Hello, pumpkin. How are you?"

For fuck's sake. Miranda was going to reach through the phone and strangle him.

"Are you dying?" she asked after a long pause.

"Why do you and your brother keep asking that?"

"Wishful thinking," Miranda and I said at the same time.

Through gritted teeth, he said, "I'm being inducted into the Rock & Roll Hall of Fame. I'd like for you, Chord, and Alice to be there."

Silence stretched over the phone. It ended up being so long, he looked at the phone, checking to make sure he hadn't lost the call. "Well?"

"I'm thinking."

"Well, I'm going to need to know soon. It's on Saturday. I

will understand if you can't come due to it being short notice," he rushed out.

I held back a laugh. I knew exactly what he was trying to do. Only he didn't know my sister like I did. She was too smart to fall for that. She was about to call him out and do exactly what he didn't want her to do.

"We will be there," she said then hung up.

A dazed look painted the great Jimmy Ray's face. "They are coming."

I smiled broadly at him. "Guess you will have all your family there."

Looking down at my phone, it told me I'd better get a move on it to make it back in time. I wiped off my mouth then threw down my napkin.

"Thanks for lunch. It was a real blast. Gotta get back to work before the toddlers glue Mary to her chair." I stood and turned to walk away but stopped and said, "See you Saturday, Dad."

With pep in my step, I left the café just in time for the few people who recognized my father to rush him for an autograph. I may have won but Saturday was going to suck no matter what happened.

I walked into the dark restaurant at close to 6:30. Looking around I didn't see my mother right away. There was a haze that hung in the air giving it a gloomy feel. Vaping was allowed in this restaurant because it was the trendy thing to do. When I didn't see my mother after a few more minutes I walked up to the hostess stand. The ultra-skinny woman looked at me.

"That bitch needs to eat a cheeseburger," Queen B said.

I shook my head then asked. "Has Aurora Cinderella arrived?"

The woman gave me a bothered look. She looked down at the tablet in her hand then said, "What was the name?"

I sighed. "Aurora Cinderella." My mother insisted on using aliases at all times.

She checked her list again but before she could say anything I heard something that made me cringe. "Little Beaver! Little Beaver! Over here, sweetie."

My shoulders slumped at the screeching of a nickname that made me want to crawl into a hole and die. I looked over at the woman wearing a T-shirt, leather pants, and a boa. On top of her head, she wore large sunglasses holding back her mane of wild curls. Subtlety was not my mother's forte.

"That's her. Thanks."

Navigating between tables, I found my way to my mother who had worked herself up so much she was bouncing on her toes as I approached. I glared at her but she either ignored it or didn't see it through the haze.

"Mom! Sit down," I whisper-yelled.

"I'm so happy to see you, little beaver."

"Good God! Will you quit it with that nickname? It was never cute or funny."

She waved her hand signaling for another drink. "Oh stop. It is adorable. You had the cutest buck teeth when you were little. Thank goodness your grandmother got those fixed for you." She made a face imitating a beaver.

I sighed. "Why am I here, Mom?"

"Don't you want a drink?" She noticed my lack of alcoholic beverage.

"I have to work in the morning. I will stick with water," I said smoothly.

"Live a little, Rhapsody. I can't believe I have such a boring daughter. Your cousin Cassie is so much fun."

I rolled my eyes. "Then why didn't you ask her for dinner instead of me?"

She squinted her eyes at me. "Because you're my daughter, and I need something specific from you."

"Of course you do. What is it now?"

The waitress approached and asked for our order. My mother ordered a steak and potato. I stuck with a salad with dressing on the side. My stomach wasn't doing well with the mixture of smells, and it seemed like a safer bet to have a salad.

"Watching your weight?" she asked.

"Sure. So, what was it you need from me?"

My mother leaned forward. "Blue Vengeance is getting inducted into the Rock & Roll Hall of Fame."

I took a sip of my water. I'd already heard about them getting the nod this year. It was a hell of an accomplishment for them. It always surprised me they were able to stay together for over twenty-five years, but my mother couldn't put forth the effort to care when I was growing up.

"Congratulations, Mom," I said flatly.

"You need to be there."

When she said that I was drinking my water and managed to inhale some. The water had nowhere to go but out of my nose. It burned, making my eyes water. I grabbed a napkin to wipe my face. My mother cackled at me.

She wiped a tear from her eye then said, "You're always a good time, Rhapsody. So, you're going."

It wasn't a question. "Why the hell do you want me there?"

"You're my daughter. How would it look if my only daughter wasn't there?"

"It would look like we don't have a relationship." I crossed my arms.

"We have a relationship," she snapped.

"Oh really? Where do I work then?"

My mother blinked at me. "How would I know that? That doesn't mean anything."

"Yeah, well it means something to me. I am not going. Why don't you just pretend Cassie is your daughter? I know you've done that before."

I stood from the table. My emotions started to take over my body. I felt out of control. I needed to go home to a pint of B & J and some trashy TV. Throwing my napkin back on the table, I walked away from my stunned mother. A weight lifted from my shoulders as I exited the restaurant and hailed a cab.

———

A soft knock on my door had me pausing a spoon to my lips. My grandmother eased the door open. She shuffled in and sat on the edge of my bed.

"Are you okay, sweetie?" She patted my knee.

All I wanted to do at that moment was crawl in her lap and tell her everything. Tell her about how horrible my mother, her daughter, was to me. Tell her how she was going to be a great grandmother. Tell her how I didn't even really know the baby's daddy. Instead, I shoved the spoonful of ice cream in my mouth to stop those things from spilling out.

"Your mother called," she said, taking the remote and shutting off the TV.

I sighed. "I'm not going, Grams."

"Why not?"

I snorted. "There are too many reasons to count."

"Don't sass me, Rhapsody," she snapped.

"Fine. Why should I be there for her when she hasn't been there for us?"

My grandmother nodded. "You're right. My daughter has not been the mother I would have liked her to be to you. But that doesn't mean you act like her. You are better than that." Grams sighed. "Her entire life has been to make it as a star. Now, she is getting recognized for it. I want you to be there for her. She wouldn't say this, but I think it would break her heart if you weren't."

I pinched my hand to keep from rolling my eyes. "Grams, she didn't even invite you. Her own mother. Aren't you hurt at all about this?"

A sad smile crossed her face. "Your mom and I have our own issues. It's okay if she only wants her daughter there. I'm actually quite proud that she wants you there."

"I'm just a trophy for her to show off."

She reached up and pushed a stray hair behind my ear. "Then be the shiniest trophy you can be."

I smiled and felt my unruly emotions roaring back. "All right, Grams. I will go."

She stood and leaned over, placing a kiss on my forehead. "That's my girl."

My grandmother shuffled out of my room, shutting the door quietly behind her. With a sigh, I put my pint of ice cream on my nightstand and grabbed my phone.

Me: I'll go.

Mom: Thanks, little beaver! This is going to be a blast!

I seriously doubted that statement.

12

CHORD

"I can't believe you conned the old man into bringing us," Miranda said, straightening her dress.

"If he can blackmail us all the time, why can't I flip the script on him?"

Miranda shot me a look. "I hate when you try to use hip language. You are not hip."

Alice looked between us. She wore a pretty pink dress with shiny white shoes. Her curly hair was bouncing in a halo around her head. Ever since she put on the dress, she'd had a permanent smile on her face. She was going to dazzle everyone with her cuteness. I looked back to Miranda, wearing a slinky black dress with faint designs that you could only see in a certain light. Her hair was swept up in an artful updo.

"You can't tell me you two don't love that you are dressed up right now and getting to see some big-time rock stars," I said.

Miranda glared at me, but Alice chose that moment to put her two-sense in. "I'm so excited. Will Grandpa be playing?"

"I think so."

The limo slowed outside a tall upscale apartment building. I watched the limo driver jump out of the car and run around to the door. I looked at Miranda whose leg was bouncing nervously. As much of a tough front she put up our father could still make her nervous. I hated that he did that to her.

"It'll be cool," I whispered.

She glared then pointed to me. "You're not hip." With an eye roll, she nodded to me.

The comment had the desired effect and took her mind off the man entering the limo. He had to duck his head to keep from hitting the spikes of his trademark mohawk on the roof. Dressed in a T-shirt, with a leather jacket over it, leather pants, leather spiked cuffs, and boots, our father was *the* Jimmy Ray at that moment.

"Hello, kids," he said, reaching over to the limo's mini bar.

"Not in front of Alice," Miranda quipped.

Our father snapped his eyes to her. It looked like sadness crossed his features. He didn't seem to recognize her. He put his hands up and slid back in the seat. The limo lurched forward. Silence weighed heavily in the air. Alice coughed, and my father finally noticed the little pink cuteness that was seated between me and my sister.

I watched as Miranda tensed. Alice smiled at him. For the first time in my life, I saw my father's face soften as he took in Alice. He smiled back at her. I knew that little girl would be the one to charm him.

"Your hair is pointy," she said.

My dad smiled and rubbed one of the spikes. "Yep."

"Can I feel?" Alice leaned forward, stretching out her hand.

"Alice!" Miranda pushed her back into her seat. "It's not nice to ask that."

I looked at my sister. She was shaking. "She can feel one if she wants," our father said but then revised it. "That is if you will allow her to do so."

My sister and father stared at one another. A silent conversation with no one but them was going on in front of Alice and me. Miranda gave a weak nod.

Jimmy Ray leaned forward. Alice took her small hand and touched one of the spikes. "Ew. That's weird." She wrinkled her nose.

Her grandfather let out a light laugh. It was a laugh that *the* Jimmy Ray would have never been caught dead doing.

In another unprecedented move, Alice unbuckled her seatbelt and moved to sit next to my father.

"Alice don—" Miranda started.

"I'm going to sit next to Grandpa, Mommy." Alice smiled up at my father after buckling her seatbelt. "Don't you need to buckle your seatbelt too?"

My father quickly buckled his seatbelt then turned to Alice. "All better?"

Alice nodded and took my father's hand in hers. "Your hand feels funny." She must have felt the callouses on his hands from the years of playing guitar.

"I know. It is because I play guitar. They make it easier to play."

She nodded as if she understood everything he just said then she lit up. "Do you play music like Terry the T-Rex?"

He furrowed his brow. "I don't know who that is."

"He's a singing and dancing cowboy dinosaur. He plays the guitar too. Mama says he plays better than you," Alice said offhandedly.

A snort escaped me when I saw how red Miranda was becoming.

"Oh, does she now." He looked at Miranda.

"Yeah, but I don't think he's playing tonight so I guess you are going to have to do." Alice sighed.

This time it wasn't a snort that came out. Instead, I bent over laughing so hard tears were sliding down my face. Alice watched me laughing at the joke she didn't understand.

Alice turned to my father and asked, "Can I tell you a secret?"

"Sure." He leaned in as if conspiring with her.

She giggled then said, "I heard Uncle Chord tell Mommy that he was only really coming to see his favorite band."

My father looked at me with an "I knew it" look. "Did Uncle Chord say who his favorite band is?"

"Yep. He has a picture of them on his wall."

"Does he now?" My father glared at me.

"Yep, he loves Blue Vengeance."

My blood froze. In that moment, you could only hear the clinking of the liquor glasses clanking against one another. Fury cast dark shadows over his face. A muscle ticked in his jaw.

"Blue Vengeance," he growled at me. "You fucking traitor."

"Oooo…you said a bad word. Mommy is going to have to wash your mouth out. Don't worry, I will hold your hand when she does it." She tapped his hand.

Right when my father would have screamed at me for loving the one band that was never to be uttered in his presence the limo door opened to flashing cameras. We'd arrived at the ceremony. My father glared at me, put on a pair of sunglasses then exited the limo.

He leaned close so only I could hear. "We will talk about your decision to betray the family."

I pursed my lips. Good thing he didn't know that under my tux I wore a Blue Vengeance T-shirt. Watching him walk through the throng of photographers, I exited the limo with Miranda and Alice right behind me.

Miranda was laughing. "That was great. I love when she weaponizes her cuteness."

"Shut up!"

That sent Miranda off into another laughing fit. "Oh my God! This really has turned out to be a great night."

"I'm so glad I can entertain you," I grumbled.

She smacked my shoulder then took Alice's hand as we began walking to the entrance for family. "You really are good for that, Chord."

Sisters really were the work of the devil.

13

RHAPSODY

I sat at the table with my cousin and my mother's band. All of them were dressed in exactly what you would think someone in a band would wear. Leather, lace, and too tight clothes were everywhere. My mother was no exception. She wore a skimpy halter top with clear visibility of wearing no bra, a leather mini skirt, fishnet stockings, and sky-high heels. I was actually embarrassed for her. She was in her fifties dressing like someone in their teens. Compared to my mother, I was dressed extremely conservative. That meant I wore a bra under my strapless dress.

"You look nice, cuz." Cassie leaned toward me.

I smiled at her. "Thanks, Cass."

"You could have dressed more appropriately," my mother said while glaring at me.

I chose to ignore her comment.

"Leave her alone, Em. Rhapsody looks gorgeous." Dan Waters, my mom's lead guitarist and lifelong best friend, winked at me.

"She is definitely a delicious little nugget." Q, her skeevy drummer, looked at me a bit too closely. It made me feel gross.

"God! You're such a perve, Q. Leave her alone." Imogen

Good, Mom's bassist and my godmother, leaned toward me. "You are a vision, Rhapsody. I'm so proud of the woman you've become."

"Wonder if she'd say that knowing you were knocked up." Queen B popped up.

I really hated that bitch.

"Thanks, Imogen."

"Shh…" Mom shushed me as they talked about another rock band. I watched as my mom sat forward in her chair. A giant screen showed pictures of a band that wasn't hers. In fact, it was the one band she'd had a feud with for years, Furious Storm.

"Now, for the first of our two iconic bands being inducted tonight, Furious Storm!" the emcee said into the microphone.

I began to stand and clap when my mother grabbed my arm, yanking me back into my seat. "Ow." I pulled my arm out of her grasp.

"How dare you stand and clap for that no talent group of clowns? You're Emmerson Lee's daughter. You should know we don't acknowledge them. Especially, Jimmy Ray." She sneered.

"I was being polite, Mother," I barked.

"I never want to see you clapping for him again." She grimaced and sat back in her seat.

Looking around the table, I blushed. The rest of the band were clapping politely and giving me a sad look. Furious Storm took the stage with a flourish. Their table was standing and clapping. I saw a little girl with bouncing curls standing on a chair being supported by a beautiful woman. The little girl made me smile. She was clapping and hooting for a group there was no way she'd know. I covered my stomach with my hands wondering if I would have a little girl like that or maybe a little boy with Chord's dimple.

"Why do you have a sour face? Cheer up. Those blowhards are almost done. Then it's time for the real stars to shine." She adjusted her boa and sunglasses.

To my mother's dismay, they paused for an intermission

before announcing her band. I escaped the table and found my way to the bathroom. My stomach was beginning to twist again. I managed to keep it together as I entered the bathroom. Rushing to the stall and making it just in time to dry heave. When my stomach stopped feeling like it needed to jump out of my body, I leaned against the wall. With a few deep breaths, I exited the stall and approached the sinks. My reflection told my story. Makeup covered my pale face with dark circles. Thanks to the dry heaving I had to touch up my makeup.

Pregnancy was a real bitch.

"Excuse me are you Emmerson Lee's daughter?" a woman in a Blue Vengeance T-shirt asked.

I finished washing my hands then said, "Yes. I am."

"Oh my God! Your mom is everything! She is so deserving of this honor. It's a shame that Furious Storm got inducted with her. They aren't even half as good."

I just nodded and reached for one of the hand dryers. The whir of the dryer drowned out the nattering of the girl. Thanks to the dryer I didn't notice another girl with short blue hair and wearing a Furious Storm shirt enter the bathroom. I turned toward the door and found it blocked by the two women.

"Furious Storm can suck it!" Mom's fan spat.

"Well, Blue Vengeance is just a glorified pop band and Emmerson Lee is a wannabe rock star. Every time I see her, I think "try much"." Her high voice cut off when the other girl grabbed her blue hair.

I shimmied past the brawling women in the restroom. Leaving the restroom, I noticed my mother talking with some fans. With a sigh, I went to stand near the doors and hoped I could become invisible. I wasn't ready to deal with going back in quite yet. Other people gathered around in groups, chatting and waiting for the lights to blink. Watching them helped to distract me from my thoughts.

"Where did you go?" My mother's voice hissed next to me, and she grabbed my arm again.

"I had to pee. Geez. Let me go." I snatched my arm from her grip and stepped away from the door.

"Let's go, Rhapsody."

This was the mother I knew. A fifty plus year old spoiled brat. Before I could say anything, a deep voice drew our attention.

"Hello, Em." Jimmy Ray's voice was like melted butter.

"Jimmy," my mother hissed.

His eyes drifted to me and took me in from head to toe. "This your daughter?"

She grabbed my arm, pulling me to her again. I bit the inside of my cheek to keep from snatching my arm away.

"Yes. Isn't she gorgeous?"

That must have killed her to say.

He gave me a leer and said, "Yes, she looks delectable." He ran his tongue over his teeth.

My stomach heaved but I couldn't move because my mother dug her nails into my arm to keep me pinned to her.

"You stay away from—" she spat but was cut off.

"Dad! What are you—" A familiar deep voice caressed me. "Rhapsody?"

"Chord?" I said when I saw him step next to Jimmy Ray.

"How do you know my son?" he asked.

Chord and I looked at each other and blushed.

"Em, we need to get back to our seats." Cassie appeared next to us.

"Jimmy, we need to finish this." Another familiar looking guy stood next to Jimmy Ray. He looked at me then recognition lit his features. "Holy shit! That's the vomiter!"

Chord looked from me to the guy. He looked like he was about to ask a question when the cute little girl I saw earlier walked up and was holding a woman's hand. She linked hands with Chord and pulled.

"Let's go," the little girl said.

I couldn't take any more. Sickness came over me in a wave. I managed to pull far enough away from my mother to find the fern next to the door and proceeded to empty the contents of my stomach.

Between heaves, I heard the obnoxious asshat say, "Thar she blows."

14

CHORD

Rhapsody was Emmerson Lee's daughter. Son of a bitch. The one woman in the whole world I shouldn't be attracted to made my dick hard in a matter of seconds. My ass of a cousin just stood there pointing and laughing as she got sick. I dropped Alice's hand and went to Rhapsody, but I was cut off by another woman who had a furious look on her face.

"I think you need to go," she spat.

"Come on, cuz. We need to be seen back at our seats." Alec pulled me away.

I watched as Rhapsody crumpled to the floor and the angry woman knelt next to her, handing her a tissue.

"Come on, Uncle Chord." Alice took my hand, making me smile.

"Okay. Let's go."

Over Alice's head, Miranda caught my eye. "How do you know Emmerson Lee's daughter?"

"Long story," I answered.

She nodded and sat Alice close to Alec, which allowed her to sit next to me. I looked around trying to find my father. I didn't see him, so I took a deep breath. Miranda did a quick look too and leaned toward me.

"He's at the bar. Looks like Emmerson Lee really does have a hell of an effect on him."

I glanced toward the bar and saw him pounding a shot. Shaking my head, I said, "Well, there goes your no liquor rule."

"If he stays away long enough for me to get this story out of you, I don't really care."

I let out a laugh as the lights flashed. "All right."

In a quick hushed tone, I told my sister about the wedding two months ago. The horrible table we were at and saving her from the creepy guy. Miranda smiled when I got to the dancing part. I tried to skate over the bedroom part, but she said she needed to know everything. I just think she's nosy as shit. She let out a snort-laugh when I let it slip about everything being a bit too quick.

"Oh my God! My brother is a one pump chump." The guests at the table next to us turned to us with horror on their faces.

Fantastic. "Keep it down, Miranda."

She waved off my embarrassment. "Continue, chumpy."

I rolled my eyes and finished with leaving the note and never hearing from her again. It was just in time to hear them start talking about Blue Vengeance. Instead of watching the screen I looked over at the Blue Vengeance table. It took me a few covert glances to finally land eyes on Rhapsody. She looked just as beautiful as I remembered. Perhaps a bit green around the edges but the poor girl just puked in a fake plant.

I was so lost in thought I didn't know my father was back until the slap on the back of my head. "Ow. Why'd you do that?"

"You will not associate with that girl, Chord."

A laugh escaped me. "Are you fucking kidding me, Jimmy?"

"No. I mean it. That girl is trouble. We don't associate with them, and they don't associate with us. Period. End of story."

It felt like my jaw had dropped to the floor. How did he think he was going to stop me from seeing Rhapsody?

"You're funny. I'm a grown man. I can do whatever I want."

A cold look frosted his eyes as the audience stood and clapped for Blue Vengeance. He leaned toward me, speaking so only I could hear. "Who do you think pays for your grandfather's medical bills? That house that your sister, niece, and grandfather live in is mine." He snapped his fingers. "Just like that, they could be on the street."

Fear coursed through my veins. "You'd put your own father, daughter, and granddaughter on the street."

The son of a bitch threw back another drink while meeting my gaze. "I'd do it without a moment's pause. So, Chord, just try me by seeing that girl again. I hold all the chips. You can't support them being a fucking librarian." He sat back crossing his arms. "Now, watch your favorite band get inducted into the Rock & Roll Hall of Fame."

Everything sounded like it was in a tunnel. I watched as Emmerson Lee spoke into the microphone and waved her arms. My eyes drifted back to the Blue Vengeance table and clashed with Rhapsody's eyes. She looked like I felt.

Seeing Rhapsody was a mix of surprise, excitement, sadness, and confusion. There were so many questions that needed to be answered. We just couldn't answer them here. I needed to talk to her and if that ended with me between her thighs, all the better. My gaze traveled back up to the stage to watch Blue Vengeance play one of their biggest hits. While the music played, I began to formulate a plan. By the time the song ended, I knew exactly what I was going to do and who I needed help from.

———

"Come on, Alec," I begged.

"Fuck no. I am not crossing your dad. He would have kittens if he knew you were trying to see Emmerson Lee's daughter."

I followed Alec around our apartment. "He doesn't even need to know."

"He has ways of finding out, Chord." Alec shook his head.

"For fuck's sake, Alec, just give him something so he can stop obsessing about this. He's fucking with my game," Benny said from the couch, wearing a gaming headset.

Alec walked back to the kitchen and paced. I bit my lip. It was a good sign that he stopped saying no. He was just not saying anything. When he pulled out a piece of paper and wrote something on it, I knew I'd broken him.

"Here. You didn't get this from me and if your father ever asks I will deny everything."

With a whoop, I hugged my cousin who then promptly punched me in my stomach, which caused me to double over. The fucker had a wicked jab. I should've known better than to hug him, but I was so happy I'd won, I'd forgotten about it.

"Thanks, Alec," I wheezed out.

After a few minutes, I was able to compose myself. Leaning against the kitchen island, I unfolded the note.

Anderson Accounting

Good luck, fucker.

You're gonna need it.

My nervous butterflies went into overdrive. I rushed over to the door and grabbed my keys. The door opened, almost hitting me in the face. I ran past Oscar and out to the elevator. Without having to wait, the elevator door opened, and I entered the confined space. My leg bounced as I watched the numbers move lower. Finally, the doors opened, and I squeezed past them and ran into the lobby.

"Mr. Reedy!" Wesley, the daytime security guard, yelled as I ran past.

I slid to a stop. "Yeah?" It came out breathlessly.

Wesley looked uncomfortable. "Uh, sir, I'm not sure you

want to leave the building like that." Motioning with his hand to my body.

I looked at the mirrors mounted over the desk. In only a pair of boxers and high socks, I stood in the lobby. I felt my face flame as I quickly put my hand over the opening of my boxers. Of course I had to be wearing a pair of novelty boxers too.

Shuffling back to the elevator, I said over my shoulder, "Thanks for looking out, Wes."

He nodded with a grin that was barely holding back a laugh. As the elevator doors opened, an elderly woman stood next to me.

She glanced over at me and looked surprised. "You know you're almost naked?"

I nodded with a smile. The elevator saved me from more conversation when it opened. I walked onto the elevator hoping she'd feel too uncomfortable to ride with me. She only grinned and stood only a hair's breath away from me.

When she pushed the button for the floor below me, I sighed. She continued to smirk. I watched as she looked at my boxers. On the butt it read Cock-a-doodle Doo. Where my hands covered was a cartoon rooster with an eyebrow raised.

The elevator chimed to let her off on her floor. As she walked past me, I felt a pinch on my butt. I jumped then faintly heard, "Mmm...nice. Bakery fresh."

I felt my eyes bulge while my face blushed again when she gave me a wink and a small finger wave. I bit my tongue and waited for the elevator to give me privacy again. When the door opened on my floor, I ran down the hall and threw open the door.

"Finally realized you were pretty much naked?" Alec said, reading the paper.

"Wes stopped me."

"You're an idiot." He took a sip of his coffee then looked at me. "When are you going to figure out it's Sunday and nothing but churches are open."

Fuck me.

With that being pointed out, I realized I didn't need to cover my junk anymore. Stan was out of commission at least for the day.

While walking back to my room, I mumbled, "Sorry, buddy."

Before entering my room, I heard Alec yell, "Stop talking to your cock, you weird fucker."

15

———————

RHAPSODY

Monday morning came with a vengeance. The horrible scene at the induction would be something that would stay with me forever. Who would have thought Chord was Jimmy Ray's son? After the ceremony, my mother refused to talk to me the rest of the evening. The band left for an after party while I went to the bathroom, leaving me to get an Uber home. I made sure I wasn't seen by anyone. Anyone being Chord and the beautiful woman he was with. Did he have a family already? Was I really only a one-night stand? How could I tell him that he had another kid on the way?

I dropped my head to my desk.

"You are so fucked," Queen B said.

"Shut up." My voice was muffled from the desk.

"I haven't even said anything yet," Daniel said, dropping a large coffee on my desk.

"You are a God," I said taking a sip then grimacing. "What the hell is this?"

"It's decaf. You're pregnant remember." He sat across from me with his caffeinated goodness.

"I hate you." I pouted.

He slurped his coffee and sat back in the chair. "You gonna tell me what happened on Saturday?"

I groaned. "No."

"Come on, it will make you feel better." He prodded.

"Fine. I saw the baby daddy on Saturday."

Daniel started coughing then grabbed a tissue to wipe his mouth. "What? How? Are you sure?"

"First question: yes. Second question: his father was getting inducted too. Third question: very sure." I ticked off each answer on my fingers.

"Holy shit! Well, at least you can tell him now. You won't have to carry this around by yourself anymore."

"Wrong." I took a sip of the nasty coffee. My face was going to have a permanent grimace thanks to that crap.

"What do you mean wrong? Tell him." Daniel hit my desk.

"Hey! No banging on the desk," I shouted.

A devilish grin crossed his face. "And that is exactly why we didn't work out."

"You're horrible. I'm going to tell Izzy."

He stuck out his tongue. We both started laughing. It helped lift the weight that seemed to be permanently sitting on my shoulders since I took those three tests.

"Seriously, why won't you tell him?" He stared at me.

I let out a sigh. "He's Jimmy Ray's son."

Daniel stared at me blankly. "Is that supposed to mean something to me?"

"Come on. You're one of my best friends and you don't know who Jimmy Ray is."

He shook his head. "Enlighten me."

"He is the lead guitarist for Furious Storm."

"Oh." Things were finally connecting for him. "He's in your mom's band."

Or maybe not.

"Damn he's hot but sure as shit doesn't know a thing about you," Queen B piped in.

"Wow! You really know nothing about me."

Daniel threw his hands in the air. "Rhapsody, you never wanted to talk about your family. All I ever knew was you lived with your grandmother and your mom was a singer."

"Fair enough. My mother is the lead singer for Blue Vengeance. There is a very well-known feud between Furious Storm and Blue Vengeance. Me hooking up with the son of Jimmy Ray, who my mom has a very particular hatred toward, would kill her."

"Is it really that dramatic?"

I opened my mouth to respond but my phone rang first. I held up a finger.

"Rhapsody Bell," I said into the phone.

"Ms. Bell, you have a delivery. Can I send it up to you?" the building security guard asked.

"Sure thing." I wasn't expecting a delivery but maybe it would be a good surprise today.

I hung up the phone and stared at Daniel, who was clearly enjoying his coffee. With a glare, I said, "I really do hate you."

"Yeah, yeah. So, you can't tell him because of some stupid feud between your parents? That sounds ridiculous."

I shrugged. "It is what it is, Daniel. Looks like I will be going this alone."

He shook his head. "I think you're making a big mistake. But it is yours to make." He stood and I stood with him. "I'm here for you no matter what, Rhapsody."

Walking over I hugged him. He was always great with hugs. "Thanks, Daniel." I paused then said, "For the talk not the coffee. That shit sucks."

He laughed and put one arm around me. Then his attention snagged at something in my doorway. "Shit!"

I looked and saw an enormous bouquet of flowers filling up the doorway. As the bouquet lowered, someone dressed like Harry Potter smiled at me. I just blinked and felt the world spin.

The Harry Potter delivery boy's smile fell as he saw Daniel's arm around me.

"Chord?" I asked.

"What the hell is going on here?" he snapped.

Queen B munched on popcorn and said, *"Well, this should be good."*

Fuck my life.

16

CHORD

I've always had piss poor timing. First, when I was five, I woke up and found my grandfather posing as Santa on Christmas Eve. Then when I was ten, I ruined my own surprise party by being too early. When I was fifteen, I walked into our living room and found my sister losing her virginity. That one still gave me nightmares. More than once in college, I walked in on different roommates having sex with different girlfriends. Now, I walk in on Rhapsody having a too cozy moment with a man that could probably kick my ass. Like I said, piss poor timing.

"I'm gonna go, Rhapsody. Let me know if you need anything." Tough guy scooted around me and the flowers then said, "Love your books, man."

He left, leaving me to stare at a very surprised Rhapsody. "Surprised?" I said.

"Yes." She had a pinched expression on her face. "That's only one of many things going through my head right now. What are you doing here?"

"These are for you." I shoved the giant bouquet at her.

She hesitated but then took them. Placing them on a table in the corner she turned back toward me. Rhapsody sighed. "What are you doing here, Chord?"

I bit my lip. "I needed to see you."

"Uh…okay."

I attempted to shove my hands in my pockets to hide their shaking. Unfortunately, the damn Harry Potter robe didn't have any and I found myself trying and failing twice to put my hands in pockets that were AWOL.

"It was good to see you Saturday." My voice sounded like I was a twelve-year-old wizard.

"Which part? The part where we found out who our parents were? Or was it the part where I puked in the fake fichus?" She crossed her arms.

"How about the part where I saw you?" I said weakly.

She sighed. "Okay. Thank you for the flowers, Chord. But it's not a good idea for you to be here."

"Why? Will your boyfriend be upset?" I didn't mean to get snippy but this surprise was starting to suck and that really pissed me off.

"Boyfriend?"

"Yeah. The monster that just left." I crossed my arms.

She let out a laugh. "Daniel is not my boyfriend."

"Well, he sure looked like it to me." I couldn't help the petulance that laced my tone. I sounded like a child.

"Well, he isn't. In fact, though it's none of your business, he is married with a cute little girl who I'm godmother to."

"Oh."

"Yeah. You should go. Go back to the beautiful woman and your baby that you were with on Saturday."

What the hell was she talking about? "Who?"

"You know who, Chord. I will not be a homewrecker." She crossed her arms managing to push her breasts up.

I couldn't help it, but I totally checked out her rack. It was a wonderful rack. I shook my head to focus on the subject at hand. "Are you talking about my sister and niece?"

A pretty blush rose up her neck then to her cheeks. "Your sister and niece?"

"Yep."

"Fuck me," she mumbled.

Taking two steps, I placed myself in her personal space and said, "I'd love to."

Her tongue slid out and wet her lips. My eyes lasered on that one movement. Stan was getting embarrassingly hard. The khakis I wore under the robe did nothing to hide it.

"Why do you want to see me, Chord? Why reach out now? It's been over two months since Jane and Rufus's wedding," she whispered.

"I could ask you the same thing. Why didn't you call me?" I stared at her. Her pouty lips were beckoning me.

"Call you? How?"

"The note I left that morning had all my contact information and pretty much begged you to call me. I had to leave early that morning because I was competing in a charity mud run."

Rhapsody became pale. "I never got a note. Where did you put it?"

"I left it on my pillow."

"Son of a bitch." She cursed, and it was the cutest damn thing I'd ever heard. "When I woke up that morning all the pillows were on the floor. I must have knocked them off and apparently the note you left me. Sorry." Embarrassment had her avoiding my gaze.

Using one finger I tilted her head up. "It's fine. Now, I get to ask you out in person."

A smile came and went so quickly if I had blinked I'd have missed it. "We can't do this, Chord."

"Yes, we can. We've already done it."

"You know why we can't. Our families and that stupid feud."

Lifting one hand, I caressed her cheek. She leaned into my touch as I stroked her soft skin. This woman was going to be my undoing. My hand slid to the back of her neck, pulling her close.

When our lips met again, the same visceral reaction shot through my body. Rhapsody was going to unman me with just a kiss. It didn't help that she also had one of the sexiest moans I'd ever heard.

When I broke the kiss all too soon, I said, "Just one date, Rhapsody. They don't need to know anything right now. It can just be you and me."

Her kiss haze cleared with her chewing on her plump bottom lip. I watched as she debated with herself. She was having one hell of an internal argument. The moment she decided to throw caution to the wind I smiled.

"Okay, Chord. One date. There is something we need to talk about."

I smiled. "Fantastic. I will pick you up tomorrow night after work."

She nodded then leaned in and kissed me softly. I allowed my hands to hold her waist, pulling her closer to feel my hard-on. A squeak escaped her, and her eyes flew open. I grinned at her.

"All right. I gotta go, Rhapsody." I reached out and hooked an errant piece of hair behind her ear. "See you tomorrow, love."

She smiled. "Okay, Chord."

Relief and excitement filled my body as I walked away from her. I had a date with a woman I thought would always be the one that got away. Now, I just have to convince her that we'd be better off together rather than apart.

"Chord."

I stopped and turned before leaving the office. "Yes?"

"What in the hell are you wearing?"

"It's Harry Potter day," I said then left her office.

Faintly, I heard, "Of course it is."

I bit back a laugh and strode away from her office.

17

RHAPSODY

Pacing was all my nerves would allow me to do. The past two days were hellish at work. Mr. Boswaker was in such a mood that we avoided him at all costs. I hid in my office with only the occasional visit from Daniel. My mind had been spinning ever since my visit from Chord. When he walked into my office, I didn't even realize it was him. He was dressed ridiculously. I thought it was some new themed flower delivery service. But his reaction to Daniel hugging me told me exactly who he was.

I shook my head as I stood outside of Anderson Accounting's building. In the past half an hour I had gone between running home and diving head first into a pint of ice cream or biting the bullet and telling Chord the moment he picked me up that I've got his bun in my oven.

"What are you doing, Ms. Bell?" A voice broke into my thoughts.

"Oh, uh hello, Mr. Anderson," I stuttered out.

"Are you waiting for someone? I sure hope you aren't still on the clock." He looked down at his watch.

I smiled. "Yes. I am waiting for my date to pick me up. I am most assuredly not on the clock."

He smiled then said, "I am going to have Sandra set up a meeting with you. Do you think you'd be available early next week? I apologize it isn't sooner, but I have to be out of town until then."

"That should work."

"Good." He said softly to me, "I didn't want you to think I'd forgotten about our discussion. I've got big plans." His gaze caught on something and he smiled. "I think your date is here."

I spun around. Chord stood at the doors of the building wearing dark pants and a light blue shirt with a matching tie. He made Queen B stand up and pay attention.

"Look at that scrumptious piece of manmeat. Yummy!" Queen B purred.

"I believe you are right, sir."

With a smirk, he patted my shoulder and said, "Have fun."

Chord watched as Mr. Anderson walked past him. Smiling, he started to walk toward me. His eyes scanned me from head to toe. I'd brought something to change into. It was a simple black dress that managed to accentuate my best assets while hiding my worst. I paired it with a long jacket and high boots. From the look in his eyes, he liked what he saw. I doubted that he'd like what I would have to say during dinner though.

"Wow!" he breathed out.

"Oh, he likes it all right. Look at that bulge." Queen B started to pant.

Queen B was such a slut. Though I did also take notice of the growing bulge that made him adjust his package more than once. Was it a bad thing that I liked knowing he enjoyed what he saw?

"You don't look so bad either." I snickered.

He handed me a single pale pink rose that he'd been hiding behind his back. "This is for you."

"Thank you." I put the rose to my nose, taking in its aroma. Closing my eyes, I enjoyed the soft scent. When I opened my eyes, Chord was watching me with an unfathomable look.

"Wow," he said again.

Blushing, I said, "What no gigantic flower arrangement this time?"

His lips cocked up on one side. "I didn't want to overdo it. Are you ready?"

With a deep breath, I said, "Yeah."

Chord offered me his arm and I hooked mine with his.

We began to walk away from the building. He didn't give me a clue as to where we were headed so I followed his lead. Quiet surrounded us as we passed people talking in small groups. Chord pulled me to a stop outside of a small door that didn't even look like it was open. I looked at Chord and he smiled. Dear Lord I was going to be murdered tonight.

"Yeah but at least it would be a hot killer." Queen B sighed looking at Chord.

I cleared my throat and asked, "Where are we?"

He winked. "It's a surprise."

I felt my eyes bug out. "Is this where you're planning on murdering me?"

The smile on his face was replaced by a look as if I'd slapped it. "What? We're going to dinner." He waved his hand toward a door next to the closed one.

"Keep your shit together! You're embarrassing me," Queen B huffed.

"Oh. I saw the boarded-up door and got worried," I said quickly.

An amused chuckle escaped him. "I've been accused of a lot of things by women but trying to murder them has not been one of them." He pushed open the door to the hole in the wall restaurant. "Come on."

Nodding, I followed him into the small area that posed as the waiting area. It was a very small restaurant. I counted only six tables. Three of those were occupied by lone customers.

I looked at Chord. "Where have you taken me?"

Chord walked into my personal space then softly said, "Trust me."

My heart did a little flip. These damn horny pregnancy hormones. The reminder of what I needed to tell him was as good as a bucket of ice water. His touch on me still made me hot but it was now under control.

"Okay."

"Chord?" A pretty woman about our age walked toward us.

He smiled then let my hand drop and picked her up in a big hug. The woman squealed.

"Time to cut a bitch." Queen B sharpened a shiv.

The jealousy I felt wasn't something I was used to. Clearly, this woman was a girlfriend. The question was if she was current or past.

"Quinn, let me introduce you to Rhapsody." Chord led the woman over to me.

"Hello."

The woman blinked and looked between us. Then with a raised hand said, "Wait a minute. The Rhapsody? Emmerson Lee's daughter?"

I nodded though the question was posed to Chord.

"The one and only," he said, linking our hands again.

She raised a brow at the gesture. "Miranda did tell me you had a thing with her. Didn't know it was still going on."

"Well, it's just one date. Please keep this to yourself. Our parents would have hedgehogs if they knew we were even seen together," I pleaded then looked to Chord. He had a hurt look on his face.

Quinn waved her hand. "No worries, sweetie. My lips are zipped." She paused a minute, looked at Chord, then stuck out her hand. "Since this little ass isn't going to be polite, I will introduce myself. I'm Quinn Pendergrast. The owner and proprietor of this place."

"Nice to meet you. Rhapsody Bell." I shook her hand.

Chord stood there watching the two of us interact. "Sorry," he mumbled.

Quinn looked at me with a smile. "I've been best friends with his sister since we were five years old. Unfortunately, that means I've known Chord for just as long and if his grandpa knew he wasn't going to introduce me, he'd take a switch to his ass."

Chord nodded in agreement. "I can count on you to keep that our little secret?"

Quinn bit her lip. "Maybe. I will let you know before you leave." She clapped her hands together then said, "Now, let's get you seated and eating the best food you'll ever have in this city."

I followed Quinn to a nearby table. The heat of Chord's hand on my lower back felt like a brand. The walk was too short for me to truly enjoy the small touch though. When we reached the table, Chord moved to hold out the chair for me. I sat while Quinn placed a piece of paper in front of me.

"The way my restaurant works is that we offer a four-course meal. It is one option. There is a different option every day so take a look while I get you some water."

Chord glanced down at the paper for a second then continued to stare at me. "I have never had anything bad from Quinn. Her husband is a highly regarded chef. They don't do any substitutions unless you are allergic to something."

I nodded and read the menu. It was like every food I'd been craving in one meal. My stomach chose that moment to grumble loud enough that the couple two tables over gave me a shocked look. Well, at least it was an "I'm hungry" grumble instead of the "I'm about to puke my guts out" grumble.

"Sorry," I whispered.

Chord winked at me. "No need to be sorry, Rhapsody. I'm surprised it wasn't my stomach that grumbled."

Quinn arrived with their waters and asked, "Everything good for you?"

"Yes!" I said enthusiastically.

"Fantastic. Wine for you two?"

Chord looked at me, waiting for my answer.

I looked at Quinn and said, "No, thank you."

"Okay. Chord, for you?"

"Water is fine with me too."

Quinn nodded. "I will be back with course one."

Chord shook his head but kept his gaze on me. He was making me squirm and not in the panty melting way. Breaking his gaze, I took in the restaurant around us. It looked like a set from a movie. The setting was as if it were a Victorian salon. There was every modern convenience disguised as Victorian décor. It felt warm and inviting. I could understand why this was such a gem.

"Here we go." Quinn placed salads in front of us.

Thankful for the opportunity to focus on anything but the damn sexy looks Chord was giving me, I dug in. I am not normally a salad girl. Shouldn't be too surprising considering the shape that I am in. However, the salad was scrumptious. A tiny moan escaped me, drawing a familiar look from Chord. It must have been one of the looks he gave me during our bedroom Olympics.

"What?" I said after swallowing.

Chord looked from me to the occupied table near us seemingly to confirm they were focused on their own conversation. He leaned in and began, "You make eating a salad sexy as hell. I hate fucking salads." He paused, grimacing. "Sorry. I hate freaking salads but if I could get you to make those noises with just a salad, I'd only take you to places that sold salads."

I felt heat on my cheeks. "I hate fucking salads too." I winked. "This happens to be a particularly good one. If this is any indication of the food here, you may have to wheel me out of here after I fall into a food coma."

Chord laughed. We finished our salads and Quinn was there in a flash taking our plates. It was my turn now to stare at the gorgeous man in front of me. Damn, but I hoped our kid looked like him. I bit my lip wondering when I should tell him. While I was trying to plan how I was going to shatter his world, he reached across the table for my hand and began to stroke the top of it with his thumb.

"Thank you for agreeing to go out with me," he whispered.

I shrugged then made a silly face. "Well, it really was a tough decision." I pretended to be contemplating something. "Go out with a sexy guy I've already seen naked or stay home and eat another pint of ice cream."

"That's a tough decision. I'm glad you chose me." He cocked his head then asked, "What kind of ice cream?"

I huffed out a laugh then grabbed his hand. "Right now, I've been craving death by chocolate, but my go to is usually black raspberry."

"Good to know." He acted like he was memorizing my answer.

"What about yours?"

He shrugged. "I'm not really into sweets. But if I am getting ice cream it is usually vanilla."

I grimaced. "I guess this date is over now." Pretending to stand to leave, I looked at him.

The look on his face caused me to fall into giggles. I plopped back into the chair as the panicked look began to melt away.

"You were joking?" His statement came out more like a question.

"Of course. What person would leave a date because someone said they liked the most boring ice cream in the world? I may be petty sometimes but not that petty." I winked. "Plus, I'm pretty sure you're creative in other ways but that is kind of a blur."

He let out a laugh as Quinn placed the next course in front of us. "You're something else, Rhapsody Bell."

I bowed my head. "Glad you noticed."

The rest of our meal was wonderful. Easily one of the best

dinner dates I'd ever had. Conversation flowed without effort. Thinking back to the wedding reception, our connection was easy then too. It baffled me how things could be so easy with someone you'd had sex with. When our final course came, we shared a large fruit pastry. Thank goodness it was the final course because my moaning was getting out of hand. A loud clang brought my attention from the pastry to Chord who'd dropped his fork.

Leaning close to me he said, "You need to stop that before I scandalize everyone in here and take you on this table."

A girlish giggle came out of my mouth.

"What the hell is that? Is that a new thing you're doing now? If so, stop. We are not one of those girls." Queen B grimaced.

I sucked in my lips to suppress another giggle.

"I like when you giggle. It's cute."

"Eww. Cute? Quick flash him the boobies. He won't think you're cute then. He will want to put his face between them," Queen B offered unhelpfully as usual.

"Glad one of us finds it cute."

Before Chord could answer, Quinn approached the table. "Here is your check. You better tip well, Chord, or I will be spilling the beans about you two." She glared at him then turned to me, giving me a wink he couldn't see.

"Of course, Quinn. I was going to do that anyway."

"Uh-huh. Now, pay so you can take your little love affair somewhere else. Don't need the two of you catching this place on fire with your sexual tension."

"Thanks again, Quinn." Chord dropped money on the check and stood. "Shall we leave this mighty fine establishment?"

Quinn rolled her eyes, taking the cash and check. "It was nice meeting you, Rhapsody."

I stood and linked my arm with Chord's like before. We exited the restaurant and found the streets bustling with activity. Chord walked me back toward my work. As our date was coming to an end, I felt my tension ratcheting higher. I needed to tell him tonight. I would not be a chicken shit about this. If he decides he wants nothing else to do with me, then I would deal with it by becoming the most kick ass single mom. I was prepared for his rejection.

We stopped in front of Anderson Accounting's building. He turned toward me. "I really want to see you again."

I bit my lip. "Okay."

He squeezed my hand. "Does that mean you want to see me too?"

I closed my eyes for a minute steadying myself. "Before I answer that question, there is something I need to tell you."

A grin curved his lips. "I'm listening."

Unlinking our fingers, I took a step away from him. His touch made making coherent sentences difficult. I would not chicken out. I would tell him. Wanting to tell him and having the words to tell him were two different things.

"Rhapsody?" Worry tinged my name on his lips.

"I'm going to be honest. I had an ulterior motive to going out with you tonight." All of a sudden, my mouth was dryer than the Sahara.

He relinked our fingers and gave them a squeeze. "What is it, Rhapsody?"

"Oh, just spit it out already." Queen B had the patience of an errant toddler.

"Fine," I mumbled.

"What?" Chord asked.

"I'm pregnant," I blurted out.

Chord blinked at me. Moments passed by. It began to feel like an eternity when Chord finally shook his head. "That's fine, Rhapsody. I love kids. I still want to see you."

It was my turn to be confused. What the hell kind of reaction was that? I only managed to articulate one word. "Okay."

He nodded then asked, "Is the baby's daddy in your life? Are you seeing him? Is that why you were hesitant to go out with me?"

I couldn't believe the words I was hearing. The dumbass thought I'd gotten knocked up by some other guy. Closing my eyes again, I readied myself to upend Chord's world.

"It's your baby, Chord. I haven't been with anyone since you, and it had been close to two years before you."

"My baby?" Chord squeaked.

I watched as Chord took in the enormity of what I'd just said. He continued to blink at me as if he were waking from a dream. He didn't immediately run away screaming. That was a good sign. What I didn't expect was for his eyes to roll back in his head as he crumpled to the ground. I moved quickly to make sure he wasn't hurt.

He fucking fainted.

Fantastic.

"I told you to tell him not to kill him. You really know how to pick 'em, Rhapsody," Queen B said shaking her head.

18

CHORD

I fucking fainted.

That's right. I dropped like a rock in front of the woman who just told me she was pregnant with my baby. I was going to be a daddy. Holy fuck! Blackness threatened to take me back when I saw Rhapsody's face in front of me. How long had she known about this? If we hadn't seen each other at the induction ceremony, would she have ever told me?

My head began to pound from landing on it when I fainted.

"Chord? Are you okay?" Her soft voice helped to ease the pain a bit.

Rhapsody's face was fuzzy around the edges. I blinked my eyes trying to focus. "My head hurts."

"Miss, do you need help?" a voice asked.

"We're fine," Rhapsody said then looked at me. "We are fine, right?"

I managed a nod but closed my eyes to the sharp pain. I needed to man the fuck up and get off the damn sidewalk. With a groan, I heaved myself into a seated position. The world wavered and darkened at the edges. I was a man dammit. I was not going to pass out again.

"Chord?" Rhapsody's voice sounded funny.

Forcing my eyes open I looked at her. She was looking a little green around the edges. Was she really or was that my possible concussion?

"Fuck." She jumped up and ran over to the side of the building.

People walked around my still seated form. I watched as she vomited in the sketchy alley. I made an effort to stand but my head felt like it was going to explode. Dammit! Stand up, Chord. You will not be a pussy while your baby's mama was puking her guts out next to a dumpster. Closing my eyes I stood on wobbly legs. People moved away from me as I walked over to Rhapsody who was now dry heaving.

"Are you okay, babe?" I gagged on the last babe. Vomit made me vomit. I had to look at a bag of rotting garbage to keep from puking right next to her.

"What does it look like, Chord?" If she had laser eyes, I would have been toast.

"I'm sorry." I rubbed her back.

She wiped her lips with the back of her hand and stood straight. "For what? For not using a condom? For passing out when you found out you were going to be a daddy? For asking me stupid questions?"

Each venomous question felt like a punch. Pregnancy really made Rhapsody a bitch. I hoped it was just the hormones but the glare she shot me made me think it could just be her.

"Uhm…all of it?"

She rolled her eyes and walked away from the alley and back toward the building's entrance. I followed behind like I was a baby deer following its mama. Frustration and anger spiked through me. She had no right to be pissed right now. She just dropped this bomb on me and expected no reaction. Did she think that I'd just be happy about it? This chick was crazy.

"Hey!" Rhapsody stopped and turned toward me. "You aren't allowed to be angry right now. You just dropped this news on me like it was nothing. Did you expect me to be jumping up and down about this? I assume you've known about this for a while. Were you just going to hold onto this until the kid needed something then finally come to me? Did you even think to try to contact me?" I pointed my finger at her. "You don't have a right to be angry."

Rhapsody stared at me. Her face revealed nothing. It was a little scary. But in the next breath her hand whipped out and slapped me so hard my head snapped to the side. I literally spun in a circle then fell on my ass again.

"Fuck you, Chord!" Rhapsody walked away as I watched from the sidewalk.

What the fuck did I just do?

———

"What the fuck happened to you?" Alec's voice came from my bedroom door.

"Go away." My head was still spinning thanks to my possible concussion.

I heard my door close. I relaxed into my bed but felt the mattress dip. Dammit. Now was not the time for Alec to become a caring cousin.

"Seriously, Chord, what's up? You look like hell. Ben said you came in like a zombie. Apparently, he tried to talk to you but you just came in here. That isn't like you."

"Can you just go away, Alec? I probably have a concussion so now is not the time."

"A concussion? What the hell happened on your date?"

I lifted my head off my pillow and looked at him.

"Yes, I knew you were going out with Emmerson Lee's daughter. Do you really think I'm an idiot?"

"Did you tell my dad?" I sat up, piling my pillows behind my back.

"Do I look like I have a death wish? I am definitely not going to be the person who tells him you are "betraying the family"." He put the last bit in air quotes.

"All right." I bit my lip contemplating whether or not to tell him. I needed to talk to someone. I guess Alec was a someone. That was debatable. "If I tell you this, it can't leave this room. I'm deadly serious, Alec."

"Oh shit! Is she really a man? Did she give you the clap? Are you two really brother and sister?"

I hated my cousin sometimes. With a weak punch, I said, "I'm serious, dickface. Promise me."

He grimaced. "That was a weak ass punch." I swung again but he easily dodged it. "Fine. Fine. Just stop with the bitch punching. It's getting embarrassing."

I shut my eyes. Rhapsody floated in front of them. She was still the sexiest woman I'd ever met. The vision of her round with my child crossed my mind, and it made me feel warm all over. I looked at Alec and told him everything. From the wedding to two hours ago when she changed my life forever. When I'd finally gotten to my temper tantrum he winced.

"Oh fuck, dude." He shook his head.

"I know. I can't believe I'm going to be a dad either." I stared down at my hands.

"Did you hit your head harder than you told me?" he asked.

"No, why?"

"Because you just told me that you had a big ass tantrum accusing your baby's mama of purposely hiding the baby from you then went onto being an even worse lunatic by saying she was using you. I'm surprised she didn't push you in front of a bus. I would have totally done that."

I blinked at him.

"Please tell me you understand that."

"She lied to me, Alec. I would have thought you'd be on my side."

He shook his head again. "I'm not on a side with this, Chord. Everything I know about Emmerson Lee tells me she was never the most caring or attentive mother. I'm guessing that Rhapsody hasn't told a soul about this. She probably just found out herself. So, you accusing her and lashing out was a dick move." Alec stood.

"Where are you going?"

"I need to get out of this room. If I don't I may beat the crap out of you myself. It's disappointing knowing my best friend just did that to the woman carrying his baby. Fix this, Chord, or you are going to end up making the same mistakes Jimmy made. Do you really want your child to have the same kind of childhood you had?" He shrugged, stopping at the door. With his hand on the knob, he said, "Something to think about, Chord."

Alec left quietly shutting the door behind him. Human-like Alec was not the Alec I was used to dealing with. Callous and obnoxious I knew how to handle. Borderline emotional and caring felt like an alien had taken over his body.

I leaned back on the pillows and stared out the window. That was how I sat the rest of the night. Watching the path of the full moon as it crossed through my room. By the time the sun was rising I was still no closer to a solution to my problem. However, I knew one thing. My child would have a better fucking father than I did no matter what.

19

RHAPSODY

"Rhapsody?" Cassie's voice called through my door.

I held my breath hoping she'd go away.

"You know that holding your breath hoping I go away won't work, right?" Cassie whispered to the door.

Exhaling a watery breath, I said, "Come in."

Cassie slid into my room, closing the door quietly behind her. The darkness enveloped us. She was quiet as a cat as she walked to where my bed was. The bed dipped as she sat on the edge.

"You gonna tell me what's up?" she asked.

"I wasn't planning on it." I curled into a tighter ball.

I'd been laying in my bed since I came home from my date with Chord. What a freaking disaster that turned out to be. How could he possibly think I planned on using him? I wasn't my mother.

"We can find better. One that doesn't dress in strange outfits." Queen B buzzed in my head.

"Not now," I mumbled.

"What?" Cassie asked.

"Nothing. Is there something you want, Cassie? If you're

bored, I'm sure my mother could find something or someone to do." The venom that spewed from my mouth even stung me as I said it.

Her soothing motions on my back stopped. Guilt rose up inside me.

"I'm so—" I began.

"I know your secret." Cassie blurted out.

I sat up. "What secret?" Please just say it's the Chord thing. There would be no way she'd know I was pregnant. I was like a ninja with that secret.

"You're pregnant." Cassie's voice was soft.

"Wha? How did you…" I trailed off trying to figure out how she could have possibly found out when I had been so good at keeping that bit of information close to my chest.

"I found these, and I knew they weren't Grams." Soft thuds fell on the bed.

Reaching over to the lamp next to my bed, I clicked it on. The soft light temporarily blinded us. I blinked the spots out of my vision and saw my positive pregnancy tests on the bed. Fuck me!

"How did you find these?" I snatched them up.

Cassie gave me an exasperated sigh. "You left them on top of the wastebasket. I snatched them up before Grams could spot them. You're welcome. So whose is it?"

"Ninja? Yeah right. Don't quit your day job," Queen B snarked, refilling her martini.

I stared down at the tests then rested my hand on my belly. Tears blurred my vision as Chord's vicious words repeated. My heart dropped again. Did he want nothing to do with our child? He didn't have to like me, but he wouldn't just turn his back on our child would he?

"Rhapsody? Do you know whose it is?" Cassie placed her hand on my leg.

I let out a watery laugh. "Yeah, but you aren't gonna like it."

She furrowed her brow. "Why?"

"It's Jimmy Ray's son."

"What? Jimmy Ray knocked you up? Emmerson is going to have hedgehogs."

"Wait what?" Her words weren't making sense.

"You do know the feud she has with him, right? If that is his son…I don't know what she'll do." Cassie pointed to my belly.

"The baby isn't Jimmy Rays. It's Jimmy Ray's son's kid. Chord Reedy."

Cassie paled. "Oh shit. That might be worse. At least if it were Jimmy Ray's kid then maybe Emmerson would be willing to bury the hatchet or in the least call a truce. This might just make everything explode. How did this happen?"

I bit my lip holding back my words. Cassie had been my best friend at one time. We'd grown up together. Both raised by Grams while our wayward parents lived their own lives. We told each other everything. However, when Emmerson made one of her rare visits, she happened to catch Cassie singing one of her original songs. She managed to persuade her to drop out of high school and go on tour with Blue Vengeance. Cassie and I had a huge fight the night she told me she was leaving. I felt betrayed and jealous. I'd noticed the pride my mother had shown at Cassie's natural talent. I'd never seen her give me that look. When I gave Cassie an ultimatum of choosing Emmerson or me, I fractured everything we had. With tears streaming down her face, she packed her bag and left. I ignored her as she tried to say goodbye. That was almost fourteen years ago. The memory still hurt.

"I don't know if I can trust you." My words were flat.

Cassie blanched. The hurt I'd seen those years ago was on her face but this time she managed to hide it in a blink. "Look, I know we've had our differences." I scoffed but she continued. "However, I've never stopped thinking of you as my sister. You don't know how many times I wanted to pick up the phone and call you about something cool that happened. I didn't call though. I didn't think you'd pick up."

First Chord and now Cassie with the fucking guilt.

"This girl is good. Top notch guilt tripping here. Hope you brought your passport because you are going on one hell of a trip." Queen B saluted with her martini.

"Bitch," I said softly.

Queen B smirked and shot me with finger guns.

"Excuse me?" Cassie sat up straighter.

Shit! Guess I wasn't as quiet as I'd thought.

"Sorry. Queen B." I'd said like she knew what the hell I was talking about. I shook my head then said, "All right, I will confide in you, but you cannot tell Emmerson or Grams."

Cassie crossed her heart. Despite my reservations, I told her everything. The wedding, the unremarkable sex, the presentation fiasco, the hall of fame, and then my date with Chord. When I got to the part where Chord accused me of lying, Cassie balled her fists. I felt a bit vindicated in my anger with her reaction.

"That son of a bitch," she mumbled.

I shrugged. "I did kind of drop the fact that I was knocked up and it was his kid on him."

"Yeah, but he immediately thought you were a hanger on. If he even knew you for a moment he'd realize that isn't you."

"We have only been around each other a grand total of four times. It isn't like we've been dating for months, Cassie."

She glared at me. "Stop defending him to me. Let me be righteously angry for you."

We looked at each other and started laughing. We fell into such a laughing fit that Cassie fell off the bed with a thud. It made me laugh even harder.

"Oh my God! Stop! I'm going to pee my pants," I said between giggle fits.

Soft knocks froze us.

"Rhapsody? Cassandra? Are you two all right?"

Cassie grabbed the pee sticks and shoved them under my blankets. Moving over so she could sit next to me, I looked at her and hoped she'd see my pleading face. She did and nodded in agreement. She was going to keep her mouth shut.

"Come in, Grams," we said together.

Well, that didn't sound like we were up to something.

Grams walked in and looked at the two of us. She looked around the room. Stooping down she peered under the bed too.

"Are you looking for something, Grams?" Cassie asked.

"No, but I haven't seen you two like this in ages. Something must be up. Are you hiding young men in here?" She crossed her arms while staring the two of us down.

"Of course not, Grams. Plus, we are both almost thirty. I'm pretty sure we'd be allowed to have young men in here."

Gram's smacked Cassie with her cane. "Just because you can doesn't mean you should, Cassandra. Now, what are you two doing?"

"Just some girl talk. We're catching up. We've spent too many years not talking. A lot of stuff happened in that time," I said with a stiff smile.

A warm smile lit up her face. "It's about time. I'm going to go get some cookies and you are going to include me in this girl talk." She left faster than I thought she could move.

"Great, now we have to talk about your baby with Grams."

I shook my head. "Nope. Not the time. However, we can talk to her about how many rando men you slept with while on the road."

"Hey! I'm not the one that got knocked up after shitty sex. I at least know to have him wrap it up." She shoved me with her shoulder.

"When I fuck up...I don't do it halfway." I tried to laugh.

Cassie grew serious. "You know you have choices, right?"

I nodded. "Yeah, but something tells me this is the path I'm supposed to go down. Plus, this baby needs to be a terror to its Aunt Cassie."

Cassie laughed then rubbed her chin. "I wonder how young is too young for a drum set."

I pushed her out of the bed, and she landed on the floor with a thump. We erupted into a fit of giggles again. That was exactly how Grams found us along with the pregnancy tests laying scattered on the floor.

"Like I said. Don't quit your day job." Queen B put her head in her hands.

20

———————

CHORD

I stood in front of the unfamiliar door. My hands were clammy, and I couldn't help but twitch nervously. The small home in front of me felt ominous. I was there to grovel and hopefully redeem myself. The doorbell rang for the third time as I waited for someone to answer. A thundering came from behind the door. When a bang and cursing came next, I wanted to flee.

"This better not be one of those religious traveling salesmen. I swear to God I will open the damn door naked and give them something to repent about," a muffled voice said.

"I'd be open to a sex cult where they worshipped my body," another voice said.

"Of course you would, you're a slut," the first voice said then I heard an "Ow!"

"Will one of you girls please see who is at the door?" an older voice shouted.

"Sorry, Grams," the first two voices said in unison.

The door swung open, and I saw a disheveled Rhapsody. She wore a long T-shirt with a barely there pair of shorts. Her hair was pulled up on top of her head in a messy bun. She was a dream.

"Chord?"

The girl from the hall of fame night poked her head over her shoulder. "Damn. No sex cult, Grams. But we've got the one who knocked up Rhapsy."

I felt my face flush. "Hi."

Rhapsody crossed her arms in front of her. "What do you want?"

"Rhapsody! Don't talk that way to the young man. Let him come in and grovel properly." An older woman appeared in the doorway and pushed her out of the way. "Come in. The carpet in the living room is perfect for groveling."

I passed Rhapsody and the other girl whispering. The older woman sat on an overstuffed chair and gestured for me to have a seat on the matching couch. The other girl, who I now recognized as one of the younger members of Blue Vengeance, sat flush against me. Rhapsody stood in the entryway of the room with her arms crossed. This was not going to be easy.

"Uhm…could I have a moment with Rhapsody alone?" I asked tentatively.

"Nope," all three of them said.

"Son, you can say what you need to say in front of all of us. I'm Grandma Leah and next to you is Cassandra. Of course, you're already acquainted with our Rhapsody."

Rhapsody snorted.

"Nice to meet all of you." I swallowed. All of a sudden my mouth was the damn Sahara. I turned toward Rhapsody and said, "First, I need to apologize. I didn't react well."

"That's the understatement of the century," Cassandra said next to me.

"Cassandra! Let the boy speak," Grandma Leah scolded her. "Keep going."

"What made you come to that conclusion, Chord?" Rhapsody asked.

I stood from the couch and took a step closer to her. Her

laser gaze warned me to not take another step closer. "I had a conversation with my cousin."

"Your asshole cousin, Alec?" Cassandra asked.

"Uhm…yeah. Do you know Alec?"

Cassandra scoffed and crossed her arms in front of her.

"How did a conversation with your cousin change your mind?" Rhapsody drew my attention back to the issue at hand.

"He showed me exactly how much of an idiot I was being. When I finally took a moment and the world stopped spinning, I realized I was acting just like my father. I never want to become him." I walked over to Rhapsody. "I want to be here for you and the baby. I know I fucked up. I don't deserve one ounce of forgiveness from you. However, if you can find it in your heart to give me another chance, I will never stop making it up to you."

I dropped to my knees in front of her. Rhapsody covered her mouth with her hands. Tears glistened in her eyes. Oh dear Lord! I made her cry again.

"I'm so sorry, Rhapsody. Please don't cry."

She sniffled. "You really are an idiot." Rhapsody knelt in front of me and kissed me. I pulled her to me feeling her curves against my body. It was a really poor time for Stan to get any ideas, but he decided to stand at attention. Feeling her against me was the most perfect thing in the world. I wanted nothing more than this woman with me for the rest of my life.

"Good. That's handled. Who's hungry?" Grandma Leah asked, standing from her chair.

"Me. I'm not sure if Rhapsy can handle food since she was puking all morning." Cassandra walked past us still on the floor.

"You've been sick?" I asked Rhapsody.

She shrugged. "It's just morning sickness." Rhapsody grimaced then continued. "I'm not entirely sure why they are calling it morning sickness. I get sick any time of day."

"Well, do you want to go for a drive and maybe grab a coffee? I borrowed Alec's car." I asked tentatively as I helped her stand.

She gave me a bright smile. My heart grew when that smile was aimed my way.

"Absolutely. Let me get dressed then we can go." Rhapsody disappeared from the room.

I watched her go and enjoyed every inch those shorts didn't cover. My mind was so focused on Rhapsody that I didn't realize Cassandra had come back into the room. She was standing where Rhapsody had been earlier. Her earlier jovial look was replaced with a look that could very well kill me.

"You and Rhapsody heading out?" she asked.

"Yep."

She nodded. "Look, Chord, I'm going to say this once and you take it for what it is. If you pull some more shit like you did last night and hurt my cousin and her child, I will castrate you." I opened my mouth to object, but she continued, "I'm sure you're wondering why I would castrate you instead of kill you. Well, I feel that if you are dumb enough to do something to Rhapsody and baby bean then you should never procreate in this world. Make sense?"

I nodded.

"Good. Also, your father and her mother do not need to know about any of this yet. It is going to be a shit storm when that happens. Got it?"

"Yeah. But aren't you in Blue Vengeance? How are you gonna hide that from Emmerson Lee?"

"You don't need to worry about that. You just worry about making Rhapsody happy and making sure your douche of a cousin doesn't spill the beans about baby bean."

I nodded again.

Cassandra handed me a piece of paper. "Here is my number. If anything ever happens, call me and I will be there as soon as humanly possible." She turned to walk away from me then said, "Oh and you can call me Cassie. Grams is the only person who calls me Cassandra."

All I could do was nod again. I was slightly scared of that

chick. Rhapsody found her way down the stairs while I was still staring into the empty hallway.

"You okay?"

With a strained smile, I said, "Yep. Ready to go?"

She gave me that brilliant smile again then linked her arm with mine. "Let's go."

I leaned over and kissed her cheek. This day was finally beginning to look up.

21

RHAPSODY

"Told you he wouldn't show," Queen B said, sharpening her nails.

"Shut it," I mumbled.

My day with Chord had ended with me stupidly asking him to come with me to my first doctor's appointment. When I'd asked him, he got so excited he looked like he was going to go to something exciting instead of a place where someone was going to look at my vag.

Looking down at my phone I saw I only had five minutes until my appointment. With a shrug, I walked into the building where my doctor's office was located. Taking the stairs to the second floor, I entered the sterile office. A screaming child made me blanche. Sitting in a chair against the wall was a haggard looking mother who was holding the wailing toddler over her distended belly.

"Guess no one told her about birth control," Queen B whispered.

Ignoring the bitch, I continued to the counter and passed other women in the waiting room. There was a small line, so I tried to wait patiently. Unfortunately, my nerves and patience weren't cooperating, and I found myself moving side to side showing my irritation. The little old lady that was holding up the line finally moved away from the window, giving me a smile as she passed by.

"Wonder what she's here for? Think it's to get the cobwebs removed?" Queen B cackled, kicking her legs in the air.

"Can I help you?" a young woman called toward me.

"Uhm yes. Rhapsody Bell to see Dr. Minnow."

The young woman typed furiously on the computer. She obnoxiously chewed gum, popping it loudly. I drummed my fingers on the counter nervously. The door to the office opened, and I looked over my shoulder hoping it was Chord. No such luck. A cute little elderly couple shuffled in arm in arm.

"Is this a geriatric gyno? Are you at the right place?" Queen B asked.

"Shut it," I gritted through my teeth.

"Excuse me?" the girl asked.

I cleared my throat. "What?"

The girl gave me the crazy look I always got when I was caught talking to Queen B. She slid a small plastic cup on the counter. "Pee in this. Leave it in the designated area in the restroom when you're finished. We will call you shortly."

"Okay."

I took the cup and strode over to the empty bathroom. Locking the door behind me, I placed my purse on the back of the door and proceeded to attempt to fill the cup. Unfortunately, I was having problems going. My bladder was not cooperating. Moments before I knew I had to go. The handle jiggled at someone's attempt to come in. Dammit. I reached over to the nearby sink to turn on the water, but it was a motion sensor. There was only one thing to do. Stretching toward the sink I managed to activate the sink. The cool water flowing over my fingers was just enough to activate my bladder. I sat back down on the toilet and filled the cup. With the cup in my hand, I stood but the jiggling of the handle made me jump again which caused me to spill some of the contents on my gray pants.

Queen B started cackling again. *"Now you look like you pissed yourself. Way to go, Rhapsody."*

"Son of a bitch." I cursed as I pulled up the stained pants.

Great. Oh well, I'd just have to walk with my purse discreetly in front of me. After placing the cup in the designated area, I quickly washed my hands. Holding my bag in front of my wet pants, I opened the bathroom door and passed a woman who was looking at her phone and leaning next to the door. I gave her a small smile then took the closest seat.

Digging out my phone, I chanced a look to see if Chord had contacted me. No message. Son of a bitch. He was doing it again. I gritted my teeth and began plotting his death both gruesome and swift.

"Ms. Bell?" A nurse broke through a particularly interesting torture using a pineapple, a taser, and a pair of pliers.

I stood too quickly, and my purse fell from my lap. All heads turned toward me. All eyes got a good view of what my purse was covering. Swiftly, I retrieved my bag and rushed over to the nurse. She kindly ignored the stain on my pants while she took my height and weight. After I slipped my shoes back on, I followed her to an exam room.

Closing the door behind her, the nurse said, "We are going to need you to put on a paper gown. The open part is in the front, leave it loosely tied. The doctor will be in shortly."

"Okay. Thank you," I said.

Once again, I stepped out of my flats and made quick work to remove my clothes. While I dressed in the gown provided, I couldn't help but think about Chord. My heart sank as I came to the only conclusion I could. He had second thoughts and decided to back out. He was just too chicken shit to tell me.

A knock jarred me from my spiraling thoughts. "Ms. Bell? Are you ready?" an elderly voice asked through the crack in the door.

"Yes."

"Wonderful. I'm Dr. Minnow." She held out her small hand

to me as she entered. With a smile, I took her hand in mine, giving it a little shake.

The doctor nodded to me then strode over to the corner, sitting down on a little rolling stool, and logged into a computer as I sat awkwardly on the exam table. I watched as her fingers moved swiftly over the keyboard. She looked to be in her sixties with salt and pepper gray hair styled in a pixie cut. The white lab coat she wore dwarfed her small stature. Her appearance seemed more like a child playing dress up rather than a woman who had probably delivered hundreds of babies.

While she focused on the computer the nurse snuck back in holding a tray with an array of objects. A shiver made me shake, rustling the weird paper draped over the exam table. The room was like a freezer. It had to be the temperature of the room and not my frayed nerves that made me shake. They always made these damn rooms so cold. My headlights were on, so I crossed my arms hoping to calm down the girls.

"You're scared shitless. Your shaking has nothing to do with the temperature," Queen B quipped.

I ignored Queen B. If I answered, they wouldn't be checking on the baby but shipping me to the psych ward. The doctor continued to type a few things on the computer then rolled over to sit in front of me. She gave me a toothy smile. I knew it was supposed to be comforting but it looked a little like a shark.

"So..." She paused as her eyes wandered appraisingly. "We have a little bun in the oven?"

"Well, if the three different pregnancy tests aren't correct, I'm suing those bastards."

Dr. Minnow and the nurse laughed. What they didn't realize was I was one hundred percent serious. If those fuckers were wrong, I was going to be a billionaire.

"I'd say there could have been a chance of a false positive if it were one or maybe even two. However, three is pretty definitive. We'll make sure though. Why don't you lay back so I can check you?" She stood from the stool and walked over to the counter where I watched as she put on latex gloves.

I scooted back on the exam table, well and truly destroying the paper covering. Laying back I looked up at the ceiling and blinked. "Is that a half-naked picture of Jason Mamoa?"

"Yes. We find that women are more relaxed if they have something nice to look at." Dr. Minnow winked at me as she pulled out retractable stirrups attached to the table.

"That is definitely good scenery."

"Certainly is. Now, just relax, Rhapsody. This will be a quick pelvic exam to make sure everything is in working order. Then we are going to do an ultrasound. Is that okay?"

I tried to swallow around the lump in my throat then decided words weren't necessary and just nodded. The doctor disappeared between my legs. Just as I relaxed staring at Jason Mamoa, I heard a ruckus coming from outside the room. I sat up and looked toward the door. Dr. Minnow didn't seem to notice and continued with the exam. When the door slammed open and a man wearing a pirate costume complete with a stuffed parrot on his shoulder stepped in everyone froze.

Chord looked down at Dr. Minnow. She stared back at the invader while continuing to be wrist deep in my lady bits.

"What the hell is going on here?" Chord looked down at the doctor then at me.

I rolled my eyes and laid back down staring at the scenery above me while Chord, the nurse, and Dr. Minnow talked over one another.

"Well, you did it, Rhapsody. You managed to find the one man who didn't know better than to burst into a cooter doctor appointment. Your child is doomed." Queen Bee swung her legs while watching the weird exchange between my baby daddy, my cooter doctor, and the cooter nurse.

"Shut up and let me focus on some Mamoa," I mumbled while counting the ridges on his perfect abs.

Everything was better with a dash of Mamoa.

22

CHORD

I stared down at the black and white picture in my hand. Awe had overcome me when I got to see the little pod with a heartbeat. That little pod was going to be my everything. As long as I didn't keep acting like an idiot and pissing off her mother. I was convinced it was a she. Rhapsody ignored my ranting about our little girl. She had been pissed after I burst into the examination.

That day hadn't started out well. The electricity in our building had gone out, and my alarm never went off. By the time I'd woken up, I had only an hour to get ready for pirate day at work and meet Rhapsody in time for her appointment. I'd made good time but knew I would be late if Alec wouldn't give me a ride.

"Alec! Can you give me a ride over to Church Street?" I hopped on one foot trying to get on my pirate boot.

Alec sipped his coffee while staring at his phone. "Nope."

"Why not? It's not out of your way." I adjusted the fake parrot on my shoulder.

"None of that is getting in my car. Bike it," he said, waving at my costume.

"Are you fucking kidding me?"

"No, I am not, Chord. Take your bike or I don't know tap that wealthy pops of yours to get your own mode of transportation. You'd look great on a moped."

I stared at my asshole cousin. "You know why I won't do that." Huffing out a breath, I said, "Fine. Be a prick."

Storming out of the apartment, I remembered to grab my keys and my phone. My anger at my cousin consumed my thoughts as I rode the elevator down to retrieve my bike from the bike rack outside. It had clouded my vision so much that I found myself on automatic pilot. By the time I realized I had ridden all the way to work, I was five minutes late meeting Rhapsody. Cursing myself I turned my bike around and proceeded to weave recklessly through traffic. When I finally arrived at the doctor's office, I was drenched in sweat and the stuffed parrot hung limply from my shoulder.

After the nightmare of my morning, I may or may not have been a bit belligerent to the front desk girl when I insisted she take me to see Rhapsody. That was my first mistake. Barging into a gynecologist doing an exam was my second. Only Rhapsody could convince them I should be allowed to stay, which kept me from getting arrested.

Now, I had a picture of my little pumpkin seed and couldn't be more overjoyed.

"What's that, Chord?" Mary, the other children's librarian, asked as she rounded the children's section circulation desk.

I flashed it toward her.

"Aww. Are you gonna be a dad?"

All I could do was nod. The idea of being a dad still seemed surreal.

Mary must have seen the look of fear on my face. "Scared?"

I nodded again.

"My husband, Tim, was terrified when I told him about our first. He told me once that all he thought about was how would he be able to protect something so small from the horrors of the world." A small smile curled her lips as she recalled the memory.

"Exactly. How did Tim get past it?"

She shrugged. "I don't know if he ever got past the idea but as time goes by your fear will be replaced with excitement and happiness. You have a long way to go but it will go by fast. How is your girlfriend doing?"

How do I answer that question? Rhapsody wasn't my girlfriend, yet. I wanted to change that, but I kept messing up. Why would any woman want to be anything with me if I kept fucking up?

"It's complicated."

"It always is." Mary gave my shoulder a squeeze. "Well, I'm so happy for you and your little one, Chord. You're going to be a great dad. If you or your girlfriend need anything, please let me know." Mary's eyes went to something behind me. She gave me a small smile and walked over to the table we had crafts set up on.

"Uncle Chord!" Alice's high-pitched voice came running toward me.

I placed the ultrasound picture on the desk then rounded the desk and kneeled down to catch the mini-tornado. Her cloud of curls bounced around her head. My mind immediately wandered to what my daughter would look like. Alice's arms wrapped around my neck, giving me a squeeze.

"I've missed you," she whispered in my ear.

"I've missed you too, sweetie." I looked up to see my sister walking slowly with Grandpa Lew. She had a strange look on her face.

I let go of Alice and watched as she walked over to Mary and the craft station.

"Everything okay?" I asked Miranda.

Before she could answer, Grandpa Lew said, "She's being dramatic."

"No, I'm not, Grandpa," Miranda protested then turned to

me. "We just came from the doctor. They are worried about his sugar levels again. Apparently, they were so high he could have gone into a diabetic coma."

"Those damn doctors don't know their ass from a hole in the ground." He pulled away from Miranda and leaned against the circulation desk.

"Grandpa, are you taking your medicine?" I asked.

He shrugged.

"He's sneaking sweets again," Miranda ratted out Grandpa Lew.

"Grandpa..." I began but was interrupted.

"What's this?" Alice held up the ultrasound printout.

I felt my face heat. "That's uhm..."

"Let me see that, sweetie." Miranda took the paper from Alice.

She looked at it then at me with large eyes. Before she could say anything, someone snatched it out of her hand. My stomach dropped to the floor as I watched my father look at the first image of my little pumpkin seed.

"Did you knock up someone, Chord?" Jimmy Ray asked.

I looked over at Miranda.

"He came with us to Grandpa's appointment. He just showed up at the house." She mouthed sorry to me.

"What are you doing here, Jimmy?" I snapped while trying to deflect his question.

"I was just checking in on my pops to see how he was feeling. Color me surprised when I learned he was on his way to the doctor. I decided to tag along to spend some time with my daughter and granddaughter." He gave me a smile usually reserved for his fans.

I looked at Miranda, who was rolling her eyes.

"Papa J, come see my pirate." Alice grabbed Jimmy's hand while Grandpa Lew snatched the ultrasound out of his hand.

Jimmy glared at me but let Alice pull him along. A mixture

of dread, anger, and fear spread through me. We watched as Alice chattered to my dad in front of the craft table.

"You're going to be a daddy," Grandpa Lew stated.

I sighed. I wasn't ready for this conversation. With a glance back to Alice and my dad, I said, "Yes."

A beat of silence built between us. Then Grandpa Lew and Miranda gave me huge smiles. Miranda pulled me into a big hug while Grandpa slapped my back.

"I can't wait to meet my little niece or nephew." Miranda spoke soft enough for our ears only.

"I can't wait to meet the mother of my great-grandchild. Sunday dinner, Chord." Another statement.

"Grandpa, that might be a bit—"

"No excuses. I want to meet this girl, Chord. I'm sure your sister and niece want to also."

I nodded reluctantly then said, "Jimmy can't know."

Grandpa looked at his son still standing with Alice. "He doesn't need to know. However, he will eventually need to know he's going to be a grandpa again."

"Just not right now." Or ever if I had a say in it. He'd blow a gasket knowing that I'd knocked up his mortal enemy's daughter.

Miranda and Grandpa nodded together. She called over to Alice. Alice dragged Jimmy back to our small group. He had a fake smile plastered on his face.

"We gotta get going, Alice." Miranda took the pirate picture she was holding.

"Okay." Alice turned toward me, opening her arms.

I picked her up, and she wrapped her arms around my neck. She leaned back and looked me in the eye. "Are you coming over for Sunday dinner?"

"I am, sweetie."

"Good." She kissed my cheek then squirmed to get down.

"Sunday dinner?" Jimmy looked at the three of us.

"Come on, kids. I'm getting tired." Grandpa Lew held out his hand for Alice to hold it.

Jimmy looked at them then at me. His scrutiny made me uneasy. Without saying a word, he turned then followed behind Grandpa, Miranda, and Alice. I watched them leave and leaned against the circulation desk. A feeling of exhaustion overcame me.

"Everything okay, Chord?"

"Sure." I gave Mary a strained smile. My phone vibrated in my pocket.

Jimmy Ray: I know something is up. I will figure it out.

I deleted the message but then a cold finger of fear slid down my spine. Looking around I noticed the ultrasound picture wasn't on the desk. I rifled around the desk.

"Did you lose something?" Mary asked.

"No. I'm sure it will turn up."

Mary walked back to the craft table to help a few children that had come in. My mind whirled. Could Jimmy have taken the ultrasound? I felt sick wondering what he would do if he found out Rhapsody was pregnant with my baby. My phone vibrated in my pocket again. I pulled it out expecting to see another text from Jimmy.

Rhapsody: Wanna hang out tonight?

My heart flipped in my chest.

Me: Definitely! What did you have in mind?

Rhapsody: Pizza, ice cream and a movie.

Me: Sounds perfect. I will pick up the pizza and ice cream.

Rhapsody: Make sure it's sausage with extra cheese and cookie dough ice cream. I've already got the movie.

I smiled at her bossiness.

Me: I will be over at 5.

Rhapsody: Great. See you then.

I smiled as I put away my phone. I had a date with my baby mama.

23

RHAPSODY

"I didn't expect you to be so squeamish," I said to Chord, who had his head buried in my chest.

His mumbled response was muffled thanks to my ample bosom.

"What?"

Chord lifted his head then said, "I didn't know you'd be a horror aficionado."

I smirked at him. "I didn't know my baby's daddy would be such a wimp."

He looked offended then grinned. "How do you know I'm actually scared and not using this to bury myself in one of my favorite places?" Chord burrowed back into my breasts.

"Hey!" I pushed his head away.

Chord started laughing and fell against the pillows on his side of my bed. I smacked his shoulder. He moaned and rubbed it.

"Ow! That hurt. Does being pregnant give you superpowers?"

"You're such a big baby." I started rubbing my non-existent baby bump. "You need to be tough like your mama."

Chord eyed me then in a swift movement rolled on top of me. "Tough like her mama, huh?"

I licked my lips when I felt his hardness against my core. This was exactly how we got in trouble the first time. "Yeah. You got a problem with that?"

He watched my mouth as I talked. A grin curled his lips. "Absolutely not. I've always liked my women tough." He paused and leaned so close I could feel his breath on my lips. "Can I do the one thing I've been dying to do for months?"

"What's that?" I played coy.

"Kiss you. I've dreamt about your lips and the feel of your body just like this. Your soft curves under my hands, lips, and tongue."

My body involuntarily reacted by rolling my hips against his. We both groaned.

"Yes," I breathed out.

His eyes flared with a heat I hadn't seen since the wedding. As he slowly lowered his mouth those few scant inches, it seemed like an eternity. When I finally felt his lips against mine it felt so good. Our last time on a bed led to the predicament we were in. Just like before, kissing Chord felt like coming home. My heart flipped in my chest as our tongues met and tangled with an increased level of passion. His hand slid under my shirt to my breast. When he squeezed, I pulled away with a yelp.

"Are you okay?" Chord had a worried look on his face.

The grimace on my face probably told him everything he needed to know. But he was a dumb guy and didn't know what came along with pregnancy. "My breasts are really sensitive thanks to the bun in the oven."

"Oh my God. I am so sorry, Rhapsody. I didn't know." He petted the breast he'd squeezed.

"It's okay. Just take it easy with the milk jugs."

He stopped his petting and looked down at my breasts. "Milk jugs? Are you gonna start squirting milk at me?"

It was a good thing he was pretty because sometimes his brain cells weren't firing on all cylinders.

"Do we need to get you the book *What to Expect When Expecting?*"

Chord's face lit up. "That's a great idea."

"You really know how to pick 'em." Queen B shook her head.

I ignored her. She'd been quiet thanks to her love of the blood and gore of horror movies.

With a shake of my head, I grabbed his shirt, pulling him to me effectively shutting him up with a kiss. This kiss ignited the passion between us instantly. Curling a leg over his hip, I ground my core against the hardness threatening to burst through his jeans. I moaned into his mouth as he ran his hands over my body. Everywhere his hands landed left a heated imprint on my skin. All I wanted to do was get naked and feel him inside me again. Hopefully this round he wouldn't be a minute man.

"Good luck with that one," Queen B quipped.

Letting her words float out of my brain, I broke our kiss and began pulling his shirt over his head. Unfortunately, it was a collared shirt, and it got caught on his head. We struggled to get it off but when a knock on my door interrupted us, Chord moved off me and directly onto the floor.

"Hey, Rhapsody, can I borrow—" Cassandra began as she pushed open the door but froze as she looked from my disheveled form on the bed and Chord flailing on the floor like a dying fish.

"Uh…what's up, Cassie?"

She gave me a wide grin. "Well, it looks like a lot is going on in here."

"What do you want?" I snapped.

"Sorry…geez you must be in a real drought to get all snippy. I just wanted to borrow your hairdryer because mine just crapped out on me." She held up her hands.

Scooting off the bed, I stepped over Chord still tangled in his shirt. I grabbed my hairdryer off the top of my dresser and thrust it toward her.

"Here."

Cassie took it from me then said, "So, what were you two doing?"

I reached for the door and shut it in Cassie's face. Her laughter could be heard through the door.

"By the way, nice abs, Chord," she called out.

"Bye, Cassie." I banged on the door.

Plopping on the bed, I looked down at Chord who had finally disentangled himself.

"Well, that wasn't very sexy." I crossed my arms over my chest and winced at the bit of pain.

Chord moved to kneel in front of me. He gently uncrossed my arms and held my hand in my lap. "You are always sexy to me." I let out a self-deprecating laugh. "I'm serious. From the moment I saw you at that table at the wedding I knew I wanted you." Chord joined me on the bed, making sure our fingers remained linked. "At first, I thought it was pure unadulterated lust. Honestly, that first night it probably was that. I didn't expect to constantly think about you since that night. You haven't left my mind. I feel like a man possessed. And now that you are carrying my child, I really can't stop thinking about you."

"You know this won't be easy, right? Our parents hate each other with the fury of seven suns. What are they going to do when they find out?" I said to our linked hands.

Chord lifted my chin to meet his eyes. "Fuck 'em. We're adults, Rhapsody. Sooner than planned we are going to be parents. I couldn't care less what Jimmy thinks." He raised our linked hands to his lips. "I want to try to be together. I realize that we may need to keep things quiet at first, but I want this. I don't just want to be your baby daddy. I want to be your man too."

A giggle burst from me. I quickly covered my mouth. "Sorry." I started giggling all over again.

"What? What did I say that's so funny?" Chord looked honestly confused.

I shook my head. "It was probably one of the cheesiest lines I've ever heard."

Chord's face fell.

"Way to go, Rhapsody. Crush the poor guy's ego." Queen B shook her head at me.

"I didn't mean that as a bad thing. It was also one of the sweetest things I've ever heard." I squeezed his hand and prayed I hadn't just ruined everything.

Chord grinned. "Does that mean you wanna go out with me?"

I bit my lip as if pretending to contemplate the decision. "Hmmm…you know dating you would be like dating a bad boy. You're off limits."

He leaned over and kissed up my neck. "Definitely, the bad boy who's a children's librarian."

"Oh boy, this guy is getting lame with his lines." Queen B stomped with her stiletto.

Ignoring the bitch, I said, "We should probably leave out the children's librarian part if we are painting you as a bad boy."

His grin made my stomach flip. "If I can call you mine you can paint me however you want." He pulled me into his lap and kissed me.

"My life is really going to suck if I have to listen to his hallmark channel lines. Bring on the Fifty Shades! Now, that is some dialogue I can get behind. You two are lame." Queen B laid down, putting headphones and an eye mask on to drown out our make-out session.

Personally, I'd be okay with a hallmark channel life. A *Fifty Shades* life requires too many knots. I didn't even like tying my shoes.

24

CHORD

"Hello?" Rhapsody's voice was groggy.

"Hey? Did I wake you?"

"Yeah, but that's okay. I need to be awake. What time is it?" She yawned into the phone.

"It's noon."

"Damn! I closed my eyes for just a second after breakfast and now it's time for lunch. This kid is seriously draining my energy. Anyway, I'm sure you called for a reason and not to hear me being dramatic about a nap."

"It's okay. I enjoy talking to you no matter the subject."

"Uh-huh. You want something don't you."

I smiled. Damn if I didn't love when she was sassy. It was such a turn on. My mind immediately took a turn down a very dirty path.

"Chord? You still there? Earth to Chord."

Blinking away the dirty thoughts, I said, "Yeah, sorry. Uhm... I was wondering if you'd be willing to come to a family dinner with me."

Silence. A very uncomfortable and long silence.

"Rhapsody?"

"Yeah."

"Did you hear me?"

"Yeah."

"Does that mean you'll come?"

She sighed. "Is that a good idea?"

"Jimmy won't be there. It will be my grandpa, sister, and niece. That's it. I promise."

"Okay. I mean you were already put through the wringer with my family it's probably fair I go through the same."

I chuckled. "I think they will take it easy. They know you're pregnant."

"What?!" Rhapsody screeched.

"What?"

"You told them already? What story did you come up with?"

"Story?"

"Yeah. What did you say about how this happened?"

"Rhapsody, they probably know how it happened."

"Don't be dense."

"I really don't know what you're getting at."

"Fine. Are we dating? Are you the sperm donor? Were we drugged and your sperm was implanted into me by some alien race? These are details I need to know."

"What?"

"Ugh! Come on, Chord."

"I didn't tell them anything. They saw me with the ultrasound. They don't even know it's you. But I'd like to say we are boyfriend and girlfriend."

"And why haven't they met me before now?"

"You've been busy at work?" I asked.

Rhapsody sighed again. "Fine. I guess that will work. We really need to work on your ability to come up with an interesting story on the fly. Standing there with your mouth hanging open doesn't work."

How the hell did she know I did that?

"You're wondering how I know you did that, aren't you?"

I looked around my bedroom to see if there were some hidden cameras.

"I know you do that because I've seen when you're put on the spot. You stand there slack-jawed. It's really quite telling. Anyway, what should I bring?"

"Nothing. I'm bringing drinks so you don't need to bring anything."

"I'll bring a dessert. I have the perfect recipe. What time are you picking me up?"

Rhapsody was a bulldozer sometimes. She'd probably answer her own questions if I let her. My cock was perking up at her being so bossy. Everything about this woman made me hard. What was wrong with me?

"I'll pick you up at three."

"Sounds good. I'll see you tomorrow."

"See you tomorrow." I grimaced as I realized I'd just said that to an already ended call.

With a shrug, I plugged in my phone to charge it then set about gathering my clothes to do laundry. A knock made me pause while picking up a pair of underwear.

"Come in."

Alec barged in. "Hey, fucker! What are you doing?"

I looked at him while holding my dirty clothes, and I waited a minute for him to notice. He didn't. "I'm about to do laundry. What do you want?"

"Is that any way for you to treat your cousin?" Alec laid on my bed, scrolling through his phone.

"Oh I'm sorry. I meant to say, what do you want, fuckface?" I walked toward the door.

"Is that any way to talk to your cousin who you need to borrow a car from?"

I froze. I forgot I didn't have a car to pick up Rhapsody. Son of a bitch. I looked over at him. He had a shit-eating grin. Fucker.

"Ahhh…I'm guessing you forgot about that." His grin grew. "You can borrow the car. However, I'm coming with you…and I'm driving."

My dirty clothes hamper slammed on the floor. "What? Why? You never want to see Miranda and Grandpa Lew."

"You are right about Miranda. She's a shrew that only yells at me for my life choices. I don't have anything against Grandpa Lew. I miss him."

I squinted my eyes at him. Alec was up to something. "Did Jimmy put you up to this?"

"Nope." He went back to scrolling.

"Fine. I didn't want to drive anyway. We need to pick up Rhapsody by three. I'm warning you now if you fuck with her, I'm going to castrate you with a spoon while you sleep."

"Your threats don't worry me, Chord. I'll be ready by two-thirty tomorrow." Alec sprung up from my bed then left.

"Stop listening at my door, Alec," I yelled down the hall.

I was met with only laughter.

"Chord, will you come play? Oscar is totally shit at Operation Death Stomp," Benny called from the living room.

"I am not." Oscar's voice came out as if he was in a fog.

"You're fucking high right now. Unhand the controller before you mess up my high score."

I heard a controller dropping.

"I'll play as soon as I start my laundry."

"Good. Hurry up though. My life depends on it."

I shut my eyes and shook my head. Then a thought crashed into my mind. How the hell could I bring my little pumpkin around these people? They would be horrible role models. Mentally, I'd started a list of things I needed to do before my little bean was born. Well, the list only had two things so far but they were huge.

Number one: Get car

Number two: Find new place

"Hurry up, Chord!" Benny shouted, making me jump.

"I'm coming. I'm coming."

"That's what last night's bar bunny said." He laughed at his own joke.

I took a deep breath then mentally moved *find a new place* to the number one spot.

25

———————

RHAPSODY

I paced in front of the door. Pulling out my phone, I looked at the time. Two fifty-eight. He was going to be late again. If this was a thing with him, I really hoped our kid got my on-time genes.

"You're not always on-time. Just look how late you are on your period," Queen B said as she kicked her legs up on an ottoman.

"Where did you get an ottoman?" I mumbled.

Queen B just shrugged.

"Who are you talking to, Rhapsody?" Cassie asked.

I jumped then said, "No one."

"Uh-huh. Are you doing that crazy thing you do?" she asked.

"Crazy thing?"

"You know. Talk to the voices in your head. It's pretty creepy and weird."

"Whatever."

I looked down at my phone. Two fifty-nine.

"Cassie, leave your cousin alone. She's nervous." Grams walked into the foyer, holding a foil covered pan. "She's so nervous she almost forgot my famous apple cobbler."

"Dammit. Thanks for looking out, Grams."

I took the pan from her. Holding it against my hip, I looked at my phone again. Two fifty-seven. What? How the hell was time moving backward? Was I seriously going crazy?

Queen B opened her mouth.

"Don't say it," I grumbled.

Queen B smirked.

"There she goes again, Grams. Talking to those voices in her head."

"Shut up, Cassandra."

Grams caressed the back of my head. "It's okay, sweetie. We all have a little crazy in us. Yours just comes out more often."

Cassie snorted a laugh. I glared at her just as the doorbell rang.

"I got it!" Cassie pushed me out of the way nearly knocking the apple cobbler out of my hands.

"Watch it, Cassie!"

Cassie opened the door then froze. "What the fuck are you doing here?"

"Oh great, another shrew. Chord! You didn't tell me she lives here."

"That's because you were supposed to remain in the car, asswipe," Chord said breathlessly, approaching the door.

"I'm not staying in the car as if I'm your damn chauffeur."

"You didn't have to act like your ass was on fire to get here either." Chord railed back at him.

Cassie shook her head then turned to me. "Sure, you want to go knowing *that* will be along?"

"Who are you calling *that*?" the annoying third wheel asked.

My eyes met Chords. I held back a smile as I watched him scan me from head to toe. Gooseflesh pebbled my skin. Heat flared in his eyes. Who would have thought that jeans, boots, and a flattering blouse would get him all hot and bothered?

"Ew! Will you stop eye fucking my cousin?" Cassie scrunched up her face in disgust.

"He wasn't doing any such thing. And even if he was it's his right to do so." Third wheel crossed his arms.

"Cassandra, did I just hear you use a certain four-letter word?" Grams asked.

Cassie deflated. "Sorry, Grams."

"The jar is in the kitchen. With the way you're going, you're going to fund my bingo habit for the whole year." Grams smiled.

Cassie glared at the third wheel who had a Cheshire grin curving his lips. She walked away but lifted a middle finger as she did so.

"I see that, Cassandra. Double the fine."

I heard a loud huff then coins hitting coins as Cassie dropped change in the jar.

"Are you ready to go?"

"Yep. We should probably move fast before Cassie comes back and your friend gets a black eye or swift kick to the nether region."

"He deserves it." Chord grinned. "I'll take that for you." He reached for the pan in my hands.

"Hey!" Third wheel protested and stepped between us before I could hand the pan to Chord.

"It was nice seeing you, boys. Have fun, Rhapsody!" Grams gave me a little shove then shut the door behind me.

"Well, that was fun." Third wheel smirked then held out his hand to me. "I'm Alec. The donor's cousin."

I looked at his outstretched hand then to Chord. "Why is this asshat here?"

Chord choked. "I didn't invite him."

"What my cousin isn't saying is that he doesn't own a car, and he needed a ride. I generously offered so you wouldn't have to balance on his handlebars. It probably isn't good for the baby."

"You fucking told this turd." I waved my hand toward Alec.

Chord winced and took a step away from me. "I probably had a concussion at the time."

"You should be thanking me, mama. Without me, my fuckhead cousin wouldn't have apologized and would most likely still be crying in his pillow."

I glared at Alec then at Chord. "Let's go."

Passing through the two men, I walked toward the flashy car. It looked like a typical douchebag muscle car. If I had to pick a car that suited Alec the asshat, I would have picked the one parked in front of Grams' house.

"Wait up, Rhapsody. Let me get the door," Chord said, catching up to me.

"I was going to let you get the door anyway." I held up the cobbler.

Chord opened the door, shifted the seat forward, then took the cobbler. He gave me a small smile as I scooted past him and slid into the seat directly behind the passenger seat. I held out my hands to receive the cobbler but he shook his head.

"Move over."

"What?"

"Move over. I'm sitting back here with you."

I shrugged then shifted to the seat directly behind the driver.

"Let me take that."

Chord handed me the cobbler then got into the seat next to me. Once he was buckled, he took the cobbler from me once again. As we shut the door, Alec got in the car.

"What the fuck is this?"

"What?" Chord asked.

"Does this look like a taxi?"

"No, but it does look like someone is overcompensating for something," I said with a very angelic smile.

"Excuse me. I will have you know that is not the case."

I shrugged. "Most men who say that definitely are compensating for something."

"Chord, control your woman."

Chord laughed. "Not on your life."

I smiled then leaned over and gave him a light kiss on the

lips. Without looking at Alec, I said, "On Jeeves. We don't want to be late."

A curse laden sentence was mumbled but the loud rumble of the engine made it near inaudible. I laid my head on Chord's shoulder and relaxed. In that moment, I forgot that I was knocked up by him. It felt like we were a normal couple headed for a normal dinner with his family. That was my last thought before darkness overtook me.

26

CHORD

The angel lightly snoring on my shoulder warmed my heart. The more I got to know Rhapsody, the harder I was falling. She was quickly becoming more than just my baby's mama. We'd only been driving a few minutes when she fell asleep. According to the baby books I'd been reading, it was normal for that to happen.

"Is she snoring?" Alec asked.

"Yep. It's adorable."

"Sure, if you like the sound of a dying rhino."

"It's still adorable."

Rhapsody let out a well-timed snort then began drooling on my shirt.

"Oh God! Is she drooling now?"

I sighed. "Alec, shouldn't you be paying attention to the road and not what's going on back here?"

"I am. I'm good like that. A man compensating for something wouldn't be able to do what I'm doing."

"Oh for fuck's sake. Save it for when Rhapsody is awake or her cousin is around."

"That banshee is her cousin?" Alec screeched.

"Jesus, take it down a notch. Do you want dogs following the car? Yes, it's her cousin. She was touring with Blue Vengeance."

"Oh God! I know who that is. That's Cassandra Bash. Son of a bitch! I used to think she was so hot."

I laughed. "What changed?"

"I found out she's a horrible shrew. That really sucks. She was in the top ten in my spank bank."

The car turned onto a driveway that curved around a large tree blocking the house from the road. I smiled as Alec brought the car to a stop next to Miranda's sensible SUV. The house was a modest-sized rancher. The one good thing my father did was buy that for my grandparents. I wasn't sure if it was out of pride or guilt, but it didn't matter. Up until two years ago, my grandparents lived a blissful retirement there.

When my grandmother died, Miranda decided to move in to help take care of our grandfather. He resisted and if Miranda was correct, he was still resisting. The one thing our family continued was our Sunday dinners. Alec rarely came. Normally, his excuse was that he was busy with work. However, I knew it was because he and Miranda didn't get along.

Rhapsody snored a bit loudly and woke herself up. "Are we here?"

"Yep. Did you have a nice nap?" I brushed a strand of her hair out of her face.

"Yeah. I can't believe I fell asleep."

"I can't believe those horrible noises you were making didn't wake you up sooner." Alec smirked at her.

Rhapsody glared daggers at him then turned to me. "Definitely overcompensating."

"What? I am not—"

"Let's get out of the car before Alec blows a gasket."

Rhapsody took the dish I was holding while I slid the passenger seat forward and opened the door. As I unfolded myself from the car, I heard a squeal.

"Uncle Chord!" Alice ran toward me.

I caught her as she jumped at me. "How is my little munchkin doing today?"

"Good. I'm so excited."

"Why?"

"Mama said you were bringing a surprise. Is it a bike for me? I told Mama I thought it was a bike for me. She mumbled something about a baby doll. I don't really like those anymore. I hope you didn't get me one of those," Alice prattled on.

"Chord?" Rhapsody said as she tried to get out of the car while holding the dish.

"Oops."

I placed Alice back on the ground then took the dish from her, letting her get out of the car.

"Sorry."

"It's okay. I was just worried I was going to drop the cobbler." Rhapsody smoothed down her shirt.

"Who's that?" Alice's little voice brought their attention back to her.

"That is Uncle Chord's incubator," Alec said with a grin.

"What is an ink-a-baber? Is that a good thing?" Alice asked.

Rhapsody shot a look at Alec that told me if she got him in a corner, he'd never procreate. Which could actually be a good thing. The world didn't need little Alecs running around.

"Oh great! It's the great douche with the douchemobile," Miranda said from the steps.

"Hello, Shrew!" Alec called to Miranda.

"Mama! Uncle Chord brought us his intuberator." Alice pointed to Rhapsody.

Miranda had a confused look on her face. I shook my head at her. She stepped down the front steps and rammed her shoulder into Alec as she passed him then walked up to Rhapsody.

"I'm Miranda Reedy. It's nice to officially meet you." Miranda held her hand out to Rhapsody.

Rhapsody put her hand in Miranda's. "Rhapsody Bell."

"Your mom is Emmerson Lee, right?"

I watched as Rhapsody tensed. We hadn't really gotten into our relationships with our parents but from the look she had on her face, she must have a similar relationship to what Miranda and I have with Jimmy.

"Yep."

Miranda stared at Rhapsody for a long moment then smiled. She swung an arm around her shoulders then said, "Yeah we hate Jimmy too. I think we're going to get along great." Miranda looked back at me. "Did Chord tell you how hard he's crushed on your mom? She may have even been in his spank bank."

Rhapsody grimaced then laughed. "No. He conveniently omitted that information." Rhapsody looked over her shoulder at me. "Did you only knock me up to get to my mother?"

"What? No. How could you say that? I didn't even know you were her daughter when I knocked you up," I sputtered.

Miranda and Rhapsody shared a look then burst into laughter.

"Were you screwing with me?" I stared at them.

That only made them laugh harder.

"I don't think this dinner was a good idea," I mumbled as I walked past them.

"This should be fun." Alec chuckled. "Not for me but for me to laugh at your pain."

Miranda and Rhapsody walked between Alec and me. From one moment to the next, I barely caught Rhapsody pulling her arm forward then swinging it backward in a sharp motion. She effectively made contact with Alec's balls which caused him to collapse on the ground.

Another laugh escaped Miranda. "This is the beginning of a beautiful friendship."

———

"So, tell me how you met my grandson?" Grandpa Lew asked while he shoveled some cobbler into his mouth.

Rhapsody looked at me with an "I told you" look. Then she turned back to Grandpa Lew.

"We were both at a wedding. We were seated at the losers table together." Rhapsody smiled.

"Sounds about right," Alec added.

Grandpa Lew slid a glower toward him. "Alec, maybe you should go to weddings to meet nice women. We haven't seen you with one in a while. Well, there was that one girl that kept twitching. Stay away from the bars."

I snorted a laugh.

"Grandpa, you know Alec only likes women who have the same STDs as him. That's hard to find since he has so many."

Alec glared at Miranda. "Where is Alice's father again, Miranda?"

Miranda stood from her seat and moved to lunge at him. I grabbed her arm and pulled her down. "It's not worth it."

"Strangling him to death would be very satisfying. I even have a spot picked out under a certain tree to bury his body," Miranda offered while having a staring contest with Alec.

Rhapsody giggled then leaned toward me. "Thank you for inviting me."

"Are you sure my family isn't scaring you off?"

"Not at all. It reminds me of my own family." She smiled.

"Rhapsy, will you braid my hair?" Alice asked with a face covered in cobbler.

"Alice, I'm sure Rhapsody doesn't want to braid your hair." Miranda shook her head.

"I'd love to but why don't we clean up your face a bit then I can do your hair." Rhapsody stood from her seat.

Alice let out a squeal and ran around the table.

"You don't have to do that," Miranda said to Rhapsody.

"I want to."

Rhapsody took Alice's hand and led her to the bathroom. I watched as they disappeared down the nearby hallway. When we heard the door to the bathroom close, Grandpa Lew broke the silence.

"That's a keeper, Chord."

"I know, Grandpa."

"She's a keeper for the cobbler alone, but she's also a wonderful young woman." Grandpa Lew reached for another helping of cobbler.

"Grandpa." Miranda moved it out of reach.

"Miranda, I believe I am old enough to decide if I want another helping of dessert."

"Well, your endocrinologist says different."

Grandpa huffed then said, "Fine. You win."

"I like her, Chord. She's good for you." Miranda smiled.

"She's just so..." Words escaped me as I tried to fight the smile that curled my lips.

"If you ask me, I think she's too sassy for her own good. She needs to spend more time doing women things." Alec crossed his arms.

Miranda narrowed her eyes. "What do you mean by women things?"

"I don't know. Knitting, cooking, cleaning, and sewing socks."

I looked at Alec. What the hell was he doing? He was poking the bear. The bear was only moments away from ripping off his face. I sure as hell wouldn't be holding her back again.

"Alec, do you think we're in the nineteenth century? You're a fucking idiot and now I understand why you don't have a girlfriend."

"Any woman I'd be with will need to understand her place is either on her back or in the kitchen. There will be times both of those things occur at once."

Grandpa Lew sighed. "Boy, you are a few ants shy of a picnic. Why don't you just shut that trap of yours before I let Miranda shut it for you."

"But Grandpa—" Alec began.

Grandpa Lew raised his thick eyebrows at him. Alec slumped in his seat.

"What is taking them so long?" Miranda asked.

"I have no idea. I'll go check."

I stood so quickly I almost knocked over the chair. Fleeing from the tense atmosphere, I saw the bathroom was dark and empty. I could hear voices from a nearby room. The voices were coming from behind a door covered with stickers, so I peeked in the room.

"Mama says that Uncle Chord smiles a lot more now."

"Oh really? That's good."

Rhapsody was sitting on the floor with Alice in her lap. I watched mesmerized while Alice continued to chatter on as her captive audience braided her hair.

"I made this for Uncle Chord. He doesn't know I took it, but I think he'll like it." Alice held up a black and white photo covered in stickers.

"Can I see that?" Rhapsody asked as she finished the braid.

"Sure, but you can't tell Uncle Chord about it."

Alice handed the photo to Rhapsody after she twisted a band at the end of the braid. Rhapsody looked closely then shook while holding back a laugh.

"Do you like it?" Alice asked.

"I think it's great. Very nice." Rhapsody handed the picture back to Alice.

"What are you two doing in here?" I asked, making my presence known.

"Look what I made you." Alice jumped up from Rhapsody's lap.

I took the picture from Alice's outstretched hand. When I looked at the picture, I felt the blood drain from my face. Stickers were framing the image. A few lines of crayon turned the picture into a stick figure dog. The mystery of where my ultrasound image went was finally revealed. I looked over at

Rhapsody, who had tears streaming down her face from holding in her laughter.

Looking down at Alice's hopeful face, I smiled. "This is wonderful. Thank you, Alice."

"Yay! I got Uncle Chord to smile too." Alice ran out of the room, calling for her mother.

I sat next to Rhapsody on the floor. Her giggles finally broke free. I joined her in the laughs as we both looked down at the picture of our little bean who was turned into a puppy with a few swipes of crayon. Rhapsody leaned her face into my shoulder, and I wrapped an arm around her shaking shoulders. A sense of home overcame me. I knew at that moment I could be anywhere in the world and as long as I had Rhapsody in my arms, I'd always be home.

27

RHAPSODY

Six weeks later...

"Knock. Knock." Daniel stood in the doorway of my office.

"Hey! What are you doing here?"

"Just checking on you. How is everything going?"

I rubbed my rounded belly. My little monster was growing faster and faster with each day. Each day the little flutters were becoming stronger and stronger.

"It's going great now that the morning sickness has subsided." I took a sip of my decaf coffee.

"Coffee?"

"Decaf. So, why are you really here?" I leaned forward.

"Can't a friend come check on their friend?"

I sighed. "Yes, but when you come to check on me there is always an ulterior motive. I've known you too long, Daniel. What's up?"

He bit his lip. "I overheard Boswacker talking."

"And?"

"He's wondering if you are capable of still working while you're pregnant. I think he even mentioned going to human resources."

"He's such a fucking scumbag." I ran my hand over the spot where our little monster fluttered.

Daniel smiled. "Pregnancy looks good on you. Softens your hard edges."

"Did you just call me fat?"

"He didn't need to. It's pretty damn obvious from the empty donut box in your trash." Queen B swung her legs over the edge of the desk while looking at the trashcan.

"What? I didn't say—" Daniel stumbled over his words.

"What did my idiot husband just say?" A tall statuesque woman stood in the doorway holding the hand of what could only be described as a whirling dervish.

"Izzy!" Standing from my desk, I walked past Daniel. "I didn't know you were paying us a visit." Izzy let go of the little dervish's hand and pulled me into a hug.

"Well, even he didn't know we would stop by. We were planning on going to the library. Today is fairy tale day."

"Aunt Rhapsy!" the little girl squealed and launched herself at me.

I caught her easily and settled her on my hip. "How is my little angel doing?"

"More like devil," Daniel grumbled as he stood next to Izzy.

"Are you acting like your aunt Rhapsody again?" I couldn't fight the evil smile that curled my lips.

Olivia nodded, giving her a toothless grin.

"We stopped by to see if Daniel wanted to join us during his lunch."

"I'm sorry, sweets. I have a meeting in about fifteen." Daniel looked at me with mischief in his eyes. "Why don't you take her. She needs to go for a walk and she looooves the library especially the children section."

I glared at the ass. "I really need to work on a few things. I have a meeting with Mr. Anderson tomorrow about our project."

"Aunt Rhapsy, will you please go with us. It won't be long." Olivia, the little devil, blinked her little angel eyes at me.

"All right. I'll meet you two downstairs in five." I put Olivia down.

"Yay!" she squealed.

Izzy laughed, kissed her husband on the cheek, then said, "We'll be waiting downstairs."

I gave a little wave as they left then smacked Daniel on the shoulder. "You're an ass."

He shrugged. "Good news is you can't get knocked up again when you see him dressed as a princess."

"Out!"

Daniel laughed as he exited the office. Nervous energy made me organize the few things left on my desk. My mind wandered to who I was about to see. It made me straighten the papers a bit too hard on the desk. I shouldn't be nervous to see Chord.

"Don't be upset when Daniel is right about that idiot baby daddy. The real question is will he be a Belle, a Snow White, or an Ariel." Queen B laughed.

"Shut up!" My voice rose a bit too loudly, scaring a passing intern.

———

"Doesn't this look magical, Aunt Rhapsy?" Olivia spun around in the foyer of the lobby.

I couldn't help but be enchanted. The entrance to the children's part of the library was made to look like a castle. It even had stuffed dragons flying all over. I was so busy taking in the surroundings, I didn't hear the little feet running up to me.

"Rhapsody?"

I blinked and looked down. "Hello, Ms. Alice. How are you today?"

"I'm so excited. Do you like my dress?" Alice spun in a poofy pink dress.

"Alice! I told you not to—" Miranda said breathlessly. "Rhapsody?"

"Hey, Miranda!"

Miranda pulled her into a tight hug. "How are you feeling? Chord didn't tell us you were coming."

"It was a last-minute thing. How are you doing?"

"Good, but Grandpa Lew has been bugging us about you coming back. I hope that asshole of a cousin didn't frighten you off."

I laughed. "It would take a lot more than him to scare me off. I've actually been in the middle of a really big project. I'll be glad when it's over. Between the little monster and my job, I'm exhausted all the time." I looked to the side and realized Izzy was still standing there. "Oh my God! I'm so sorry. Miranda this is my friend, Izzy and her daughter, Olivia, is here somewhere."

Miranda smiled at Izzy. "Nice to meet you. I'm the sister of the guy who knocked her up."

Izzy grinned. "I'm the wife of her best friend/ex-lover."

Blushing, I said, "All right. Enough meeting new people. This having friends thing is really overrated. I'm going to go find the kids. They aren't determined to humiliate me."

Miranda and Izzy laughed as I walked into the castle. I smiled when I noticed that Alice and Olivia were chattering together with an older woman dressed as a princess. Looking around, I tried to see if I could find Chord.

"You just want to see if he's another princess or maybe they made him a jester like the tool he is." Queen B sipped her martini.

"Shut up," I mumbled.

"Excuse me?" A stern looking woman raked appraising eyes over me.

"Huh?"

"I thought you said—" She was cut off when someone came galloping in on an inflatable horse.

"Where, oh where is my princess?" he called out.

"I called it. He looks like a doofus. Your child is doomed." Queen B waved her arm, sloshing her martini on her tight skirt.

Queen B might have thought Chord looked like a doofus, but I thought he looked pretty cool. The little princes and princesses squealed as he galloped around pretending to search for his missing princess. Maybe it was the pregnancy hormones, but I was getting pretty horny seeing him like that.

"Uncle Chord! Uncle Chord! Your princess is over there," Alice called as she pointed in my direction.

Chord furrowed his brow then saw who she was pointing at. I gave him a little wave, and he grinned. An ornery glint flickered in his eyes, and he said, "There she is! I must save her."

He galloped toward me as the children cheered. In a swift movement, he lifted me into his arms and galloped out of the kid section of the library. I held onto him, fearing he'd drop me.

"Don't worry. I won't drop you," he whispered into my ear.

We turned a corner and he placed me on my feet. Before any words could escape me, he kissed me. I felt it down to my toes even with the inflatable horse head pressing against my vag.

He broke the kiss. "Why didn't you tell me you were coming? I've missed you so much."

"You saw me last weekend. Also, it wasn't planned. Daniel couldn't come and he somehow roped me into coming." I stepped away from him to free the trapped horse head.

Chord let out a chuckle. "Sorry, babe. Didn't realize the horse was getting some action."

"He had a good triple going." I laughed and ran my hand through his hair.

"How are you feeling today?" The back of his hand caressed my face.

"I'm okay. Just tired."

He looked at me. "Come over tonight. Let me cook for you. You can meet the guys finally."

"I don't know..." I hedged.

"Come on. Let me take care of you and little bean."

I bit my lip. I'd been putting off meeting his roommates. Granted, I already met the charming Alec but the rest just seemed like frat boys who couldn't grow up. If I was being honest with myself, I'd been putting off a lot with Chord. The whole pregnancy and work thing had me turned upside down. It was difficult to juggle and avoiding the changes in my life was easier to do than facing them head on.

"That's because you're a pussy," Queen B slurred.

"All right. I'll call you when I'm done. There is a chance I have to work late."

"Perfect. I'll be waiting." He kissed the side of my mouth. Those pregnancy hormones kicked back into gear, humping everything in their vicinity. "Are you okay? You have a strange look on your face."

I felt my face flame. Clearing my throat, I said, "Yeah. I'm great. I better get back to Izzy and Olivia. I need to head back soon."

Chord stopped me from walking away and knelt in front of me. He rubbed my rounded belly and said, "Behave for mommy, my little bean. Mommy needs a rest. I love you." He placed a tiny kiss on my blouse-covered belly. His eyes met mine and I almost swooned right there. It was that look right there that got us in this position.

"More like you're easy, and he's a one pump chump." Queen B cackled.

I really hated that bitch sometimes.

28

CHORD

"Holy shit! What the fuck is that smell?" Benny shouted with his arm around his latest piece.

"I'm cooking," I said, waving a towel around to get rid of the smoke.

"I have no idea what you're doing but it ain't cooking. Right, baby?" Benny asked the giggling girl.

"I think it tastes great," Oscar said while eating burned remains of what I'd have hoped to be a gourmet meal for Rhapsody.

"Your opinion doesn't count, Oscar," Alec said, joining everyone in the kitchen. "So, what made you want to all of a sudden cook something other than ramen?"

I sighed. "Rhapsody has been having a stressful time. I wanted to do something nice for her."

"And in turn get laid," Benny called as he shut the door behind his giggling guest.

"That's not—"

"Yeah it is. When was the last time you got laid?" Alec asked.

I felt a flush creep up my neck.

"Damn! That long? Even Oscar's gotten laid recently." Benny smacked Oscar on the back.

"Hey!" he said with a mouthful of charred food.

"It's not all about getting laid," I said and went back to searching the cabinets for something I could make quickly.

"Just 'cause you knocked her up doesn't mean you still shouldn't get action." Alec crossed his arms.

"Will all of you get out of here before she gets here?"

Just as the words left my mouth three knocks drew our attention.

"Too late." Benny laughed as he jogged to the door. He swung it open then leaned against the frame. "Well, hello, gorgeous. Where have you been all my life?"

"Is Chord here?" Rhapsody's voice was flat.

Benny blocked me from seeing her. "He's here but why have a burger when you can have steak."

Rhapsody sighed. "You know you're right, handsome. Why would I want Chord when I could have a STD riddled manwhore?"

Benny stuttered as the rest of us laughed. I pushed him aside and finally laid my eyes on her. My heart flipped when I saw her grimace at Benny. She was so damn hot when she was snarky. After I was done getting an instant hard-on from the look she was giving Benny I noticed what she was holding. She had four pizza boxes and two plastic bags.

"What is all this?"

"Does it matter? Can you just take the damn things? I had to walk all the way up here because your stupid elevator wouldn't work."

I grabbed the pizzas from her then led her into the apartment.

"Something smells good enough to eat," Benny purred next to Rhapsody.

Without looking at him, she shot her hand out and landed a solid nut punch. Benny landed on the floor in the fetal position.

She looked at me then asked, "Will there be any more assholes I need to nut punch?"

"Well, Alec is here."

"Whoa. Whoa. Whoa. No nut punches needed." Alec placed his hands over his crotch.

I leaned over and kissed her cheek. "I don't think that's necessary, babe. Why did you bring dinner? I told you I was going to cook."

Her eyes slid to Alec then back to me. "Miranda texted me saying you weren't the most experienced cook. So, she suggested I bring over a couple pies, breadsticks, wings, and a giant cookie."

"There's a giant cookie around here?" Oscar started rummaging in the bags she'd put on the counter.

"How did she even know I was cooking?"

She shrugged while pulling out paper plates.

"Alec?" I looked at my cousin.

"What? I didn't want your baby mama to starve." He opened one of the pizza boxes, letting the aroma of cheese and sauce fill the kitchen.

Feeling dejected I circled my arms around Rhapsody. "I'm sorry. I thought I could follow a recipe."

Rhapsody turned in my arms and linked her arms around my neck. "It's all right, Chord. You didn't have to make anything special for me. Hell, little monster has been craving mac and cheese with pickles."

"Ew. Even I wouldn't eat that," Oscar said with a mouthful of pizza.

She gave him a dirty look. "So, are you going to introduce me to these assholes?"

I laughed and buried my face in her neck, breathing in her scent. It made me impossibly harder than I was before she stepped into the apartment.

"Yeah. The one whose nuts you bashed is Benny, our resident gamer and manwhore." Benny glared at Rhapsody. "You already know Alec." He saluted her with a piece of pizza. "And finally, this is Oscar, our resident pothead." Oscar didn't even acknowledge I said his name.

"Nice to finally meet all of you I guess." Rhapsody grabbed a slice of ham and pineapple pizza, my favorite.

"How did you know that was my favorite?"

"Whut?" she asked behind a mouthful of pizza.

"Ham and pineapple."

Rhapsody swallowed her mouthful. "Oh...that's my favorite actually. I figured I'd have the pizza to myself."

"Great. We have two weirdos here," Alec said as he walked past us.

In a blur, Rhapsody's fist shot out and cracked him in the nuts. When he crumpled to the floor, Rhapsody stepped over him with her plate and sat at the dining room table. I shook my head and followed her. Damn if I didn't love her with each crazy moment we were together.

———

"Dammit." Benny cursed.

Rhapsody laughed. She'd managed to sneak up on him and shot him in the back.

"Damn, baby. That is some dirty play right there," I said as I continued to massage Rhapsody's feet as she played video games against the guys.

"Can you give the controller back to Chord now?" Benny asked.

"Why? Don't like losing to a girl?" she asked as she continued to mow down other players.

"Baby, he doesn't like losing period. I'm perfectly content watching. No need to go back to playing."

Benny slumped in his gaming chair. "Can we at least be on the same team?"

Rhapsody bit her lip and thought. "What's in it for me? I don't see any benefit in having you on my team."

He looked at Rhapsody then grinned. "I'll tell you what we were talking about before you came over."

She furrowed her brow. "Why would I want to know that?"

"Shut up, Benny," I said.

"It's good, Rhapsody. I promise." Benny wiggled his eyebrows.

"Hmm...sure. What were you idiots talking about?"

My hands gripped her feet as I stared daggers at Benny. His shit-eating grin was about to get smashed in by my fist.

"Ow. Chord, you're hurting me." She kicked my stomach with her foot.

"Oh. Uhm...sorry."

"It's fine." She looked at Benny. "Spill it, Benny."

Benny sat up straight and cleared his throat dramatically. "We were talking about how long it's been since our boy Chord has gotten laid."

Rhapsody blushed. "Huh. How long has it been?"

"We never found out. That was when you showed up."

She looked at me then asked, "Well, how long has it been?"

I looked around then said quietly to her, "You don't want me to answer that here."

"Oh I think I do. What are you hiding?" She snatched her foot away and sat up.

"I just don't—"

"Fine if you don't want to tell me maybe I should just leave." Rhapsody slid her feet into her shoes and stood.

"Wait! Wait! The reason I don't want to say is because you were there."

"What? That doesn't make sense unless..."

"Yep."

"Holy shit! It's been since you knocked her up?" Alec called from the hallway.

I looked up at the ceiling. "See why I didn't want to say anything around these asses."

She nodded slowly.

"Are you okay?"

"Yeah. Um...can we talk in your bedroom?"

Worry churned in my stomach, but I said, "Sure."

Taking her hand in mine, I led her down the hallway. I opened my door, led her in, then shut it behind us. I observed her taking in my disheveled room. She hadn't left screaming yet so I'd count that as a win.

"This is nice."

"I guess. I'm hoping not to be here too much longer."

Rhapsody turned to me. "Why? Where are you going?"

"I want to find my own place before little bean is born." I held back the part where I wanted her in the new place with me.

"Oh. Well, that's probably good. They are not good role models."

As if on cue, Alec yelled through the door. "Don't screw too loud in there. We are all assuming she feels bad that's why you're getting some."

"Definitely not role models," I agreed. Taking her hand, I led her to the bed. "What did you want to talk about?"

"You really haven't had sex since the wedding?"

"Nope." I swallowed the lump in my throat. "Have you?"

She let out a loud laugh. "Yeah right."

"What? You can't tell me you don't have a line of men chasing after you."

She smiled then leaned in and kissed me. Pulling back, she said, "You're so sweet."

"Oh well..."

My words were cut off as she went back to kissing me. Finally, my brain caught up to my lips, and I kissed her back fervently. I pushed her gently back against the bed. My hands explored her breasts while our tongues tangled. Breaking the kiss, I moved down her neck, placing little nibbles along the way. My hands had a mind of their own as they massaged her cloth-covered mound. She moaned with each touch. It seemed she needed me as much as I needed her. I sat up and pulled my shirt over my head. She did the same as I moved to her pants. Rhapsody lifted her hips as I slid her leggings down. I smiled when I saw the panties. Across the pink panties it said "gobble gobble" with a cartoon turkey next to them. She covered the panties with her hand.

"Sorry. I got these as a joke one Thanksgiving."

I moved her hand to the side. "I think these are fine instructions." Settling between her legs, I kissed her pussy through the cloth. As my fingers went to remove her panties there was a frantic banging on the door.

"Go away, asshole," I yelled and met Rhapsody's glazed eyes while I started to slide her panties down.

The door swung open, making me fall off the bed.

"What do we have here?" Jimmy stood in the doorway.

Rhapsody squeaked and tried to cover herself.

"What the hell are you doing here?" I stood.

"I've been thinking a lot about that ultrasound I saw. Guess I know who the baby mama is. Or weren't you going to introduce us?" He looked over at Rhapsody. "You look really familiar. Do I—"

"You need to leave, Jimmy." I placed my body between him and Rhapsody.

"Do I now? Hallway. Now." He took one more glimpse at Rhapsody then left the room.

I looked at Rhapsody then followed Jimmy out, closing the door behind me.

"What the fuck are you doing knocking up some fat chick? For fuck's sake, she's probably just after the prestige of fucking a rock star's son. Did you get a paternity test? I'm betting it isn't even yours."

"Will you shut up? It's not what you think."

"So, you're not into her? She's not pregnant? Just having a little fun with the easy girl?"

"Yeah. Okay. So, you didn't need to come barging in here like a prick. She means nothing to me."

Jimmy smiled and gave my shoulder a squeeze. "That's my boy. What I really wanted was to see if you could come with me for a week or so on tour?"

"Why?"

He cleared his throat and avoided eye contact. "Well, the hall of fame is doing something new. They want to do a documentary on the road, and they said it would be great to show some family touring with us."

I snorted. "We've never toured with you. I don't see how adding me, Miranda, and Alice would make any difference. It's not going to show how you really are."

"First, I didn't say Alice and Miranda would be coming. Second, they said it would make for a much more personal documentary. Come on. Just take a vacation and come with me. Alec will be there too."

"Perfect. It's not like I don't see him every damn day."

"Look, just try to make it happen okay."

"I'll think about it."

"Good." He winked then said, "I'll leave you to your big girl. They are always so grateful to get some."

I watched him walk away then turned back to my room. When I opened the door, Rhapsody was getting dressed.

"What are you doing? He's gone."

Her tear-stained face looked at me. "I need to go."

"Why?"

"I figured the fat girl could leave since she doesn't matter to you." She moved toward the door.

"Wait a minute. You didn't believe what I just said did you? I had to say that to get him to go away. He can't know whose daughter you are."

"Yeah, well that answer came a little too easily for my

comfort. Goodbye, Chord." She pushed past me, leaving the room.

"Rhapsody! Wait!" I followed her down the hallway, but she just ran out the door.

"Did you fuck up again?" Benny asked.

"Oh, he royally fucked up," Alec offered.

"Thanks for the help, Alec."

Alec pushed off the counter he was leaning against. "Who the fuck do you think banged on your door? If you'd have listened, then you wouldn't have had to say that bullshit to Jimmy. Why does it matter if he and Emmerson Lee know? You two are adults and are about to have a child. The stupid feud doesn't matter anymore." Alec marched off.

"Yeah, he screwed the pooch," Benny said into his gaming headset.

Feeling at a loss, I went back to my room. Falling into my bed, I stared at the ceiling and wondered why what I felt for Rhapsody and our little bean needed to be a secret anymore.

I typed furiously on my laptop as I put the finishing touches on the report for Mr. Anderson. It was the culmination of the many months of work I'd dedicated to the project. It had the potential to skyrocket my career. Sitting back in my chair, I rubbed my rounded belly. I was officially six months pregnant. That's right, six months pregnant, avoiding the baby's daddy and my mother like the plague while throwing myself into my work. My life was incredibly busy.

"Ms. Bell. I need you in my office now," Mr. Boswacker yelled into my office.

"Yes, sir."

I hefted myself out of my chair and followed him down the hall to his office.

"Close the door then have a seat."

After doing as he asked, I made eye contact with Daniel, who was talking to a junior associate.

"I need that report you've been working on for Mr. Anderson."

I furrowed my brow. "Why?"

"It isn't your job to question me. I need it and expect it in my inbox the minute this meeting ends."

"I'm going to need to run that by Mr. Anderson."

"No, you don't. Send me the report or send me your resignation."

"Excuse me?"

"I'm sure there is nothing wrong with your hearing."

"You're giving me an ultimatum."

"You are quite clever, Ms. Bell. Now, please leave and get me that report."

I stood and left his office. A fog came over me, and I felt dizzy.

"Rhapsody! Are you okay?" Daniel's voice sounded far away.

"Yeah. I just need to get back to my office."

"What's wrong?" He put an arm around my waist and assisted me to my office. Closing the door behind him, he sat across from me.

Plopping into my chair, I sighed. "Boswacker said if I don't give him the project I've been working on for Mr. Anderson then I'm fired. My other option is to resign. I can't afford either one. I'm six months pregnant and can't lose my job now. How can I support myself and little bean?" My words came out so quick I felt lightheaded.

Daniel blinked at me. "Okay. Relax. It will be fine."

Daniel slid a cup across my desk then sat in the chair facing me. "All right, now what did Boswacker say?"

After a few sips of water, I explained once again the short conversation with my boss. The words floated through my mind. When I was finished, I took another sip of water, trying to stave off the feeling of getting sick.

"He's outright trying to steal your work?"

"Looks like it."

I placed my hand over my protruding belly. Little monster was kicking up a storm. It seemed like he or she was pissed off at Boswacker too.

"You've got to be kidding me."

"Nope."

"You aren't thinking of handing your project over are you?"

I shrugged and opened my laptop. "I don't know, Daniel. I've got little monster to think about."

"I understand but you can't let him get away with that. If you quit there will be loads of companies coming after you. You can't give in to him."

Staring at the report in front of me, I contemplated my next move. The idea of losing my job made me sick. However, the idea of just handing over that work made me want to vomit all over Boswacker.

"Rhapsody?"

"Hold on a second. I'm thinking."

"I hope you're thinking about ways we can dispose of Ballwacker's body," Queen B said, sharpening her nails.

I ignored her as a plan began to form. I started to smile when it became fully formed in my mind.

"I've got—"

The phone ringing cut me off. I picked it up expecting Mr. Boswacker. "Rhapsody Bell."

"Rhapsody, sweetheart." Grams' voice came through the phone.

"Oh, hi, Grams. I can't really talk right now."

"I know. You're probably busy trying to take over the world. But I want to take you and Cassandra out to dinner tonight. We haven't had a girls' night out in quite a while."

I blinked then looked at the phone. "Is everything okay, Grams?"

"Of course. Why would you think something is wrong?"

"Well, we've never actually had a girls' night before."

"Oh, pish, we are starting a new tradition."

"Okay, Grams. Where am I meeting you and Cassie?"

"How about that little Italian restaurant near your work?"

"Papa Sargentinos?"

"Yes, that one. How does that sound?"

"That sounds good. I'll see you at six."

"Okay. Love you."

"Love you too." I hung up the phone.

"Something wrong?" Daniel asked.

"I get the feeling my grandmother has something up her sleeve or some bad news to share. I couldn't tell which."

"Hopefully, it's nothing. Maybe Chord contacted her."

I glared at Daniel. "I hope not. Though I doubt it. I haven't heard from him since that disastrous night when Jimmy Ray burst in on us."

Daniel looked down at the floor. "I know I shouldn't say it but maybe you should talk to him. I mean maybe he really didn't mean it. How would you have reacted if Emmerson showed up?"

"It doesn't matter anymore. I haven't thought about him since I left that night."

"Haven't thought about him my ass. You only count the days and minutes since you've seen him. I think you're up to sixty-five days, sixteen hours, twenty-two minutes and thirty-nine seconds." Queen B tapped her watch.

"None of that matters. Do you want to hear about my plan or not?"

Daniel smiled, sat back in the chair, and said, "I'm all ears."

———

I wove my way through the crowded restaurant. I'd run late after my meeting with human resources. I attempted to suck in my stomach but soon remember that I was pregnant and no amount of sucking in would lessen the protrusion of the very obvious baby bump.

"I know a kind of sucking that wouldn't have caused that," Queen B said as she made a rude gesture with her mouth and hand.

"Shut it," I mumbled, drawing the attention of an elderly man from the table I was passing.

"Rhapsody! Over here!" Cassie called.

"I see you, Cassie. You don't need to yell. It just takes me a bit longer to get places."

"I know. I just wanted to make sure you saw us." Her voice continued at the loud pitch.

"Why are you still yelling?"

"Yes, Cassandra, please stop that. You're making my hearing aids ring," Grams said as she gave me a hug. "What's wrong with you, Rhapsody? You don't look yourself."

"I'll tell you later. I just need to relax and get this little monster fed." I rubbed my belly then sat at the table.

Taking the menu that was on the setting in front of me, I opened it. I'd been to Papa Sargentinos many times before and had a favorite dish, but little monster was craving something different. When I finally settled on eggplant parmesan with a side of boneless buffalo wings, I noticed Cassie was staring at me with a stressed look on her face.

"What's going on?"

"What do you mean?" Cassie asked with a strange smile on her face.

"You're acting weird."

She shrugged then I watched as her eyes went over my shoulder. I turned and watched my mother strut through the restaurant toward us.

"What the hell is going on? Emmerson is here. Why didn't you tell me?"

Grams took in a deep breath. "I'm tired of all this cloak and dagger stuff, Rhapsody. Your mother needs to know she will be a grandmother."

"Grams..." I whined.

"Hello, everyone! I'm here." She whipped off her jacket with a flourish.

"Mother," I mumbled.

"Don't I get a hug, Rhapsody?" Emmerson Lee stood with her arms outstretched.

I stood from the table and watched as she took in my form. The moment she realized I was pregnant, her demeanor changed.

"You're pregnant?"

I opened my mouth to confirm her suspicions when Grams interrupted me.

"With Jimmy Ray's son's child."

"Boom! Now that's how you ruin a family dinner." Queen B did a slow clap.

"I can't believe you're finally living on your own," Miranda said as she unpacked a box labeled kitchen.

"It was bound to happen." I carried two boxes into my bedroom.

"Yeah, but we had odds that you'd be living with those idiots for the rest of your life," Miranda called out.

"Who is we?"

"Grandpa and me."

"Seriously? You really thought I'd bring my little bean into that apartment?"

Miranda shrugged as she put away the last of my mismatched glassware. "Speaking of your little bean, have you talked to Rhapsody?"

I took a swig out of a water bottle and sat on the counter to buy time to figure out what answer I was going to give.

"I take it that's a no."

"I needed to get my life together before I called."

"Why are men so dense? Please tell me you didn't listen to Alec or Benny or that pothead, Oscar."

"What's a pothead?" Alice asked.

I grinned at Miranda as I snatched up my niece. "Yes, what is a pothead, Miranda?"

Miranda glared at me then looked to Alice. "A pothead is someone who likes plants a little too much."

Alice worried her little lip thinking about what her mother had just said. "How can you like a plant too much?"

"Yeah, how?" I asked unhelpfully.

"Well, if you like plants too much then you can get dirty and smelly. That's why you never want to become a pothead."

Alice scrunched up her face. "I don't like to be dirty. I don't ever want to be a pothead."

"Good. Now, go sit on the couch and play on your tablet while I finish helping Uncle Chord."

"Okay, Mama." Alice wiggled out of my grasp.

"Nicely done." I smiled.

Miranda flipped me the bird. "Get back to explaining why you haven't talked to Rhapsody after being an idiot around Jimmy."

"Fine. I'm scared."

"Don't you mean chicken shit," Alec said as he walked through the door to the apartment carrying a box.

"What the hell are you doing here?" Miranda demanded.

"I'm here to help my dear cousin. Plus, I have some things that he left."

I furrowed my brow. "I didn't leave anything."

"Check it out." He placed the box on my small kitchen table.

I opened the box. There were boxes of tissues lined across the top of the box. Looking over at Alec, he smirked at my confused look.

"These aren't mine."

"Keep going."

I glared at Alec. My gut told me he was up to something. He was way too excited about a cardboard box that contained tissues. However, if I ever wanted him to leave my apartment, I needed to go through the stupid box. I removed two of the tissue boxes and felt my face flame.

"What is it?" Miranda looked over my shoulder into the box. "Ew…ugh…you two are perverts."

"These are not mine," I protested.

Alec bent over laughing. I stared at him as I pushed the box away. Beneath the tissue boxes was an assortment of porno magazines and sex toys. The top porn magazine was a granny fetish magazine. It made me shudder.

"What? So, it wasn't your stuff really. It is now though. The guys and I thought since you royally fucked up with Rhapsody, you're going to need to…" he cleared his throat then continued, "to…uhm…entertain yourself."

Miranda scrunched up her face. "You two are disgusting."

I looked at my sister. "Don't lump me in with him."

"Well, if you would just fix things with Rhapsody, I wouldn't be forced to lump you in with him."

"I will as soon as—" My phone vibrating in my pocket interrupted me.

Rhapsody: Emmerson knows.

I blinked at the phone. Frantically typing back, I felt a mixture of happy excitement and cold dread.

Me: What?

That's me. A master of the English language.

Rhapsody: CALL ME NOW!!

"Everything okay, Chord?" Miranda asked.

"I'm fine. I need to make a call. I'll be right back."

Walking to my bedroom, I sat on my bare mattress. Organizing my bedroom hadn't been a priority yet. Boxes filled with sheets, clothes, and miscellaneous goods were piled around the room. I scrolled to Rhapsody's contact. With a deep breath, I pressed the number.

It rang twice when I heard a click then, "What do you mean what? What don't you understand about me telling you Emmerson knows?"

"Um…hi," I said reluctantly.

Rhapsody blew out a breath then said flatly, "Hello, Chord." It couldn't be any clearer that I was the last person she wanted to be talking to.

Though I knew she was pissed, I couldn't fight the smile that curved my lips. I'd missed her so much it hurt. With each passing day, I didn't think I could miss someone any more than I already did but each day the pain in my chest got worse. "I've missed you."

"Focus, Chord. She's going to contact Jimmy."

"What?"

"Seriously, Chord. You really need to find a way to keep up with conversations."

"She's going to call Jimmy about little bean?"

"No."

A breath escaped me as I collapsed against my bed in relief. "Good. That's good news."

"She's calling Jimmy about you."

Going from laying to standing is never a good decision for anyone. The world spun as the words she'd said hit me like a sledgehammer.

"Fuck me."

"That's how we got into this position."

"Okay. Okay. This will be fine."

"Jimmy's going to find out that your baby mama is the fat girl. I don't see how that's good for you."

The precision in which she threw my stupid words back at me caused physical pain. Not only pain but anger. I hated that she felt that way because of my idiocy.

"I'll handle it."

"Uh-huh. Sure, Chord. Well, I thought I'd warn you that hurricane Emmerson was headed your way."

"Thanks for the heads up. Um…would you like to have dinner tonight?"

Silence. So much silence met me with that one question. It

felt like an eternity of silence went by. I even glanced at the phone to make sure we hadn't lost connection.

"Rhapsody? Are you still there?"

"I don't think that's a good idea. Goodbye, Chord."

This time I knew the silence indicated she'd hung up.

"Dammit!" I threw my phone onto the bed. I watched helplessly as it bounced off the mattress, somersaulted through the air, and embedded itself into the wall. Damn. There went my security deposit.

"Everything okay?" Miranda poked her head into the room.

I shook my head. "Jimmy is about to find out that Emmerson Lee's daughter is carrying my little bean."

"Fuck. What are you going to do?"

"I'm not sure but honestly I'm tired of hiding Rhapsody. Who our parents are and their stupid feud shouldn't matter. Only Rhapsody and little bean matter."

Miranda smiled then pulled me into a hug. She planted a kiss on my cheek then let me go.

"What was that for?"

"I'm proud of you. You finally grew a pair and realized that none of their rock star dramatics matter."

"What if he tries to get rid of the house? Where will you, Alice, and Gramps live?"

"Relax, Chord. I've got it covered. Let the prick try to take the house away from Gramps. I've been saving up enough money in case that happened. Ever since I had Alice, I've been preparing for Jimmy to be a giant dildo. I just wasn't sure what he would do or when he would do it."

A snort-laugh escaped. "Well, then I think I'm ready to royally piss him off."

"Sweet. Just video it so I can enjoy it too." She smiled and hugged me once more.

"Mama! Look at my new belt." Alice stood in my doorway.

I choked on a laugh while holding Miranda tightly. She was not prepared to see the vision I saw.

Alec ran to the doorway behind Alice. "I swear I didn't even see her get into it."

Miranda continued to have her back to where Alice and Alec stood. She asked, "Is my daughter wearing a strap-on?"

"Yep," I choked out as Alice danced around with her new "belt".

"Jesus. Just being around you and Alec makes me a bad mom." Miranda broke free from my hold and turned around. Finally, she saw what Alice was wearing. It was just in time to see her daughter pretending to fight an invisible foe using her new "belt". "Alice, sweetie, that is Uncle Chord's special belt. I don't think you can have it."

Alice stuck out her lip. It began to quiver, and I was only a moment away from giving her anything she wanted. However, Miranda was immune.

"Tuck in that lip, young lady. You will remove that belt and hand it to your uncle."

In an instant, Alice's quivering lip and watery eyes dried up. She unbuckled the belt then handed it to me. "Sorry, Uncle Chord."

"It's okay, Alice. How about we go get you a sparkly pink one next time I babysit?"

Her eyes lit up and she bounced on her toes. "Yes."

Miranda shook her head. "All right, I think we need to go before your uncle promises you a pink Cadillac." She turned back to me. "Have fun unpacking. Call if you need anything." Miranda grabbed Alice's hand and left the room.

I laughed as I heard Alice ask, "What is a cod-ill-duck? Is that an animal? Is it a pink animal?"

Alec moved out of reach when he saw the pissed off look on Miranda's face. He even made the wise decision of covering his junk just in case. I watched him relax as soon as we heard the door shut behind Miranda and Alice.

"Whew! Dodged one there. So, did you make up with

Rhapsody? If you had some phone sex in here you really are a one pump chump."

I glared at my cousin then grinned when a devious thought floated through my mind. "I haven't made up with Rhapsody yet but when I tell Jimmy that she is carrying my baby, I think it will help."

Alec clapped me on the back. "Finally growing a pair."

"I think telling Jimmy she is Emmerson Lee's daughter and that you knew all along will hopefully let me grovel for forgiveness."

"I'm sure that—" Alec turned to me with his eyes as big as saucers. "You're telling him I knew?"

I winked. "Thanks for the box of goodies. Now, get the hell out of my apartment."

Shoving him out the bedroom door, I locked it then retrieved my phone from the wall. It was time I finally stood up to my asshole father. I just hoped it wouldn't be too late to win back Rhapsody and little bean.

"Rhapsody." Cassie's voice gently floated into my darkened room.

I snuggled further into my bed. It had been a little over a month since I quit my job and told my mother I was pregnant with her archenemy's son's baby. Well, technically I didn't say anything. Grams was the culprit there. It had also been just as long since I spoke with Chord. I shouldn't be sulking because of that. I had a lot of other things I could've been sulking about like the aforementioned info bomb to my mother or the demise of my sole ability to care for my little monster. Instead of mourning my career, I'm hiding in my dark room under covers because I turned him down.

"Rhapsody." Cassie's voice came closer.

I held my breath and hoped Cassie would buy I was sleeping.

"You know holding your breath only makes people think you're dead. Not sleeping." Queen B shook her head.

The breath whooshed out just in time for Cassie's face to be inches from mine when she lifted the comforter.

"Jesus, Rhapsody. Your breath is rank. Is that how you drove that book nerd away?" Cassie waved her hand in front of her face.

"Leave me alone, Cassie." I rolled over, pulling the blanket with me.

Instead of leaving, Cassie yanked the covers toward her and crawled in with me. I grumbled under my breath.

"Hey! Enjoy it. It may be the last person you get to crawl into your bed." Queen B snapped her gum and thumbed through a magazine.

"Shut up," I mumbled.

"Don't get me wrong. Your cousin is pretty hot. I'd do her." Queen B wagged her eyebrows.

"When you're done having an argument with your inner demons can you please get up, take a shower, brush your fucking teeth, and get dressed."

"It's just one demon or rather a queen bitch."

Cassie shook her head. "I seriously worry about you sometimes. Anyway, it doesn't matter if you have a demon, a bitch, or thirty chihuahuas inside your twisted brain. What does matter is what is on our front lawn right now."

I turned toward her. "What's on the front lawn?"

"I'm not telling until you pull yourself together. And believe me, you want to see this."

"I don't think I'm up for human interaction."

"Ever. You forgot the ever," Queen B added.

"Come on, Rhapsy. I'll wait for you downstairs."

Cassie left the bed and only a few moments later I heard my bedroom door shut. Rolling onto my back, I kept my comforter over my face. I scrunched my nose when I got a whiff of my breath bouncing back at me. Maybe Cassie had a point. I needed to get my shit back together. No more sulking over some guy. Throwing off the cover I rolled out of bed.

"Sure. Listen to her but not to me. You know if you keep treating me this way one of these days I'm just going to leave," Queen B huffed.

"If only," I mumbled.

I grabbed my stuff and headed to the bathroom across from my room. Before I could even start a deep clean, I went back into my room and grabbed my radio. Music was needed to drown out that bitch.

———

"Oh holy shit balls. This is the worst thing I've ever heard and keep in mind I've heard you orgasm with your vibe." Queen B covered her ears.

"How long has this been going on?" Rhapsody said flatly.

Grams and Cassie didn't answer. They continued to sit quietly in the living room. Grams was busy knitting little monster an itchy sweater or scarf or a strange looking sock, while Cassie flipped through a music magazine.

"Hello!" I waved my hands in the air to get their attention.

They both looked up and smiled."

"I see you saw the front lawn," Grams yelled.

"See what's on the front lawn?" Cassie's voice rose above Grams.

"Yeah. How long has he been out there?" I pointed toward the window.

Grams and Cassie gave me a questioning look then each pulled clear pieces of plastic out of their ears. I blinked at them when I realized they'd been wearing earplugs. Each grimaced as a particularly bad screeching filled the room.

"How long have you had earplugs in?"

"An hour and a half...give or take." Grams shrugged. "Are you going out there?"

"Yes. Please. For the love of all music, go out there and make it stop," Cassie begged.

I sighed then crossed my arms over my growing belly. "I have nothing to say to him."

"Get the hell off my lawn while spraying him with a hose would make a statement," Queen B suggested.

Grams placed down the yarn and stood from her seat. She walked over to me then pulled me into a tight hug. Her arthritic riddled hand cupped my cheek. "I love you, darling. You know I do. However, if you don't get him off my front lawn, I'm going to go out there with a baseball bat. I can't guarantee he won't be a casualty. So, for everyone's sake please make it end." A phone in the kitchen rang angrily. Grams sighed. "I'll get that. I'm sure that's another neighbor calling to tell me I have something dying on the front lawn."

"I'll go with you, Grams. Hopefully, it's quieter out there." Cassie jumped from her seat and followed. A few feet away from me, she turned back. "How the hell is he related to Jimmy Ray?"

Right then there was a screech from a mic getting too close to an amp. Cassie and I winced together. With a deep breath, I approached the front door. The thumbs up from Cassie wasn't as helpful as she thought it was. Opening the door, I got the full effect of the scene on the lawn. Chord stood with a mic, next to a portable amp, some sort of light mechanism flashed weird Christmas images on him while what looked like a huge silver boombox from 1985 spit out one of my favorite songs. Now, if that was all it was, it would be annoying but not something that would drive Grams homicidal.

Along with his elaborate electronic setup, he wore a powder blue tuxedo while holding an inflatable guitar. Even that I could ignore. Unfortunately, his voice was the biggest problem. It was horrible. Not just bad but unbearable. Mix the sound of a dying cat with the mating call of a walrus and only then would that noise be even close to what was coming out of Chord.

Opening the screen door, I stepped out onto the small brick steps in front of the house. "What in the fuck are you doing, Chord?"

"I'm trying to win you back." He held up his hand when I

opened my mouth to shut him down. "Hold on, I need to finish this chorus. We're coming up on the best part."

Chord's horrendous voice rose and destroyed my love for the song he was covering. I'd never be able to hear that song again.

"Just the song? He's ruined music entirely." Queen B shoved in earplugs.

Shaking my head, I descended the brick steps. While Chord got into the song, he did some tribal dance, which I'm pretty sure was some sort of cultural appropriation. I wanted to stop him, but I knew stopping the music was the real issue. It didn't matter what he was doing. I need to be the bad guy. Marching over to an extension cord I hadn't seen before, I unplugged it. Chord's voice immediately only became audible to us. He stopped when he realized there was no music accompanying him.

Blissful silence rained down upon us. The only sound was the blood pumping in my abused ears. I shook my head trying to dislodge the horrible caterwauling. As my hearing came back, I heard clapping. I looked around and saw many of my neighbors along with Grams and Cassie applauding.

"Are they applauding me?" A confused look colored his features.

Whew. Clearly, he was aware of his heinous singing ability. At least I wouldn't be breaking his heart about that. Maybe his balls but not his heart.

"Applauding him? Is he high? That's the only explanation." Queen B flung herself on a chair.

"Nope. That is all for me. I may even get a neighborhood award."

"They have awards?"

"Well, no, but I'm sure they'd make one up just for me in this moment."

Chord breathed out a laugh.

"Why are you here, Chord?" I stared at his lips and

immediately regretted it when my horniness went into overdrive.

"I've come to win you back." He smiled.

"You thought dressing like that and singing like a horny moose during mating season was going to win me over?"

He shrugged. "I was hoping that if I humiliated myself enough you'd be willing to have dinner with me."

A breath whooshed out of me. "Chord…" I began.

"Wait. Just hear me out. I want to sit down and talk. I have some news and wanted to pretend like we are civilized adults who can have a meal and talk."

"*He. He.*" Queen B giggled.

"Not gonna happen."

Chord nodded. "I figured you'd say that. Onto plan b." He moved to plug his equipment back in.

"What are you doing?" I stepped in front of him, blocking his access to the cord.

"Well, since you won't go out with me then I will continue to play until you agree."

"Are you trying to fucking blackmail me?"

He shrugged. "I need to start playing dirty."

"You dick."

"If you will excuse me, I need to get back to it. I think I'm getting better at this song."

I placed my hand on his chest. "Hold on. Have you only been singing this one song?"

"Yep. Over and over and over. Now, please move, Rhapsody. I have to get back to convincing you to go out with me."

I opened my mouth but was cut off.

"Rhapsody, if you don't go out with that boy, I'm officially kicking you out of this house," Grams called from the door.

"Go out with him," the neighbors began to chant.

Chord grinned. I was torn between punching him in his stupid face and tackling him right there on the front lawn to have my way with him.

"Fine. I'll go."

Another round of applause echoed around us. I watched Chord take a bow. Smug asshole.

"I'll give it to Mr. One Pump. He just outsmarted you." Queen B stood and clapped.

32

CHORD

Rhapsody sat across from me in the plastic booth at the fast food joint. The same silence filled the air between us as it did in my car. I watched her dip fries in a pool of ketchup while averting her eyes from mine.

"Are you going to talk to me?" I crumpled up my empty burger wrapper.

"You forced me to come to dinner. You didn't say anything about me having to participate in any conversation."

Rhapsody dipped another fry in the ketchup pool. This was going to be the longest fast food dinner in the history of fast food.

"Will you please talk to me?"

Rhapsody sighed and looked at me with raised eyebrows.

"All right. Since you're at least looking at me now, I'm going to say what I want to say."

She stared at me blankly.

"I want us to be an us again."

She snorted then went back to dipping a fry into the red blob.

"I know I fucked up."

"Yup." She slurped on her soda.

"I want to make things better."

"How do you plan on that, Chord? I don't know if I can trust what you say?"

"I know I have a lot of work cut out for me but—" I was cut off by the buzzing of my phone. Glancing down, I noticed it was Alec. Pressing ignore I flipped over my cell. "What was I saying?"

"You were telling me about how—" Rhapsody was cut off by her ringing phone. She opened her bag and pulled out the offending phone. She had a weird look on her face.

"Everything okay?"

She looked at the phone then back to me. "Was that Alec who texted you?"

I blanched. "Yeah. How did you know?"

"Cassie just texted me."

"Okay. I'm not seeing the connection."

"Look at your phone, Chord."

I flipped over my phone and immediately regretted it.

Alec: You're needed at the Central PD.

Alec: Chord? Pick up your fucking phone.

Alec: This is serious.

Alec: Don't make me talk to the dragon shrew.

Alec: I had to talk to her. I hate you.

Alec: CHORD!!!

Me: What the hell is going on?

Alec: Fucking finally. What the hell have you been doing?

Alec: Never mind. Get down to the police department now.

Me: Why?

Alec: You'll see when you get here.

Me: You better not be fucking with me.

Alec: I wouldn't do that.

Me: Yeah you would.

Alec: Yeah I would but this isn't that. I'll see you in ten.

I sighed and looked at Rhapsody. She was standing and

holding her purse. While I'd been texting my idiot cousin, she'd cleaned our table and was ready to leave.

"I'm so sorry. It looks like there is some kind of emergency."

"Alec wouldn't tell you either?"

I stood from the booth. "What?"

"Cassie wouldn't tell me anything, but I have a feeling this has to do with our parents."

"Fuck me," I muttered as I held open the door for her.

Rhapsody grinned at me. "That might be why they are in jail."

"I doubt it. I'm sure it's just a coincidence."

We got into the car, and I pulled away. Rhapsody drummed her fingers nervously against her purse. The tension between us became thicker. I didn't think that was even possible.

"Do you really think something happened between our parents?"

She shrugged. "This wouldn't be the first time."

"What?"

"Apparently, a few decades back when this whole feud started there was something with a television through someone's hotel room and a stolen giraffe."

"A stolen giraffe?" I looked over at her.

"Yep. Though it could be some other animal. I was probably five when I heard the story, and I wasn't listening that closely. The only thing I was supposed to get out of it was to stay away from anyone associated with Jimmy Ray. How was I supposed to know the one time I get drunk and have sex with a hot guy it would be Jimmy's son."

I bit my lip then said, "You think I'm hot."

Her face flushed then she straightened in her seat. "You know you're hot. I also think you're an idiot. You should probably focus on that part."

A laugh bubbled out of me as I pulled the car into a parking spot in front of the police department. I glanced up and the thought of me taking the pregnant mother of my child into a police department because of our parents struck me as hilarious. My loud laughter drew the looks of nearby officers getting into their squad cars.

"Did I break you?"

Holding up one finger I put my head on the steering wheel and continued to laugh until I was heaving in breaths. Finally, the laughs stopped, and I glanced at Rhapsody. Her look almost made me start all over. She reached over and twisted my nipple.

"Ow! Why did you do that?" I rubbed my poor injured nipple.

"I figured giving you a purple nurple would keep you from laughing all over again. I saw the look on your face. You were headed down the laugh track again."

I crossed my arms. "How would you like it if I did that?"

She let out a frustrated sigh. "Can we just find out what the hell is going on? Then we can go our separate ways."

Her words were like a bucket of ice water. "I don't want to go our separate ways."

"Dammit, Chord. Focus. Let's get things handled then we can figure out our junk."

I gave her a long look then nodded. "Let's go."

We exited the car then walked up to the double doors of the police station. We could see Alec and Cassie having an argument with an officer standing between them. If we didn't get in there we'd have to bail them out too.

"Jesus. I don't have money for two bails tonight," Rhapsody quipped.

"It's your aunt's fault that any of this happened," Alec yelled, pointing a finger in Cassie's face.

"Are you fucking high? You've got to be high. Officer, I think you need to check this asshole for drugs. He's saying ridiculously stupid things that only someone on an illegal substance would say."

"I'm high? I'm high? You're the one that got busted a few years back. You aren't one to talk."

"What?!" Cassie screeched.

"Cassie!" Rhapsody yelled.

"Alec!" I approached my cousin.

"Rhapsody! Finally! I'm sorry I had to drag you from your alone time, but this is something you need to handle."

Rhapsody rolled her eyes. "Thanks. Now, if you shut up and go sit over there I can talk to this nice police officer about Emmerson." She moved past Cassie and the other officer to speak with someone at the desk.

"What the hell is going on, Alec?"

"I told you I didn't want to talk to the dragon shrew." Alec crossed his arms as if that sentence made any sense.

"I have no idea what the hell you're talking about. Why do I need to be involved when you are Jimmy's manager?"

"I had to talk to her." Alec pointed at Cassie. She stuck out her tongue at him. "She's impossible."

"Focus, Alec."

"The agency won't let me handle Jimmy's troubles anymore. They said you or Miranda needed to."

"You didn't call Miranda because…"

He gave me a horrified look. "I already had to deal with one shrew. Did I really need two?"

A tension headache built behind my eyes. "Fine. Go sit over there and act like a civilized adult."

Alec glared over at Cassie then sat in a chair across from her. I shook my head then went to the desk where Rhapsody was talking to the officer.

"…she can't just burst into a hotel room and pour Jell-o all over someone's bed," the officer explained.

"I understand, officer, but I didn't realize a prank was an arrestable offense."

"It's not but when she broke into the room and effectively stole Mr. Ray's guitar strings and condoms it was."

Rhapsody rubbed the bridge of her nose. "How much will this cost?"

"Seven hundred."

I cringed. "I can take care of it."

"No. Emmerson is my problem. I think you have your own problem with Jimmy."

Looking at the officer, I asked, "What did he do to get himself in here?"

"Well, when Mr. Ray discovered Ms. Lee was the culprit he burst through the hotel room door and assaulted Ms. Lee with a pillow then absconded with her...uhm..."

"What?" I asked.

"Her sexual assistant devices." The officer blushed.

"Her what?"

"Emmerson has an extensive collection of vibrators and dildos." Rhapsody's voice was matter-of-fact.

"What the hell is wrong with them?"

The officer shrugged. "It will be seven hundred for you too."

I wanted to bang my head on the counter, but I figured if I did that, they'd send me to the asylum or worse in the jail with Jimmy. "All right. How does this work?"

"I need you two to sign these then I can go get them."

Rhapsody and I signed identical papers effectively taking responsibility of our parents.

"Thank you. I will have someone bring them out now." The officer took the papers then began typing on his computer.

I looked at Rhapsody. "I guess we wait."

"I guess so." She winced as she rubbed her belly.

"Are you okay?"

She closed her eyes and took a deep breath. "Yeah. I'll be fine. We better sit with them before they decide to go another round."

"Good idea."

I walked over to Alec and sat next to him.

"Did you fix it?" he asked.

"Yeah. They are bringing him out now."

"Not Jimmy. Did you fix your issues with Rhapsody?"

"What?" I furrowed my brow then I understood what he said. "Oh. No. I was in the middle of trying to convince her that I wouldn't act like an idiot any longer, but this happened."

"Sorry, man. If I could have handled it, I would have."

I leaned back in the chair and closed my eyes. The fluorescent lights were making my headache worse. It was only a few minutes later when a commotion drew all our attention.

"You miserable son of a bitch." Emmerson Lee's voice echoed through the police station.

"I'm miserable? You're the miserable one. You have all those sex toys because you need to get laid. Maybe then you won't be obsessed with me," Jimmy yelled.

"Obsessed! Obsessed? The only thing I'm obsessed with is making your life miserable. Next time I'll cut off your cock. Maybe then you'll learn," She screeched.

"Did you hear her, officer? She's threatening me. I feel threatened."

I watched as Jimmy covered his junk with his bound hands while Emmerson tried to kick him as the officer tugged her away from him.

"Mother!" Rhapsody's voice snapped.

In that moment, I envisioned Rhapsody using that voice to correct our little bean.

"Rhapsody?" Emmerson asked.

"Chord?"

I met Jimmy's eyes.

"If you don't knock it off, I'm not..." Rhapsody stilled.

"Rhapsody, are you okay?" I stood from the chair.

She nodded but I watched all the color drain from her face. With a speed I didn't know I possessed, I made it to her just in time to catch her before she hit the floor.

"Fuck! Rhapsody!" Cassie slid over to where I was sitting with Rhapsody's prone form.

"Rhapsody? Sweetie?" Emmerson's voice wavered then she

turned to Jimmy. "See what you did? I swear if anything happens to her…"

"How the hell are you blaming this on me? I didn't do anything to her," Jimmy protested.

Emmerson Lee reared back readying herself to go at Jimmy again.

"Will you two knock it off?" I yelled.

Everyone froze. By the looks on Jimmy's and Emmerson's faces, it had been a long time since anyone yelled at them.

"I'm taking Rhapsody to the hospital." I picked her up then turned toward Cassie and Alec. "I need you two to handle these two."

Cassie and Alec nodded as I walked past them. Worry cooled the blood in my veins. If anything happened to Rhapsody and little bean, our parents would feel what wrath really felt like.

33

RHAPSODY

An incessant beeping pounded in my head. It had to be my damn alarm. Why the hell would I set my alarm? I didn't have a job anymore. When did my phone get such an annoying ringtone? It didn't matter. I rolled over to turn it off, but my arms felt heavy. Fuck my life. It would be just my luck to get sleep paralysis or something.

Peeling my eyes open I shut them again immediately. I never kept my blinds open. What the hell happened last night? My fuzzy brain started putting together the previous night's events. Dinner with Chord. The texts from Cassie. Emmerson and Jimmy in jail. Then nothing. I hoped no one spiked my drink. It could endanger the baby. Fear rushed through me. Forcing my eyes open I blinked until the floating spots left my sight.

I was in a strange sterile looking room. The lone window in the room let in the horrible sunshine. Sitting on the ledge by the window were the only bits of color. A bouquet of gerbera daisies was in a vase next to a stuffed octopus.

"What the hell?" I mumbled.

I felt something squeeze my hand. My eyes landed on someone holding my hand while laying their head on the bed. It was Chord. A rumbling sound that was reminiscent of a bear hibernating came out of him. How did I not know he snored?

"You only slept with him once, dummy. And you didn't do much sleeping." Queen B shook her head.

The head moved. An eye opened and met my gaze.

"Rhapsody?"

"Hi."

He shot to a sitting position then climbed onto the bed and pulled me to him. His strong arms held me tight. I took in a deep breath as I wrapped my arms around him. We sat like that for what seemed like an hour. He pulled away, and his eyes roamed my body.

"You scared me, baby."

"Why? What happened?"

A quizzical look passed over his handsome features. "You passed out. We're in the hospital."

"The hospital?" I tried to remember.

"Yep. You gave us all a fright."

I tried to remember what happened, but it was all blacked out.

"Sounds like someone roofied you if you ask me." Queen B swirled her martini.

"How long have I been in here?"

He sighed. "Two days."

I nodded then slapped my hands on my stomach. "Is everything okay? Nothing happened to little monster did it?"

"No. She's fine." Chord grinned.

"You mean he."

He shook his head. "No. It's officially a she. The doctor kind of spilled the beans."

"A girl."

"A little girl that is going to be the spitting image of her beautiful mother."

I felt the heat rise up my neck. Chord lifted my hand to his lips, placing a light kiss on the palm.

"I'll be right back. I need to tell the nurse you're awake." He stood and left the room.

The crumpled clothing he wore told me he'd been with me for the past two days. I hope he told Grams about everything. She'd be worried to death when I didn't come home.

"Look who's awake," a cheerful voice said.

"I didn't mean to take such a long nap." I tried to crack a weak joke.

The young woman in a white coat looked at my chart. "How are you feeling, Rhapsody?"

"Rested?"

She let out a little laugh. "Well, it seems your sense of humor is still intact. Let's take your vitals."

I sat up in the bed. She adjusted the stethoscope that hung around her neck. I stared at the wall while she listened to my heartbeat.

"Do you know what happened to me?"

"It looks like your blood pressure spiked to dangerous levels. Also, you were incredibly dehydrated. You need to drink more water. Over your long nap," she smiled at me, "we were able to get your vitals under control. It was touch and go for a bit when you first got here."

I stared down at my chipped nails thinking over what the doctor had said.

"You know that young man hasn't left your side."

"What?"

"Your husband."

"Oh, he's not my husband."

The doctor looked at me. "Boyfriend?"

I bit my lip and agreed. I wasn't sure what made me want to lie about the state of Chord's and my relationship. All I knew was I didn't want this pretty doctor getting ideas. He may only be little monster's dad, but I didn't want some successful doctor to come in and snap him up.

"He's a keeper." She finished up her tests then smiled. "Well, it seems everything is normal."

"Even with the baby?"

She smiled. "That little girl is just as strong as her mama. However, I'm recommending bedrest for the remainder of your pregnancy. We don't want you passing out again and injuring yourself or the baby."

"You mean in bed 24/7?"

"No, but you will need to be in bed most of the day. When you do get out of bed it can only be for short periods of time."

"This sounds like it's right up your alley. You get to initiate your sloth mode." Queen B cackled.

"This isn't going to work. I need to find a new job."

"Rhapsody, for the sake of yours and your baby's health you will need to job hunt from the comfort of your bed. Do you have someone who can take care of you? If not, we can connect you with a visiting nurse."

"I…"

"She does." Chord walked over to the bed, grabbed my hand in his, then took his place sitting on my bed.

"I do?"

He looked at me then to the doctor. "She does. I'll take care of her."

My jaw dropped open.

"Oh great. You're doing your slack-jawed yocal thing again. Shut your mouth before a bug flies in there." Queen B grimaced.

The doctor smiled. "Fantastic. Now, I think you're ready to get out of here. I will have your discharge papers processed so you can head out."

I watched the doctor disappear behind the door. Once the door was closed, I turned toward Chord.

"What the fuck do you think you're doing?"

He avoided my gaze by busying himself with putting random items in a bag to leave. "I'm getting your things ready to leave."

"You know damn well I'm not talking about that." I sat up

further on the bed. "Why would you tell the doctor you would be taking care of me?"

Chord sucked in a deep breath then turned back to me. "I plan on taking care of the woman I love and my unborn child."

I blinked at him. "The woman you…what?"

He came over and took my hands in his. The blue in his eyes drew me in. "I know you don't trust me right now. My fuck ups have been epic. I don't deserve you to give me a second chance."

"Aren't we on your fourth or fifth chance?" I asked.

"Yeah probably, and it seems I will probably fuck up again. However, I want to show you how much you mean to me and how I will stop at nothing to make you understand that no one will love you and our little bean more than I will. Let me take care of you. If after a few weeks you want to go back home, then I will take you back to your Grams' house. Just give me those weeks." His eyes pleaded with me.

"What do you have to lose? Grams won't be able to wait on you hand and foot. Cassie would really fuck it up. Let the loser have his chance." Queen B shrugged.

My thoughts swirled around in my head. Doubt, fear, and worry flowed through me. But when I looked at Chord all those feelings calmed. Though my trust has been bruised by him, I still had a feeling of safety when I thought about being with Chord.

"Fine."

Chord's face lit up. "I swear you won't regret this. I promise this will be the best thing—"

"Hold that thought. I have a few stipulations. First, I will not be living in that den of nasty you share with those three idiots. Second, I will need to stop at home to get a few things. Third, we are not sharing a bed. If that means you sleep on the couch, then that's what that means. Take it or leave it."

He grinned. "Sounds great. I forgot to tell you that I have my own place now. So, no more idiots." I raised my eyebrows at that. "Well, no other idiots but me. Everything else is doable.

We can stop at your Grams' place then head over to mine. I have a spare room that I can sleep in."

I sighed. "All right. I guess that's all set. We just have to wait for the paperwork."

"I give you a week before he has his head planted between your thighs." Queen B slurped her martini.

"Are we ready to go?" A nurse entered the room.

"We are so ready," Chord said enthusiastically.

The nurse and I looked at Chord then shook our heads. This setup was going to blow up in my face.

34

___

CHORD

We were back in the car headed toward Rhapsody's Grams' house. I was so excited that I was finally going to get six plus weeks of uninterrupted time with her. My mind was so focused on that fact I almost missed the house. The car screeched to a halt.

"Holy shit, Chord. I thought the whole point of me being with you was to take care of me not perform seatbelt checks. I know you haven't had your own car for a while, but let's not crash your new one." Rhapsody loosened the seatbelt.

"Sorry. My mind wandered and I almost missed your Grams' house."

"It's fine. Let's go."

"Wait. I can go in and get what you need."

"Uhm...no. I think I can do this one thing before I become an invalid." Rhapsody opened her door.

I jumped out and ran around to help her out. Thankfully, she only sighed heavily then let me help her out of the car. We walked slowly to the house. From the outside, it appeared no one was home.

"Doesn't look like anyone's home."

"I've got my key." Rhapsody pulled out her keys and unlocked the door. "Grams? Cassie?"

Her voice echoed through the house. When no one greeted us, we continued up the stairs to Rhapsody's room. She stopped at the top step. A last-minute grab of the handrail prevented me from slamming into her.

"Are you okay? I said I can get what you need."

"Shut up! I hear something," she whispered.

"Wha—" Rhapsody slapped her hand over my mouth. I strained my ears to hear what she was hearing. Moments slipped by and I didn't hear anything. When I opened my mouth to say so, I heard something. It was a rhythmic movement along with grunting.

"Does this house have ghosts?"

She gave me a "go to hell" look then began creeping down the hall. Each step down the small hallway amplified the sound. It was clearly coming from behind Rhapsody's door.

I stepped in front of her effectively blocking her way in. "I think I should check it out. Stay out here."

"Save the chivalry bullshit. That's my bedroom and if someone is doing ungodly things on my bed, I want to be the one to bust them," she whispered a bit too loud because the noise ceased. Rhapsody looked at the door then said, "I swear to God, Cassie. If you are having sex with Alec on my bed because of some love/hate thing I'm putting Nair in your shampoo."

"Dammit." My shoulders fell.

Rhapsody reached behind me and flung the door open. I braced for whatever was about to happen. She screamed, and I shut the door with a slam. The sight we'd just witnessed would be burned in our minds forever.

"Was that…"

"Yep. That was your mom and my dad bumping uglies," I confirmed while rubbing my eyes.

"Rhapsody?" Emmerson Lee's voice floated from behind the door.

"Mom? What the hell are you doing?"

"You'd think she'd know being preggers with Chord's kid," Jimmy's voice answered.

"Shut up, moron. You aren't helping," Emmerson snapped.

"This is not happening," I groaned.

The door creaked open. Emmerson Lee stood in an oriental robe. Jimmy wore only a pair of low slung jeans with his arm around Emmerson's shoulders.

"Hello, sweetie. I see you're out of the hospital. How are you and the baby?" Emmerson put on the caring mother face.

"As you can see, I'm fine and out of the hospital. Not that you'd know or care considering you didn't visit."

She blushed and Jimmy pulled her closer to him. "We weren't allowed to leave this house. Your Grams took over our supervision since you two were so busy."

"You act like we were on a fucking vacation," I snarled.

"Have you come home?" Emmerson asked.

"I'm just here to pick up a few things. But I can just buy what I need later." Rhapsody turned away.

"Wait! Rhapsody, are you and the baby okay?" Emmerson grabbed her arm.

With a tug, she pulled her arm from her mother, throwing her off balance. I steadied her to make sure she didn't fall. She glared at Emmerson.

"You've beat it into my head to stay away from Jimmy and anything to do with him. How the hell do you explain you fucking him on my bed?"

Emmerson had the good sense to look ashamed but Jimmy just smirked. I clenched my fists and was ready to punch him in the face the moment he opened his mouth.

"Things happen," Emmerson started to explain.

Rhapsody grunted. "Convenient. Stay away from me, Chord, and the baby. From here on out I don't know who you are. Your bullshit is no longer my problem. Goodbye."

She marched away from Emmerson Lee. I looked at the two

of them. Emmerson had tears glittering in her eyes. Jimmy continued to look smug. I turned away from them to follow Rhapsody.

"Aren't you going to say anything?" Jimmy asked.

I stopped and turned toward him. "You two are disgusting human beings that don't deserve to be around our little girl."

"A little girl?" Emmerson's voice sounded watery.

"Yes."

I left Jimmy and Emmerson in the doorway of Rhapsody's room. When I caught up to her, she was frozen at the bottom of the stairs. Grams and Cassie were staring at us.

"I'm sorry, Grams. I just can't anymore." Rhapsody sobbed.

She pulled Rhapsody into a hug. "It's okay, sweetie. Just don't close off your heart completely."

She shrugged then walked out the door. Grams looked at me and said, "Take care of my girl. She's going to need you more now than ever."

I nodded. "I plan on it."

Grams pulled me into a hug. "After I have a chat with my daughter, I will send over some of Rhapsody's things."

"Thank you."

Leaving her Grams' house, I ran out to the car. My heart broke when I saw the tears streaming down her face. Her pain made me want to go back in there and give Emmerson and Jimmy another piece of my mind. But the welfare of my daughter and her mother was much more important than two old self-centered rockers.

35

RHAPSODY

The hypocrisy of my mother burned inside me days after finding her screwing Jimmy Ray on my bed. For years, she burned it into me that he was the scum of the earth and if I ever thought of associating with him or anyone near him, I would be dead to her. Every time I thought about discovering them my blood would boil all over again. I was in the middle of another surge of anger when I heard a knock at the bedroom door.

"Come in."

Chord walked through the door holding a tray and looking mouthwateringly hot. He wore low slung gray sweatpants and a fitted white T-shirt with a college name on the front. His hair was wet. He looked freshly showered. Even if he wasn't, my pregnancy hormones were screaming for me to tie him to my bed and do unspeakable things to him.

"I brought breakfast."

I slid up the bed to a seated position. "Thanks. It smells wonderful."

He blushed. "I've been watching YouTube videos to learn the basics. It's just sausage, eggs, toast, and some tea."

My stomach chose that moment to grumble. I laughed. "It looks delicious."

Chord nodded then stood to leave.

"You aren't staying?"

He turned toward me. "I figured you'd want your peace and quiet."

"Good Lord, I've had so much peace, quiet, and alone time that I'm getting tired of my own company."

"I know I'm tired of you." Queen B opened a book while turning her back to me.

I tapped the bed near me careful not to jostle the tray. "Join me."

He gave me a long look. "I'll be right back."

I wasn't sure if he was giving me the brush off or was seriously coming back. Trying to ignore the feeling of loneliness that overcame me, I took the piece of toast and took a bite. A moan escaped me as the buttery toast touched my tongue. Who would've thought toast could taste so good? I opened my eyes from enjoying my toast to see Chord frozen in the doorway.

"What?"

He shook his head then brought over his own tray. The smell of coffee wafted over to me. I groaned again. I missed my daily coffee.

"Everything okay?" Chord croaked.

"I miss coffee."

"I'm sorry. I would have brought you some, but I read in the pregnancy book that it wasn't healthy for you or the baby to have coffee. I can get some decaf if you want."

I waved my hand at his offer. "It's okay. I can survive without it." Taking a bite of eggs, I watched him take a bite of his food. "You've been reading a pregnancy book?"

Keeping his gaze to the plate he nodded. "I figured it would be a good idea since I'd be taking care of you. I promise I wasn't trying to be creepy."

Another laugh bubbled out of me. "I didn't think it was creepy. I'm impressed. It's very sweet."

"Good."

We sat in silence and ate our breakfasts. I must have been hungrier than I thought because in a blink my plate was empty. Leaning against the propped-up pillows, I held my cooled tea close to my chest.

"Are you done?" He motioned to the empty tray.

"Does he think you're going to lick the damn plate? If he does, he knows you better than anyone else." Queen B cackled.

"I am. Thank you again."

Chord gathered the tray and moved to exit the room but stopped before leaving. He turned toward me. "Are you up for a little field trip outside of the bedroom?"

"Are you serious?"

"Yes."

"Oh thank God! I need to get out of this bed. I think your offer made me come a bit." I cringed as I realized what I'd just said.

His eyes bugged out then he laughed. "Glad I could be of service. I'll be right back."

"He totally wants his head between your thighs. It might be a good idea for you to get a little tongue lashing," Queen B encouraged while rubbing her hands together.

"Shut up." I swung my legs over the edge of the bed. The pajamas I wore were Cassie's idea of matchmaking. A pair of barely there shorts and a tank top that showed off my growing breasts and protruding belly.

"Ready?"

"Yep. Let me get my robe." I looked around for the wayward garment.

"You don't need that. If you're cold you can lean on me. I'll keep you warm." He gave me a smile filled with naughty promises.

"Okay."

Linking arms, Chord took me down the hall to a closed door. My normal impulse would have been to snoop around his apartment while he was at work. Unfortunately, I was feeling a bit down in the recent days which dampened my need to snoop. Hell, I didn't even remember he had a second room.

"Damn you're self-absorbed." Queen B shook her head at me.

"Shut it," I said under my breath.

"What?" Chord asked.

Dammit! He didn't need to see my crazy.

"Nothing. So, where are you taking me?"

"Right here." He pushed open the door.

I walked into a pink and purple wonderland. Shades of the colors swirled majestically around the room. A white dresser was in the corner next to a matching changing table. Across from them was a white crib. White frames with black and white photos of animals hung around the room. I walked over to the crib. Running my hands over the railing, I gazed down to the cutest sheets imaginable. Sloth families hugged each other in differing shades of gray. I had to swallow back the tears that threatened to stream down my face.

"Do you like it?" he asked tentatively.

All I could do was nod. If I answered he'd know I was on the verge of sobbing at the wondrous thing he'd done for our baby. Giving myself a few more moments, I walked over to the dresser. I picked up the framed picture. It was a black and white image of me laughing at something.

"Where did you get this picture?"

He shrugged. "I took it on our first real date."

"The one where you passed out because you found out you were going to be a daddy?"

Chord grinned. "Yep."

"This is wonderful. How long did this take you?" I turned around in the small room.

"I've been working on it little by little since I moved in. I didn't do the painting until recently when we found out little bean is a girl. Do you think she's going to like it?"

"If she's anything like you she's going to wish it was all black," Queen B quipped.

I ignored her and spun around the room. When something caught my eye, the spinning stopped.

"What's that?" I pointed to something sticking out of the closet.

Chord ran over to the closet and pushed it in the closet then shut the door. "Nothing."

"You know damn well I'm going to go over there and open that closet just to figure out what the hell you just shoved in there. Is it a dead body? Alec?" I said, hopeful.

He laughed. "Nothing so exciting. Though I will keep the Alec idea for a possible Christmas gift." He opened the closet and pulled out a sleeping bag.

"Why is there a sleeping bag in here?"

Avoiding my stare, he said, "I've been using it."

"Wait a minute. Are you sleeping in our daughter's room in a sleeping bag?"

He sighed then nodded.

"Why? I thought you'd sleep on the couch."

"What couch?"

"The one in the living room."

"Do you remember what my living room looks like?"

"Not really."

"Well, I don't have a couch yet. I have a hand-me-down uncomfortable recliner. Wanna know how I learned that?"

"How?"

"The first night you were here I slept in it. I could barely walk the next day. Believe me sleeping in this princess's wonderland is much more comfortable than that chair from hell."

"So, I've been sleeping peacefully in your bed while you've been in here?"

"Rhapsody, I wouldn't want it any other way."

I waved my hands at him. "Starting tonight you sleep in bed with me."

He swallowed. "What?"

"Sleep, Chord. You have a California king bed. I'm pretty sure we could fit an entire baseball team between us on that bed. No reason why you should sleep on the floor. Now, I'm tired. I need to lay down."

I marched out of the baby's bedroom and headed to what was going to be my and Chord's bedroom for the next few weeks. Closing the door behind me, I stared at the bed. Memories of our last time having sex floated through my mind. They were fuzzy, but I could still feel the way his hands felt on my curves. I closed my eyes to banish those memories when Chord in those gray sweatpants took its place.

What the hell had I just done?

"Told ya! Head between your thighs!" Queen B raised her martini glass.

36

———————

CHORD

The cold water pouring over my head wasn't helping. Finally relenting I turned off the water and stepped from the shower. I'd been in the shower so long the fog on the mirror was gone. It only reflected the idiot I was. Pulling on a pair of gym shorts for pajamas, I took a deep breath.

Since Rhapsody had demanded I join her in the bed I'd been painfully hard. Every possible sexual scenario played through my head all day long. That made cooking dinner both difficult and dangerous. Once it hit appropriate sleeping time, I fled to the bathroom to take a long shower in hopes I could take care of my raging hard-on, Stan, and that Rhapsody would be asleep by the time I was done.

It was a bust on both fronts. I pushed the door open and saw the sexiest sight in the world. Rhapsody was in bed wearing a barely there pajama top and was reading some book with a half-naked guy on the front. What took me by surprise were the glasses she was wearing.

I was frozen in the doorway when she looked up at me.

"Done jerking off in the shower?" she asked.

I blushed and looked away. "I'm surprised you're still up."

She sighed. "Little monster is riding on my spine like it's a damn slide. My back is killing me."

"Do you want me to massage it for you?" I approached the bed.

"Nah. I'm fine." Her protest was contradicted when she shifted and winced.

I shook my head. "Flip over, Rhapsody."

"Are you ordering me around?" She looked at me over her glasses.

"Yes. Now flip over before I do it for you."

Rhapsody took a few long moments to stare at me then closed her book and moved to lay on her stomach. I didn't miss the small smile she had as she rolled onto her side.

"I can't lay on my stomach."

"All right. I'll make do." My hands shook as I grabbed some lotion that was on the nightstand.

Sliding her top up a bit, I squirted the lotion onto her exposed lower back.

"Fuck! Chord! That shit is cold."

"Oh damn. I'm sorry. I wasn't paying attention." I immediately began kneading the tight muscles of her lower back.

"You're forgiven as long as you…ohhhh." She moaned.

"Feel good?" My voice was almost unrecognizable.

"Oh yes." Came out on a moan again.

This was a fucking stupid idea. All of her moaning was adding fuel to my already overloaded sex drive. I was such an idiot, but I'd do it again just to have my hand on her creamy skin.

After fifteen minutes of my mind wandering from one fantasy to another, I realized I hadn't heard anything from Rhapsody. I leaned over to check on her. Her eyes were closed while her mouth hung open. A snore indicated what I'd suspected. She was out cold, and I pulled her shirt down. Before pulling the covers over her, I took that moment to kiss her belly.

As I pressed my lips to her belly, our little bean did a quick kick, making me jump back. I froze when I thought I'd woken her up but when the snoring continued, I smiled.

A small laugh escaped, and I said, "Feisty. Just like your mama."

Pulling the covers over Rhapsody, I joined her in bed for what was going to be a really long night.

———

I blearily opened my eyes. It felt like I'd been drugged. As I finally started to come to, I felt Rhapsody fling her arm over my waist and her leg over my thigh. I was wide awake thanks to that. Her head rested on my chest. A stream of drool left her mouth and was pooling on my chest. I glanced over at the clock. My phone's alarm was about to go off. I reached for it on the nightstand but couldn't reach it. Each move closer to the phone made Rhapsody cling tighter.

When my alarm went off, Rhapsody shot off me and sat straight up. The crazed look on her face made me concerned. I reached over and grabbed my phone effectively shutting off the ringer.

"What the fuck?" She stared at me with wide eyes.

"Sorry. I was trying to get to it but you kind of had me pinned."

"That is the most annoying noise on the planet."

I shrugged as I got out of the bed. "I needed something I wouldn't sleep through."

"Where are you going?"

"Work."

"Oh."

"Is something wrong?"

"No." She looked down at the comforter she'd hogged.

I sat back on the bed and took her hands in mine. "It will be fine. Miranda is coming over with Alice. She apparently has some pampering thing in mind. Who knows?"

Her eyes brightened. "So, people are coming over? I won't be alone?"

"Nope. I promise. When I'm not here someone will come and entertain you."

"I hope Alec isn't on that list."

I bit my lip. "Well..."

"Ugh. Seriously, Chord."

"I was out of available people. But when he's here you can boss him around and make him do all the horrible chores you wouldn't want to do."

She smiled. "Dance monkey dance."

"That look in your eye is a bit frightening."

A grin curled her lips, and I couldn't help but laugh. I leaned over and gave her a kiss then stood. I froze when I realized what I'd just done. Fuck me and my idiot brain. She touched her lips tenderly then looked up at me.

"I hope you have a good day. Dressing up today?"

I let out the breath I was holding and said, "Not today. Next week is mythological week. I will be dressing up as a Greek god."

"Cupid? A diaper and wings?" She laughed mischievously.

"No. I will be Thor."

"Oh, so you wanted to wear a long blond wig and wear a cape? Hmm...starting to worry about you, Chord."

I shook my head. "I better get ready. I'll be back to check on you before I leave."

"Okay." A blush colored her cheeks.

Leaving the room, I closed the door behind me and waited a moment. My blood was rushing too fast. If I didn't calm myself, I'd end up passing out. That was not a good look for me. When I finally pulled myself together, I glanced down and saw the morning wood I was sporting.

"Back it down, Stan," I mumbled.

"What?" Rhapsody's voice made me jump.

"Fuck."

She laughed. "Sorry. I need to pee and if you don't move you're cleaning up a puddle."

Rhapsody waddled past me and into the bathroom. Instead of the cold shower I needed, I moved to the kitchen and started up the coffee. As it brewed, I popped a few pieces of bread in the toaster then retrieved fruit from the fridge.

"Aww…there you go teasing me again."

Her voice made me jump again.

"Jumpy today?"

"No, I'm just not expecting you to be wandering around here. You should be resting."

She waved my comment away as she walked toward me. "There was something I wanted to do."

"Tell me what you need, and I can do it for you," I offered.

She smiled, stood on her toes, and kissed me. For a second I froze then I pulled her against me and kissed her back. We stood like that until the beeping of the coffee maker burst our bubble.

"Well…have a good day." She grabbed the container of fruit and retreated to the bedroom.

"What do I do with that, Stan?" I grabbed my to-go cup and filled it with coffee. There wasn't any time to think about that kiss or what would happen next. If I didn't get my ass to work, I wouldn't be able to support her and little bean. That was one thing I wanted to do no matter what.

37

RHAPSODY

"So…how have things been going between you and my brother?" Miranda asked as she plopped a bowl of popcorn between us.

"Uh…okay." I looked at Alice, who was meticulously painting my toenails.

"Don't worry. She's so focused on the nail polish she isn't paying attention to us. Unless we need to plot where I need to bury him. If that's the case, we will have to ask her to go play in the living room." She popped a piece of popcorn in her mouth.

"No…it's nothing like that. Though I appreciate that you're on my side."

"Of course. I grew up with the doofus. I know better than anyone how much of an idiot he is."

I snorted a laugh and a piece of popcorn became spot welded on my uvula. I started choking, and Miranda went into immediate action by slapping my back as hard as she could. It finally dislodged after a few hard slaps. After a few deep breaths, I grabbed my water bottle and took a few swigs.

"Holy shit! Chord would have killed me if I'd killed you.

Next time try not to snort the popcorn." Miranda had her hand over her heart.

"It wasn't your fault."

"God knows you've had problems chewing food your whole life," Queen B added unhelpfully.

"I know it wasn't my fault, but would your ghost vouch for me? Come back to tell him..." She cleared her throat then said in her best ghost voice, "Miranda didn't kill me. It was my own fault."

I shoved my shoulder into hers. "Just for that I will do no such thing."

"See...I'm so screwed. The only thing we can do is make sure you don't die on my watch."

"Mom. Can you and Rhapsody please stop moving? You're making my work really difficult."

I glanced down at my feet. They were a mess. I tried to smile instead of grimace. "They look lovely, Alice. Thank you."

"I'm not done yet. I have to go get my hot glue gun." She sprinted from the room.

"Her what?"

Miranda waved her hand dismissively. "Nothing. So... something more than master and slave going on with my brother."

I sighed. "You aren't going to let this go, are you?"

"Nope."

"Fine. Nothing has happened."

"Aw man."

"Why do you look disappointed. You really wanted me to go into details of having sex with your brother. That's a bit twisted even for me."

"Ew...no." Miranda paused then turned toward me. "Wait... you had sex with him?"

Another exasperated sigh left me. "How the hell do you think I got pregnant?"

"I didn't mean ever I meant since you moved in."

"Of course we haven't had sex. We just started sharing a bed." Her eyes widened, and I rushed out, "For sleeping. For sleeping only, Miranda."

She cocked her head at me as Alice came back into the room carrying a bag almost as large as her.

"But you want to."

I looked away. It was starting to feel weird talking to her about this.

"Seriously, Rhapsody. You want more with Chord, don't you?"

"Of course I do, Miranda. I mean he's hot, sweet, goofy, and just wonderful. Have you seen the room he created just for our little bean? He's been there whenever I've needed him, but I'm wondering if any of it is a good idea. I mean remember what he did around Jimmy."

Miranda moved the bowl of popcorn out of the way, sat cross-legged, and faced her. She pulled Rhapsody's hands into hers.

"My brother is a fuck up. I will attest to that. However, there is no doubt that he loves you and that little one you're carrying. He wouldn't be doing all of this if he didn't want to atone and get you back in his life." She shrugged then said, "What harm is it to give him a chance while you're stuck here. I mean he knows if he fucks up you can castrate him in his sleep."

I laughed. "I guess you're right. You know I had an idea this morning, but since I'm shackled to this bed, I would need your help. Would you be up to it?"

Miranda smirked. "What did you have in mind?"

"Well…" I began when a searing pain shot through my foot. "Fuck!"

"What? I figured that was the end goal and there is no way I'm helping with any of that."

"No. My foot." I bit my lip and pointed to my foot where Alice was holding a hot glue gun and a large sequin.

"Alice! What are you doing?"

"I'm making Rhapsody's feet pretty." She touched my foot again with the glue gun, and I had to bite my lip to keep from screaming.

"No hot glue! Only nail polish or you're done, miss."

Alice stuck out her bottom lip in a pout. "All right, Mama. I was just trying to make them look the best so that Uncle Chord will make another baby with her."

I looked at Miranda. "Not listening, huh?"

Miranda shrugged and took the glue gun away.

———

"Rhapsody?"

I held my breath. I strained to hear Chord's movements. After the door shut, I imagined what he saw. The note with instructions to meet me in the bedroom. The beats of my heart filled my ears. I waited as minutes passed. My eyes glanced around the room as I began to second guess my plan.

After Alice completed my pedicure, I explained my idea to Miranda. As she and Alice listened intently, she smiled. She and Alice went to work right away. The once masculine room had twinkle lights strung around the ceiling. Candles of all shapes and sizes covered all available surfaces. I was slightly worried we'd accidentally set the room on fire. Pushing that thought aside, I glanced over at the small round table. It had two chairs, two silver covered plates, and a single red rose in the middle. The two champagne flutes contained the sparkling version I was able to drink.

Miranda and Alice had only left half an hour ago. I felt like I was about to pass out thanks to the little monster sucking all my energy. Even if that energy was strictly supervisory. My cell phone vibrated indicating I received a text message.

Miranda: How did he like it?

Me: He hasn't come into the bedroom yet.

Miranda: What the hell is taking him so long?

Me: No clue.

Miranda: Go see what he's doing. I swear if he is being an ass again after all my blood, sweat, and tears, I'm going to beat the blood, sweat, and tears out of him.

Me: Relax. I'm sure he's just taking his time.

Miranda: My brother is an idiot. I'm positive it's something stupid. Anyway…are you dressed all sexy? You better be showing off the preggers jugs.

I looked down at the low-cut lacy camisole I had changed into. A cami and leggings was all the sexy I could muster with my level of exhaustion. If he didn't appreciate that I was screwed. Or maybe if I don't get laid it would be un-screwed.

"Your ridiculousness knows no bounds." Queen B was doing yoga poses.

Miranda: Well?

Me: Sorta.

The doorknob began to turn. Throwing my phone on the nightstand, I attempted to lay in a seductive pose. With my gigantic whale body, I sat on the edge of the bed and dangled my legs as I propped myself up with one arm.

"Rhapsody, is every—" Chord's words stopped as he entered the room.

I held my breath as I watched him take in the bedroom. When his eyes finally landed on me, I saw a mix of emotions cross his face. Surprise, aw, and desire warred for dominance. Desire won out.

"What did you do?" he asked.

"Nothing much," I purred.

"Please don't ever do that. I think we heard that noise when we watched that wildlife documentary." Queen B tapped her chin. *"Yep. Definitely heard that when that walrus was being eaten by a polar bear."*

"Beautiful." The word came out deeper than his normal voice. It immediately made my panties wet.

"Miranda and Alice did the work. I just supervised."

"I'm not talking about the room." Chord was in front of me

in a flash. His hands cradled my face. Slower than necessary, he moved his face closer. His eyes followed my tongue as I wet my lips.

Finally, his lips crashed onto mine. My body was on fire. I groaned when his tongue slipped into my mouth. When he broke the kiss, his eyes scanned my face again.

"If you don't want to do this you need to tell me now. I don't know if I have any more self-discipline to pull away from you again."

Fisting my hands in his shirt, I pulled him toward me as I fell back against the bed. We both sighed as our lips met again. Giddy anticipation coursed through me. I was finally going to find out if he was more than a one pump chump.

38

CHORD

I was finally going to get my chance to prove that I was more than a one pump chump. Rhapsody's hands frantically began pulling off my shirt. Our kisses were frantic. It seemed both of us were in need. Thank God she was as horny as I was. A guy could only jerk off so many times in the shower. My cock was starting to get chapped thanks to the ongoing friction on my manmeat.

When I got home, the apartment was oddly quiet. I called out Rhapsody's name and heard nothing. Worry niggled at my brain. Was something wrong? I put my things on the table then saw the note.

Chord!

Come to the bedroom.

Rhapsody

My heart flipped at those words. They weren't exactly Shakespeare, but my throbbing erection didn't care. When I took two steps toward the bedroom, my sushi lunch decided to rebel in my stomach. I tiptoed quietly to the bathroom. The last thing I needed Rhapsody to envision was me taking a dump.

Fifteen minutes later. That's right fifteen minutes later, I finally left the bathroom. After an abundance of air freshener, I took a deep breath and headed to the bedroom we now shared.

"Rhapsody, is every—" Words failed me at the sight in front of me.

Rhapsody was in a sexy as fuck outfit sitting on the bed. She looked like Christmas morning. I attempted to speak but my tongue had become inexplicably glued to the top of my mouth. I watched her blush as I just stared.

"What did you do?" I could have slapped myself with that question.

"Nothing much." Her voice came out in a throaty tone that went straight to my cock.

I couldn't take my eyes off the woman in front of me. Rounded with our child and glowing, the only thing I saw was her. I needed her. And with the way she was looking at me…she needed me too. God knew Stan was ready to last longer than before.

"Beautiful," I growled.

"Miranda and Alice did the work. I just supervised."

"I'm not talking about the room." I moved in front of her so quickly she blinked up at me in surprise.

Cupping her face, I crashed my lips down on her. An electric bolt of desire shot through my body. On a moan, I slid my tongue into her mouth. My hands tangled in her hair as I moved her mouth to probe it deeper. I wanted this woman so much I was worried I'd come in my pants before we got to the good parts. Pulling back, I gazed down at her. The glazed look in her eyes told me she wanted this as much as I did but I had to ask the question.

"If you don't want to do this you need to tell me now. I don't know if I have any more self-discipline to pull away from you again."

Something flared in her eyes because before I could even think, she pulled me on top of her, and we were back to feverishly kissing. I pressed my thigh against the apex of hers.

She broke the kiss and moaned. I took that moment to kiss down her neck, placing small nips and licks along the way. Her hips ground onto my thigh. My cock was getting impossibly harder.

"You have on too much clothing," she breathed as she pulled on my shirt.

"So do you." I smiled.

With a grin, she reached for her shirt and pulled it over her head. Her abundant breasts spilled over her bra. Each movement jiggled the mounds that cried out for me to bury my face between them. I continued to watch as she shimmied out of her leggings. My mouth went dry at the sight of her tiny panties that were clearly soaked.

She blushed. "I know I don't look the same."

I blinked and stared at her as I tore off my shirt. "You look phenomenal."

"Are you sure? I feel a bit like a whale in a tutu." She rubbed her distended belly and looked away.

I turned her face toward me. "You have me so turned on right now I'm afraid I may lose it in my pants before we get to the good stuff." I took her hand and placed it on my hard cock. "See what you do to me."

She swallowed hard. "I didn't realize."

"How fucking hot you are? I don't know how you haven't realized I've had an erection around you since you came into my life." I kissed her then pulled back off the bed.

"Where are you going?"

"Don't worry, sweetheart. I'm just getting more comfortable." I dropped my pants so she could see how hard I was. My cock was popping out of the top of my boxer briefs. The things this woman did to me was like nothing I'd ever experienced.

"Oh."

"Now where were we?"

Lying next to her on the bed, I went back to kissing down

her body. I pushed one cup of her bra down, freeing the breast. Her hard dusky nipples called out for attention. Circling the tight nub with my tongue, I felt her shiver. Sucking it into my mouth elicited a moan. While sucking on one breast, I played with the other. Her wet mound searched for attention as I focused on her breasts. Switching breasts, I felt her convulse beneath me. Did she just orgasm from me playing with her breasts?

"Chord...please. I need you to touch me."

I smiled and let the breast fall from my mouth. "I am touching you."

"You know what I mean. My pussy needs you."

Nuzzling her breasts, I said, "But I like these."

"Please." She begged and lifted her hips.

"You beg so sweetly, love."

I moved down her body, placing a kiss on her belly. I dragged my lips over her drenched panties. The smell of her arousal was almost too much to bear. In a swift moment, I pulled off her panties and threw them across the room. Her pussy was calling to me and that was a call I needed to take.

Dragging my tongue through her wet folds made Rhapsody shiver and groan. I circled the bundle of nerves at the top as I slid one finger into her.

"Oh God." Her hands shot into my hair and pushed my head where she wanted it.

I took a deep pull on her clit as I added another finger into her wet channel. An erotic rhythm of sucking and fingering was driving Rhapsody closer and closer to her climax. Finally, I curled my finger inside her and she bowed off the bed.

"Oh fuck!" she yelled.

I lapped up all her sweet juices. My face was covered with her orgasm. I continued to pump and suck until she finally pushed my head away. She laid back looking completely sated. I leaned up and kissed her. Her kiss was surprisingly passionate.

She held my face and looked into my eyes. "Now, use that cock and fuck me hard."

Damn, I loved this woman.

"Yes, ma'am."

I quickly shed my boxer briefs. Positioning the head of my cock in her entrance, I pushed in quickly. Her pussy grabbed onto my cock and I had to wait a moment. The pure bliss of being inside her was almost too much to take. I took deep breaths willing myself not to be that one pump chump. Again. Her hips began to move, begging me to pump into her. After I was able to push back the rising orgasm, I began to pound into her. Her moans turned me on even more than I already was.

"Fuck me, Chord. Harder."

Slamming my cock into her made her crazier. We were building to our climax together. Her slick pussy wrapped around my cock perfectly as I pumped harder and harder into her.

"Wait."

I froze. "Are you okay? Do you need me to stop?" Internally I begged her to say no.

"Hell no. I want you to fuck me from behind."

I let out a groan as she moved out from under me and got on her hands and knees. Her puffy pink pussy lips and her round ass made me drool. I pulled on her hips and slammed my cock into her. I couldn't take much more. I fucked her harder and faster. Our climaxes were so close.

"I'm going to come," she breathed out on a moan.

"Good."

As her pussy clenched around my cock, the pressure of her orgasm made me explode. I gripped her hips tightly against mine as I came hard. I couldn't remember the last time I came that hard. After a minute or so, I was finally able to let go of her hips. We both collapsed onto the bed complete exhaustion draining our body.

"Thank God."

I pushed her hair out of her face. "For what?"

Rhapsody blushed. "Nothing."

"Oh come on. I want to know."

"Fine. Thank God you aren't actually a one pump chump."

"I told you I could do better."

"I know, but I'm glad it was true."

I fake glared at her then began tickling her. "I'll show you one pump chump."

"No. Stop. I'm going to have to pee if you keep doing that." She giggled and pulled away from me.

I stopped because something smelled funny. "What's that smell?"

"Oh there's dinner—" She stopped and looked around. "Oh fuck it's on fire." Rhapsody pointed to a mini blaze on a table I hadn't noticed in the room.

"Fuck!" I jumped off the bed and ran over to the table. An empty glass was near the fire and I ran to the bathroom.

"Hurry! Also, don't injure the peen. I'll be needing that again soon."

"Really, Rhapsody? I'm trying to put out an inferno over here." I poured the water over the fire, and it was immediately extinguished.

"My hero. What the hell started the fire?"

Pulling the burnt remains of her panties from the flames, I held them up. "Guess you won't need to wear panties anymore."

"Ahh...so it was your fault." She nodded as she pulled the covers around her, obstructing my view.

"Why are there so many candles? If there weren't all these candles your panties would have been fine."

"It's called ambiance. I was trying to seduce you. Apparently, you didn't even notice."

"Sweetheart, you in that outfit looking like a million bucks was all I needed." I leaned over to kiss her but was stopped when her phone began to ring.

She sighed and answered it. "Miranda, we just got done fucking. Can you let us bask in the afterglow please?" Rhapsody shook her head then I immediately saw the color drain from her face.

"Oh. Mr. Anderson. I'm so sorry I thought you were someone else." She cleared her throat. "How can I help you?"

I sat there and watched as Rhapsody nodded and gave one word answers.

"That would be perfect. I'll see you then. Thank you." She hung up and looked at me.

"What's going on?"

"That was my old boss. He's coming here on Monday to talk to me. Apparently, he already knew I was bedridden due to the pregnancy thanks to Daniel, and he needs to talk to me immediately. I wonder what it could be about."

"That's wonderful. I bet he's coming to offer you your job back."

"I doubt it. But he's coming here so that's definitely a big deal."

"It is. I think we need to celebrate." I wiggled my eyebrows.

"Round two?"

I nodded. "This time you're in control."

Rhapsody rubbed her hands together and said, "Oh goodie."

39

RHAPSODY

"You'll be fine." Daniel patted my hand.

"This just feels weird having Mr. Anderson here while I'm stuck in my bed." I straightened the blanket I was sitting on.

"Look, he came to me about you, and I think you're going to be pleasantly surprised."

"Wait a minute. How long have you known about this?"

Daniel looked away sheepishly. "Well...I may have spoken to him a few weeks ago."

"A few weeks—" I was cut off by knocking on the front door. "We will finish my shrieking at you when this is done. Go answer the door please."

He gallantly bowed and left the bedroom. I looked down at my casual outfit. My office attire didn't fit any longer thanks to the little monster. I ended up settling on a maternity blouse and black leggings. At least I showered. That was a feat unto itself.

"We are all grateful you showered." Queen B squirted some perfume in the air.

"Here you are, sir," Daniel said as he escorted Mr. Anderson into the bedroom.

"Thank you, Daniel. Will you be staying with us?" he asked.

Daniel glanced at me. I nodded. "I guess I am. I will pull up another chair."

Mr. Anderson sat next to the bed. It felt really weird to have the CEO of the company I used to work for sitting in the bedroom that only hours ago I was riding Chord in. Life was very strange at times.

"Thank you for seeing me, Ms. Bell."

"No problem. Though I must say I am quite surprised you wanted to visit today."

Mr. Anderson smiled at me as he placed an envelope on the bed. "Please open that."

I took the envelope and lifted the two metal prongs holding it closed. I pulled out a stack of papers. The top page said *Proposal for AeroMat Management by Charles Boswacker*. I looked at Daniel then to Mr. Anderson.

"Keep going."

Flipping through the packet of papers, I saw my work. Every word was the work I'd been doing for Mr. Anderson. It was the project I'd sent to him the day I quit. Ballslapper was taking credit for every word.

"That fucker." I glanced up at Mr. Anderson. "I'm sorry."

Daniel snorted and I glared at him.

"I said the same thing when I read this. The only original piece of it was the top page with his name on it. Thankfully, I already had this in my hands from your email. I'm unsure how he got his hands on it but it's too late to ask now. I've fired him." Mr. Anderson looked at me intently. "There's a job opening, Ms. Bell. Would you be interested?"

I blinked. "What?"

"I believe he's offering you a well-deserved promotion, Rhapsody."

"But I quit."

Mr. Anderson crossed his arms. "Yes, about that. Why did you quit?"

My teeth dug into my bottom lip. "Boswacker gave me an

ultimatum. Give him all my work so he could say it was his or get fired. I chose to quit instead. I couldn't bear giving him all that hard work."

"I can't say I blame you for quitting. You're a loyal worker. I've known that from the moment I met you. So, what do you say? Interested in coming back?"

"Uhm...yes but I'm in a bit of a bind. I can't go into the office. I'm bedridden until the little monster is born."

"Not a problem. Wesley!" Mr. Anderson called out.

A skinny guy I recognized from our IT department walked in holding a small lap desk and a new laptop. It was the top of the line computer I'd been dreaming about.

"What is all this?" I watched Wesley place the desk and laptop on the floor near the bed then leave. A moment later he entered with a small printer, wireless mouse, and a headset.

"I asked Wesley to come on my little field trip and bring all the essentials a Senior Account Manager would need to work from home. You know just in case you said you'd come back." Mr. Anderson smirked, looking very pleased with himself.

"I don't know what to say."

"Say you'll take the damn job, Rhapsody." Daniel gave my hand a squeeze.

I turned toward Mr. Anderson. "Well, I guess you have yourself a Senior Account Manager."

"Fantastic." He clapped his hands and stood from the chair. "Now, I want you back on the job starting next Monday. I knew you'd be perfect for that position. I have confidence that you are going to do great things. We will let you rest. Make sure you take care of yourself and your little one. Come on, Wesley. Our work is done here."

"Yes, Mr. Anderson." I watched them leave the bedroom. I held my breath until I heard the door to the apartment shut.

Looking over at Daniel, I asked, "Did that just happen?"

"It did, boss lady." He stood from the chair and gave me a hug.

Tears streamed down my face. "I can't believe it. They really got rid of Boswacker. I didn't think that would ever happen."

"Yeah, it's been hard keeping that secret from you."

"What?!" I screeched.

"Holy shit! Take it down a notch drama queen." Queen B covered her ears.

"Damn, Rhapsody. Are you trying to summon some dogs?"

I smacked Daniel. "Why didn't you tell me?"

"Mr. Anderson asked me not to. He had plans and wouldn't stand for me ruining his surprise."

I fell against the pillows. "I guess that's an acceptable answer. So, are you ready for me to be your legit colleague?"

"You've always been my colleague."

"Yeah but now I have the title." I smiled brightly.

"I have a feeling you will be moving up a lot faster than any of us. Mr. Anderson is a smart guy who sees potential, and his eyes are set on you. I bet in a year you're a VP."

"What? I'll just be happy with what I have."

Daniel shook his head. "Nope. Mark my words in one year you'll be a VP and have like three kids."

I punched him for that comment.

"Ouch. You have super preggers strength."

"Don't dare jinx me like that."

He laughed. "Well, with the smell of sex in this room I'd say you two made up and are going at it like rabbits."

Blushing, I looked away.

Daniel tapped my hand and said, "Don't worry. Izzy and I still go at it like that."

"Ew. I really don't need that mental image, Daniel."

"Like I wanted to smell the sex den you currently live in? We both have our scars now. All right, I'm gonna get out of your hair. Need anything before I go?"

A grin curved my lips. Giddy anticipation coursed through me. Chord and I would be doing some celebratory mattress gymnastics when he got home.

"That look on your face is creeping me out. So, I will give you another hug and split." He leaned over the bed and gave me another hug. "I'm so damn proud of you, girl." He placed a chaste kiss on my cheek.

"I go to work and come back to find you with another man in our bed." Chord's deep voice echoed through the room.

I smiled. "Someone's gotta sate my pregnancy urges."

Chord held up a bag with a pint of my favorite ice cream and a bag of pickle flavored potato chips. I looked between him and Daniel then said to Daniel, "I'm sorry, Daniel, but Chord won. He brought the ice cream and pickle flavored chips. Better luck next time."

Daniel pretended to act dejected. "I hope I will be able to rebound from this rejection."

All three of us began laughing. Chord approached the bed and placed the bag on the nightstand then gave me a sweet kiss that quickly became foreplay. A gagging sound burst our increasingly intense passion.

"Sorry, Daniel. Forgot you were there. It was the treats. They just make me so hot for—"

Daniel placed his hands over his ears while chanting, "La, la, la, la." Chord and I looked at each other then laughed.

Holding out his hand, Chord said, "Hey, Daniel. How are you?"

"I'm good if your crazy girlfriend would stop oversharing."

Chord raised an eyebrow at me. "Oversharing?"

"I'll tell you later. But I have the best news that is going to get you laid. So, be ready to rip off those pants as soon as Daniel leaves."

Queen B slapped her forehead. *"This baby can't come soon enough so you can put your filter back in place."*

"That's definitely my cue to leave. I'll see you two later. Have fun practicing the horizontal mambo."

"We will." I looked at Chord.

We listened for Daniel to leave the apartment before we

started making out again. From one moment to the next, we were naked and Chord was inside me.

"Oh God. Here come the dying moose noises. Time for the noise canceling headphones." Queen B put the headphones on just in time for my first celebratory orgasm.

40

CHORD

"Right there," Rhapsody moaned.

She was riding me awake again. Since we started having sex, she has been insatiable. I'm not complaining. I'd be an even bigger idiot if I would say out loud that Stan was getting a bit chafed from overuse.

"Come on, Chord. I'm almost there."

I grabbed her hips and rammed into her. She was getting close. I would be right behind her. Reaching between us, I found her clit. She rode me hard with each swipe of her clit, but it was the small pinch that sent her over the edge. Her pussy clamped onto my cock immediately tossing me over the orgasm abyss.

"Fuck," I exclaimed.

"Yeah. Sorry. I woke you up again."

I pulled Rhapsody down to give her a kiss. She sat back up with a dazed smile.

"I'm never going to complain about you riding me awake, babe. It's my favorite morning activity."

She wiggled her hips in encouragement. "Ready for round two?"

My eyes widened but before I could answer the bedroom

door crashed open. "Absolutely not!"

"Cassie?" Rhapsody asked.

"I told the crazy shrew to leave you two be." Alec's voice followed.

"What the hell are you two doing here?" I covered Rhapsody with the sheet. It was a good thing she hadn't taken off her nightgown to wake me up.

"It's a surprise so we don't have time for you two to get it on again. Get dressed and let's go." Cassie walked out of the room shoving her shoulder into Alec.

"Ow." He rubbed his shoulder then looked at us. "She's right. We are on a tight schedule. Oh, by the way, nice work. It sounded quite impressive, cousin." He gave us a thumbs up.

"Get out!" Rhapsody and I said together.

Cassie returned and pulled Alec away by the ear. We could hear their arguing even through the now closed door.

"I guess we have to get dressed." I stood from the bed and stretched.

"Do we have to?" Rhapsody pouted while laying across the bed.

"I don't think they'd burst into our apartment if it weren't important." I pulled on clothes but the way she was looking at me gave me all kinds of ideas. "Stop looking at me like that, Rhapsody."

She shrugged. "Well, if I can't actually fuck you right now, I'm at least going to eye fuck you."

Pulling on a shirt, I joined Rhapsody by the closet. I wrapped my arms around her then kissed her neck. "You're so damn sexy. I love you so much." I turned her around to look at me. "You know that right?"

She gave me a tense smile. "We need to get dressed."

"I'm going to keep saying it until you believe it. Now, I will take the temptation away from you and break up the fight I hear brewing in the living room." I bent down and placed a kiss on the corner of her mouth.

Leaving Rhapsody to get ready, I found Cassie holding a kitchen knife on Alec who didn't look fazed. What the hell was going on with those two?

"What is going on?"

"I'm going to castrate the asshole." Cassie swung the knife around.

"You'd never do that." Alec waved his hand around.

I saw Cassie's eyes flare. If I didn't take the knife away from her there would definitely be blood. I swiftly removed the knife just in time.

"What did you do to her?" I asked Alec.

He shrugged. I could hear Cassie grinding her teeth.

"What did he do?"

"He tried to kiss me." She crossed her arms.

"Uhm…okay." I was not good with these things. Looking toward the bedroom I sent up a prayer for Rhapsody to hurry. "I'm guessing that's something you don't want."

Cassie turned her laser gaze on me. "Why would I want any part of his disease riddled body touching me?"

"Okay. So not interested."

"She's interested," Alec added.

"Alec—" I began but Cassie cut me off.

"I am not."

Alec looked at me. "She's just pissed because I slept with one of her friends."

I winced. "Probably not helping your cause, Alec."

"Look, I don't even remember the chick. I don't see how that affects the fun we could have," Alec said to Cassie.

In all the years I've known Alec, I'd never known him to go after a challenging woman. Why was he continuing to push Cassie? It didn't make sense. Alec liked easy and Cassie was exceedingly not easy.

"Good God! What is going on?" Rhapsody finally came to my rescue.

"Lover's spat," I said.

"What?"

"No."

Alec and Cassie said at the same time.

Rhapsody rolled her eyes. "You two broke into our apartment just to fight with one another? Can you two leave so I can get back to round two?"

Cassie blew out a breath. "No you can't go back to having sex. We need the two of you to come with us. If you put up a fight, we've got chloroform, rope, and a black bag."

I looked at Alec. He shrugged. "We needed to be prepared in case you two put up a fight."

"Are you okay to be out of bed?"

"Sweet baby Jesus, yes I'm okay. I haven't left this apartment except for the damn vag doctor appointments. Let's blow this popsicle stand. Though, you guys can do the bag and rope thing. It sounds a bit kinky. I might be into it." Rhapsody grinned.

Alec and Cassie groaned then walked out of the apartment. I smiled at Rhapsody. "That was one way to get them out of the apartment. Good one, love."

Rhapsody cocked her head at me. "I wasn't making a joke."

I tried to swallow but was unable to. She winked then followed Alec and Cassie. That woman was going to be the death of me. I grabbed my keys then followed the motley crew.

———

"Surprise!"

Rhapsody fell against me as the large group yelled together.

"Holy fuck!" she said.

"Very eloquent, Rhapsody." Cassie shook her head and walked over to the bar.

I looked around the place. It was a place I'd never thought I'd see in daylight. The Cats and Cocks club was a male and female strip joint. I'd only been there once before when Alec insisted he was going to marry one of the dancers. As strip clubs went it ranked between high end exotic dance clubs and the strip joint by the airport that didn't have a name but advertised as "Live Nudes."

"Were you surprised?" Miranda came up to give me a hug.

"Yes. I really didn't have a clue why Alec was taking us to a strip club. I thought he was interested in one of the dancers again."

Miranda rolled her eyes. "Yeah. He was in charge of the venue."

"What? I got a good rate." Alec walked over holding a chicken wing and a beer. "Plus they have the best food."

"We should have never asked you to help," Cassie interjected.

Alec shrugged but a mischievous glint flickered in his gaze. "Wanna show me what you got? Maybe a lap dance in the champagne room?"

If looks could kill, Alec would have been dead right there. Thankfully, Cassie decided to be the bigger person and walked away. I watched as Rhapsody greeted all the people. A sash that said *Mom-to-be* was draped over her.

"You've got it bad," Miranda said.

I nodded. "I'm all hers if she'd let me."

"Give it time. I have a good feeling."

"Chord! Come here," Rhapsody called.

Smiling, I walked toward Rhapsody. Before I reached her the door opened shining daylight into the dark establishment. Walking through the door and holding hands were Jimmy Ray and Emmerson Lee. Aw hell. I watched Rhapsody's smile fall. Since catching the two of them in her childhood bedroom, neither of us had heard from them. It had been wonderful.

"Did we miss the surprise?" Emmerson skipped over to Rhapsody and her grandmother.

"Obviously," Rhapsody said.

Placing myself between Rhapsody and our parents, I asked, "What are you two doing here?"

"We're the proud grandparents. We wouldn't miss the baby shower for the world." Jimmy shoved his hands into his jean pockets.

"Yeah okay. You're already a grandparent and sure don't act like it toward Alice. Plus, a baby shower isn't really your thing."

He shrugged. "Doesn't matter. What my lady wants she gets."

I rolled my eyes. "So now Emmerson is your lady? You've hated each other for decades but just like that you're in love?"

"She was always the one that got away, Chord. I have a second chance, and I'm not going to blow it."

"Chord?" Rhapsody placed her hand on my arm.

"Yeah? Are you okay?"

"Yes. Wanna see the cake? Grams made it."

"Absolutely." I placed my arm around Rhapsody and left Jimmy standing there alone.

We approached a table laden with snacks. My stomach grumbled, reminding me we'd left before grabbing anything to eat. While I drooled over the goodies, my gaze landed on a three-tiered cake. Pink, white, and purple icing dotted the gorgeous confectionary. On the top tier was a pair of pink baby booties.

"Didn't Grams do a wonderful job?" Rhapsody cooed.

"She did. I didn't know she could make cakes like that."

"She used to work in a bakery when I was a kid."

"All right! It's time for some games." Emmerson clapped her hands which drew everyone's attention.

Rhapsody sighed. "Why did she have to come?"

"I don't know, babe. If they get on your nerves, I'll jump in and sweep you out of here like a knight in shining armor."

She laughed and smacked my shoulder. "Stop."

"The first game we are going to play is guess how fat Rhapsody is," Emmerson called out.

Rhapsody's face fell. "Get the horse ready."

41

RHAPSODY

I watched as Alec, Cassie, and Chord brought in all the gifts from the baby shower. Exhaustion weighed heavy on me. I'd been on my feet a lot longer than the doctor allowed. The little monster was particularly active, and she was using my bladder as a trampoline.

"Baby, why don't you go rest?" Chord said as he was bringing in a large box.

"I'm good."

"No you aren't. Get your ass back in bed." Cassie snapped. When I didn't move, she said, "Do I need to call Grams?"

"Ugh! Fine." I marched into the bedroom.

A tight pain clenched my stomach. I sat on the bed, taking deep breaths. My belly had grown so big that I couldn't see my swollen ankles. Another pain made me suck in a breath. I was still a month and a half away from my due date. I tried not to let fear enter my mind.

That little monster is fine. Relax," Queen B said as she leaned against a mountain of pillows.

"What?" I was confused about Queen B's positivity. That wasn't her norm.

"Are you talking to your voices again?" Cassie asked as she plopped on the bed.

"I have no idea what you're talking about."

"Uh-huh."

"What are you doing in here?"

Cassie fell against the bed dramatically. "I'm exhausted."

I laughed. "If you're exhausted, how do you think I feel?"

"I can't imagine. That was a pretty crazy baby shower. Granted I've only been to this one, but I didn't think most ended with a pole dance-off."

"Don't remind me. Whose idea was it to invite Emmerson?"

Sitting up, Cassie turned toward me. "The whole thing was her idea."

"Are you fucking with me right now?" Little monster gave me a hard kick, making me wince.

"You okay?"

"Yeah. She's just really active."

"As long as you're okay. I don't want to have to get Chord in here. He's busy with Alec putting together everything you got."

"I'm fine. Now, tell me what's going on with Emmerson."

"Why don't I tell you?" My mother's voice came from the doorway.

"I'll just go see if I can help Alec and Chord or more like just irritate the hell out of Alec." Cassie jumped off the bed.

"Traitor," I grumbled.

It was my mother who approached the bed. It wasn't the international superstar lead singer of Blue Vengeance. She was even dressed like a normal human being instead of the get-up she wore to the baby shower.

"Can I sit with you?"

I shrugged.

She joined me on the bed. "I'm sorry."

"For what?"

My mother stared down at her folded hands in her lap. "I'm sorry that I've been a piss poor mother."

"Yep."

She huffed out a breath. "Don't hold back, Rhapsody."

I shook my head. "What do you want, Mother?"

"I don't know. I wanted to make amends before that little one was born. That's why I insisted on throwing the baby shower. I wanted to make it special."

"Instead, you made it yet another Emmerson Lee show. For fuck's sake, you felt the need to challenge the exotic dancers to a dance off. You had to make it about you just like everything else."

"I didn't mean anything by it. I thought it would be fun."

"Fun for who?"

"I don't—"

"Look, it doesn't matter. It's done and over with. You can go back to your touring and do what you do best. Disappear."

"I'm not going back out on tour. We are taking an indefinite break."

"Sure."

"I'm serious. I talked to Blue Vengeance and we decided that it was time to take a break and spend time with our families. I'm going to be here when the baby is born. In fact, I want to be in the room with you, Rhapsody."

A vision of Emmerson Lee delivering my baby while being live on social media emerged. I really didn't need my vagina all over the internet.

"Nobody wants your vagina all over the internet. Especially a picture of the baby's head poking through like some alien bursting from a corn beef sandwich." Queen B grimaced.

"I don't know if I want anyone around when I'm giving birth."

A hurt look crossed her face. "Oh. Well, I just want you to know I will be there when my baby has her baby."

"Thanks."

A tense silence filled the air around us. I could hear muffled curses coming from the baby's room. Either it was incredibly complicated to put together a stroller or Cassie was succeeding at annoying Alec.

"Something is going on with those two," my mother stated.

"You noticed that too?"

She snorted. "I think everyone but them noticed what's going on there."

"Isn't that how it always is? You don't know what's right in front of you until you're falling on your face in front of them?"

"You don't know how right you are." She turned to me then continued. "I'm serious, Rhapsody. When the time comes and you need me, I'm going to be there. It doesn't matter when."

I nodded. "What happens when you and Jimmy implode? Will it go back to being don't associate with them blah, blah, blah? Your granddaughter will have Jimmy Ray's DNA too. If that happens neither of you will see her. You two don't have to be together but you at least have to act like damn adults."

My mother took my hands in hers. "I can't promise Jimmy and I are a forever thing. However, what I can promise is that no matter what happens, I will be able to ignore him expertly minus any kicking and spitting."

A laugh huffed out of me. "I guess that's the best thing I can ask for."

The next thing that happened made me freeze. My mother wrapped her arms around me and pulled me into a tight hug. Little monster must have been surprised too because she finally stopped using my bladder as a trampoline.

"That was beautiful," Queen B said while dabbing her eyes with a tissue.

I ignored her and just enjoyed a rare Emmerson Lee hug. I was enjoying it so much I didn't hear the commotion happening outside the door. The door banged open, making me jump.

"That's it! I can't stand his ass any longer! I'm out of here." Cassie stomped out of the bedroom.

Alec followed behind her with a smirk on his face. My mother shook her head and stood from the bed.

"Definitely something going on there," and she closed the door behind her.

42

———————

CHORD

"Lloyd was a very lonely dragon," I said holding up the book showing a picture of a sad lonely dragon.

A little hand shot up. "Mr. Chord?"

I took in a deep breath. "Yes, Seb?"

"Are all dragons green?" he asked.

"I don't know."

The little boy looked a bit frustrated with my answer. I cleared my throat to continue.

"Each day Lloyd would wake up and leave his cave in search of friends." I held up the book showing the big green dragon leaving a cave.

"Mr. Chord?"

"Yes, Seb?"

"Do all dragons live in caves?"

Giving him a small smile, I said, "I'm not sure."

Seb slumped back onto the cushion where he sat.

"Each day he tried to be friends with other animals in the forest." Flipping through the pages that showed Lloyd approaching a bird, a fish, and a bear.

"Mr. Chord?"

"Yes, Seb?"

"There are a lot of other animals in the forest. Why didn't he try other animals like a wolf or a shark or a penguin?"

There were so many things wrong with that question. Unfortunately, it was going to be the same answer.

"I don't know." I kept going hoping story time wouldn't take an hour thanks to Seb's questions. "Until one day, he looked up and saw something scary." The picture showed Lloyd staring at a shape up in the sky.

"Mr. Chord?"

Before I could give the obligatory "Yes, Seb?" another small voice said, "Will you shut up?!"

I closed my eyes then opened them slowly. Alice was glaring daggers at Seb. Her blonde curls bounced in irritation.

"I'm sorry," Seb mumbled.

"You can ask any questions you'd like, Seb." I smiled at him then looked at my niece. "Alice, we will respect everyone in the story time circle or you won't be allowed to join. Do you understand?"

Alice's bottom lip stuck out. "But Uncle Chord he"—

"Do you understand, Alice?"

My niece and I stared at one another. It was a game I was familiar with. The first person to look away lost the advantage. I wasn't about to lose. A nearby bang made her look away. I smiled when she realized she'd lost. She huffed out a breath and crossed her arms in irritation.

"Now, where were we?" I asked the small group.

"Lloyd saw something scary." Seb pointed to the picture.

"That's right. Thank you, Seb. Lloyd ran back to the safety of his cave. Past the bear. Past the fish. Past the bird." I flipped through the illustrated pictures of Lloyd's retreat.

Pausing, I waited for another question from Seb. When it didn't come, I continued. "Lloyd hid in the safety of his cave hoping the scary creature wouldn't find him."

"Did it find him?" Seb whispered.

I smiled and nodded. "The scary creature landed right outside the cave."

The group of youngsters gasped in horror as I showed them Lloyd cowering in his cave with the shadowy figure standing outside.

"Hello? Hello? A voice calls into the cave. Lloyd was both scared and curious." I held up the book showing Lloyd looking under his tail at the intruder.

"To see the stranger better he blew some fire on to some twigs." I held the book to me without showing them the pictures. "What do you think happened?"

"The scary thing attacked Lloyd," Seb said.

"Uncle Chord wouldn't read us a book about a dead dragon," Alice admonished.

"Dead? Lloyd's dead?" Another little girl screeched.

I glared at Alice then quickly flipped the book around to show a girl dragon smiling at Lloyd.

"Lloyd was surprised to see another dragon. He'd thought he was the only one around. I'm Lloyd. The girl dragon said I'm Layla. Do you live here? Lloyd nodded and showed her around his cave."

"Good. She didn't kill him. Though everyone knows girl dragons are stronger and could kill him in an instant." Alice crossed her arms.

I looked up at my sister and Rhapsody who were giggling behind one of the bookcases. I ignored Alice and continued with the story.

"Layla and Lloyd played all afternoon until the sun began to set." I showed them the picture of Layla and Lloyd watching the sunset. "Layla said I need to go home. Do you want to come with me? Lloyd looked at her with surprise and said yes."

The book showed a picture of the two of them flying to Layla's home with other dragons.

"Lloyd was scared again with all the new dragons. But all the dragons welcomed him with open wings. After a night of flying and food he laid down to rest. As his eyes began to close he knew he wouldn't be lonely again. The End."

I snapped the book closed. The group of children clapped then their parents retrieved them from their little cushions. Alice walked up to me looking put out.

"It would have been more exciting if she'd at least beat him up."

Putting my arm around my niece, I pulled her close and said, "Maybe next time I will read a book about girls beating up boys. We'll see. Now, go get your mom. I see she's still hiding with your Aunt Rhapsody." Alice made a beeline for where her mother stood.

"Mr. Reedy, I want to thank you so much for being so patient with my Seb. It's been quite difficult since his father left us. I appreciate you being a strong role model for him." Seb's mom placed her hand on my arm as she purred.

"Uhm...thank you. He's a good kid." I attempted to step away from her, but she held tight.

"I was thinking that maybe you could come over tonight and spend more quality time with us."

A blush crawled up my face. I looked past the woman and saw Rhapsody staring with her arms crossed over her belly. Uh oh. The look on her face meant someone was in danger and more than likely that someone was me.

"Uhm..."

"Chord, baby. Weren't you about to take me in the bathroom and fuck me?" Rhapsody said sweetly as she unhooked the woman's hand and replaced it with hers. She looked over at the woman. "He just can't get enough. I swear if I could get pregnant while being pregnant, I'd be having a litter instead of just this little monster."

"Hmph." The woman pulled away then grabbed Seb's hand. Seb looked back at me and Rhapsody with his mouth hanging open.

"Did you really just come into a children's book section and ask me to fuck you in the bathroom?" I nuzzled her neck.

"No. I saved you. A thank you would be appropriate."

"A thank you screw in the bathroom?" I mouthed against her neck.

"Okay, you two. She needs to get off her feet and you need to get back to work. No screwing around." Miranda came over to retrieve Rhapsody.

"Damn. She's such a killjoy," Rhapsody said.

"Hey! Next time make sure your kid is a bit less violent."

Miranda threw her hands in the air. "She didn't lay a hand on any kids. That was my gift to you. Now, let me get your girlfriend back to your apartment before she keels over."

I leaned over and gave Rhapsody a kiss. "Love you. See you when I get home."

She blushed then followed after Miranda and Alice. Something about the title of girlfriend didn't sit well with me. I mean I guess she technically was, but it felt like it was so much more. Rhapsody was the woman I wanted in my life for the rest of my life. If only I could convince her of that.

43

RHAPSODY

"This is so boring," Alec whined.

I focused on typing an email response to one of the junior executives I was working with on a project. Alec turned up a show about finding out the paternity of a child.

"You and Chord really missed out."

I sighed. "What the hell are you talking about?"

He pointed toward the television with the remote. "The two of you could have had a big paternity thing on this show." Alec sat up straight and in his best announcer's voice said, "Who is the father of Emmerson Lee's daughter's child? Could it be her archrival's son? Tune in tomorrow for the explosive reveal."

"You're an idiot." I continued to type.

"Come on. You know that would have been fucking awesome television."

I looked at the time on my laptop. "Isn't it time for you to go?"

Alec furrowed his brow. "I literally got here five minutes ago. I'm not allowed to leave until someone else shows."

"I won't tell anyone if you skip out early."

"Early would be seven hours and fifty-five minutes."

"Fifty-four," I countered.

"I'm just getting comfortable." Alec precariously leaned back on the chair.

I stared at the chair leg and willed it to slip out from under him. Fall. Fall. Fall. I chanted. A pain began to bloom behind my eye. It seemed I still hadn't acquired the power of telekinesis, but I could have possibly given myself an aneurysm.

"Fine. If you're going to sit there and watch that crap, I want your yap shut."

Alec held up his hands in surrender. It was just enough of a movement to throw off his equilibrium. I watched in slow motion as his body slammed against the floor. A whoosh of air left his lungs. For a moment, he looked like a dead possum. The visual was too much. I started laughing. Not just dainty little giggles. I was bent over laughing so hard I was crying and was afraid the little monster would make me pee myself. After about five minutes, I was finally able to pull myself back together.

While I'd been laughing, Alec had gotten back up in the chair and sat with his arms crossed. "It wasn't that funny," he grumbled.

It set me off again. I had to move my laptop so I didn't accidentally throw it on the floor from laughing. "I was wrong, Alec," I breathed out.

"Wrong about what?"

"You can stay. You're wonderfully entertaining." I grinned.

He hmphed then focused completely on the talk show. To drown out the annoying show I put on headphones and cranked up a playlist I titled "Music to Roller Skate to". They were tunes that reminded me of middle school.

I bopped along as I worked on a presentation I was expected to present in a couple of weeks. It was cutting it close to my due date, so I had to make sure it was on point in case little monster decided to make her appearance a little early. The longer I focused on my work, the more uncomfortable I became. A dull ache radiated from my lower back down my leg. When I couldn't take it any longer, I moved off the bed.

"What are you doing?" Alec asked.

"I just need to—" My words were interrupted by a splash of liquid.

"Did you just pee on the floor? Jesus, Rhapsody, I could have helped you to the bathroom." He stood from the chair.

"That wasn't pee." A pain made me double over.

"Then what..." He froze. "Please tell me your water didn't just break. Please oh please tell me that."

I held in a breath as a wave of nausea hit with a sharp pain. "I can't tell you that, Alec."

"Fuck me. Why did it have to be me? I'm not good in these scenarios. I mean I had health in middle school, but I don't remember them going over how to deliver a baby. I wonder if there is a YouTube video?" He pulled out his phone to look.

I grabbed a pillow off the bed and threw it at him. He looked up confused.

"I need to get to the hospital, you fucktard."

"Oh." He stood there.

I took deep breaths to help control the pain and anger I was feeling. He still stood there looking between me and the puddle on the floor.

"Come on! Get my bag and let's go."

"Oh! Sorry!"

I watched Alec run over to the bag I had packed the week before. All the baby books recommended having a bag packed a month in advance in case the bundle of joy wanted to join the family early. I waddled toward the door when a sharp pain made me double over. Deep breaths were coming faster than I'd practiced. Fuck the practice breaths. They didn't prepare me for the agonizing pain that would rip through me.

"Come on, Rhapsody! You're going to have a baby. We need

to get to the hospital," Alec called from down the hallway. How the hell had he gotten past me?

"Really, Alec? I didn't notice," I grunted out.

"How could you not? I mean—"

"I swear to everything that is holy, Alec, if you don't shut the fuck up and get me to the damn hospital, I am going to castrate you with my bare hands!" I yelled.

He had the sense to snap his mouth shut and wait for me.

"Damn! I was looking forward to you hurting him," Queen B chimed in.

Ignoring the homicidal voice in my head, I finally made it to the end of the hall but had to lean against the wall to catch my breath. Alec tentatively approached to wrap his arm around me to give me some needed support. I let him take my weight as we moved toward the door and just as we made our way to it, it flung open. Cassie gawked at the two of us.

"What the hell is going on here?" she demanded.

"My—" I began.

Alec stiffened then said, "None of your business. Now, get out of the way."

"Rhapsody?" She continued to block the way with her arms crossed.

"You don't need to answer her," Alec said.

"Yes she does. I think Chord would like to know too. Maybe I should call him." She held out her phone.

"Do what you want but move out of the way!"

"Not until you explain yourself, Alec. What is going on? What happened?"

"Oh for fuck's sake!" I yelled. "My fucking water broke, Cassie. I need to go to the fucking hospital before I have the damn little monster here in the doorway!"

"What?" She looked at me with a slack jaw.

"What the hell is wrong with these people? I'd much rather have that idiot that makes you make those frightening sounds instead of these two." Queen B shook her head.

"She's having the baby, Cassie. Now, if you'd move, I can assist her to the hospital," Alec said between clenched teeth.

Cassie glared at him then said, "I should be the one to take care of her. She is my cousin after all."

"Well, she's pregnant with my cousin's baby." Alec pulled me close to him as Cassie tried to grab me.

"Oh no you don't. Just because your—"

"Get. Me. To. The. Hospital. Now!" I yelled as a sharp pain caused me to double over again.

"Oh shit," they said together then finally began working in tandem to help me to the car.

It only took them ten minutes and an epic amount of bickering to get me to Alec's over-compensated vehicle. When we were finally on the way I rummaged through my purse that Cassie had grabbed without me noticing. Thankfully, someone also threw my phone in there. I pulled up Chord's texts.

Me: It's time.

Chord: Babe…we just did it this morning. I can't come home and give it to you.

I rolled my eyes as another twinge of pain hit.

Me: No idiot. It's time for the little monster to hatch.

Chord: Hahaha…you're funny. You aren't due for like three weeks.

Me: No shit, Sherlock! She's making her debut early and if you don't get to St. Francis in the next ten minutes, I'm going to name her something really ridiculous like Hashtag or Bonnie.

Chord: You aren't kidding are you?

Me: Sure, Chord. I text you all the time to tell you I'm having the baby. Stay at work and I'll let Alec deliver the baby. Hopefully my vagina won't turn him off sex.

Throwing my phone into my purse, I ignored the vibration as it continued to go off. I sat and watched the scenery go by. Alec screeched into the parking lot slamming on the brakes as he parked across two spots.

"You're really going to park it like an asshole?" I asked as I slowly got out of the car.

"We're in an emergency." He paused as Cassie helped me walk toward the emergency room doors. "Uhm…Rhapsody?"

"Yeah?"

"Why is Chord text-yelling at me about your vagina?"

44

CHORD

"Are you okay, Chord?" Mary placed a hand on my arm.

"Rhapsody is in labor."

"What?" Mary gave me a quizzical look. "Did I hear you right? Rhapsody is in labor."

I nodded numbly.

"What are you still doing here, Chord?" She pulled me into a quick hug then pushed me toward the door.

It only took me a second for all my brain cells to begin firing. I ran past the head librarian Sylvia.

"Gotta go, Sylvia. I went into labor!"

"Wha...?" I heard her comment distantly float to me as I burst through the library doors.

I ran down the steps leading to the library deftly dodging parents with their kids in tow. One thing repeated in my head as I ran. I'm going to be a father. I needed to get to the hospital ASAP. I'd be damned if Alec would be delivering my daughter. When I realized I was just running I stopped and took a deep breath. Finally, I arranged my thoughts. It made no sense for me to just run to the hospital. Luckily, I had found my way to a popular taxi stop. I waved my arm and tried to signal a taxi.

As I waved frantically, taxi after taxi buzzed by me. What the hell was wrong with these people? Couldn't they see it was an emergency? Just when I began to contemplate running to the hospital a taxi screeched to a halt in front of me.

Jumping into the cab, I said, "Take me to St. Francis as fast as you can."

The young cabbie blinked at me from the front seat then nodded. He pulled into traffic so quickly I had to grab onto the overhead handle. The cab wove through traffic like a hockey player weaving through defenders.

"Why didn't you just fly?" the cabbie asked.

"Fly? I don't think that's an option to get to St. Francis."

"Huh. So it's a mind thing then?" The cabbie's eyes didn't leave mine in the rearview mirror.

"Uhm sure. Can you just pay attention to the road?"

The cabbie, whose name was Dennis, chuckled then went back to navigating the increasingly heavy traffic. I texted Rhapsody and didn't get any answers. Her words about letting Alec deliver our little one rang through my head. I sent a text threatening his manhood if he got anywhere near Rhapsody's vagina. I didn't need him delivering my daughter like he did Alice. Miranda was still salty about that.

As the taxi began to slow, I looked up from my phone. A huge pile up blocked our way. Of course this would fucking happen to me. My knee bounced as my nerves pulled tighter and tighter. From the look of things, no cars were going anywhere. Dammit.

"How many blocks to St. Francis?" I asked.

He shrugged. "Ten?"

Fuck! I shoved the money through the partition and jumped out of the car. It looked like I would be running the ten blocks if I wanted to meet my baby girl. I ran between stopped cars as fast as I could. Shouting and honking horns urged me on faster. I could have sworn there were claps and cheers also. I shook that questioning thought out of my head and focused on the task at hand. Run ten blocks to meet my daughter.

———

I jogged into the emergency room drenched in sweat and heaving in breaths. The nurses took one look at me and rushed over.

"Are you okay, sir?" a nurse who was bent over me asked.

"I'm…having…a…baby," I breathed out.

The three nurses stood and looked at each other.

"All right, sir. Let's have a seat right here. Someone will be over," the nurse calmly said then yelled, "Code screw."

"Wait! I need to find my—"

A male orderly approached me. "We know what you have to find. We'll help you. Just come with me."

"So you're going to take me to her?" I asked.

"We sure are. Now, can you tell me what that means on your…uhm…uniform?" We walked toward a brightly lit hallway where screams could be heard.

"What?" I looked down and finally remembered that I was wearing a superhero costume for superhero day at the library. "Oh. This isn't a uniform. This is a costume. I'm a children's librarian, and it was superhero day today."

The orderly gave me a smile. "I'm sure it was. Now, let's go in here, and we'll have the doctor check you out."

"I don't need a doctor to check me out. I'm here because my girlfriend is in labor."

Another soft smile. "Yes. Please sit on the bed, and we will be able to help you."

"Look there has been a mistake. There is nothing wrong with me." I moved to leave the room.

The orderly placed hand on my chest halting me. "I don't think so, buddy."

"This is a big mistake." I did a quick evading move that did nothing.

He sighed then wrapped his arms around me and dragged me over to the bed. I struggled as he shoved me onto the bed. My struggle finally stopped when he restrained my arms in some sort of cuffs.

"What the fuck is this?"

"It's for your own good, sir." He gave me another smile.

A nurse entered the room. "I'll take it from here." She pulled out a needle. "This will help."

I tried to move away from her, but she was quick, and I felt a pinch. As the quick-acting drug began to take effect, I found my phone and attempted to type a message to Alec. When I pressed send, I saw a giant pink and purple polka-dotted tiger dancing in the room.

45

RHAPSODY

"Fuck Chord and his magical cock!" I shouted as another pain shot through my abdomen.

"Uhm...Rhapsody you may want to keep it down a bit," Cassie said as she sat in the chair next to the shitty makeshift hospital bed.

"Fuck you. Give me your hand again," I demanded.

Her face paled. "Nope." She turned to Alec, who was looking at his phone. "Alec, you're up."

"What?"

Cassie grinned at him. "Rhapsody needs your hand."

He sighed. "Fine." His hand shot out as he continued to look at his phone.

Little monster did another pass down my spine. I squeezed with all my might. "Ahhh!"

"Owwwww!" Alec squealed and fell to the floor.

Cassie giggled. "Oh, Alec, man up. Stop being a baby."

"Fuck you." He attempted to pull his hand away, but I held tight until the pain subsided.

"Whew. Thanks, Alec." I laid against the reclined bed.

"I think you broke my hand." Alec held his hand against his chest.

I just shrugged then looked around the curtained area. When we arrived at the hospital, we were escorted to a bed surrounded by curtains. The nurse said a doctor would be with us shortly. That was almost two hours ago. Chord hadn't shown up either. I was only half joking when I threatened him about not showing up. I didn't really think he wouldn't show.

"Where is the fucking doctor?" I asked.

"I'm not sure. I'll go ask again." Cassie stood to leave the area and ran into someone coming into our designated curtained room.

"Oh I'm sorry," Cassie stuttered.

When I got my first look at the man, I understood why she was stuttering. He was gorgeous. I mean if you liked the built like a bouncer with hypnotizing green eyes and perfectly just had sex black hair. I loved Chord but that man sure made my lady bits wet. Well…I think it was because of him and not just because my water had burst.

"How are you doing in here?" Dr. Wet Dream asked.

"I'm great," Cassie said.

"I think he was talking to Rhapsody," Alec said flatly.

"Oh. Sorry." Cassie blushed.

I gaped at my cousin. In all the years I've known her she never blushed because of a guy. It was something to see.

Dr. Wet Dream smiled bright, white teeth at Cassie. "I'm glad you're doing well. I hope if that changes you'd tell me.

Cassie giggled and nodded. What the hell was happening?

The doctor lasered his smile on me. I smiled back then said, "I'm not okay. I've been waiting for two hours with this little monster doing the samba on my spine. So, I'm a bit cranky and ready for this to be over with."

Dr. Wet Dream had the nerve to laugh. My hand itched with the need to throat punch him. If little monster decided to give me pain in that moment, he was going to be my first target.

"Let's see how far along we are." He took a seat on a rolling stool and positioned himself between my thighs.

I laid back against the reclined bed. The snap of the latex gloves made me jump.

"This may be a little cold," the doctor said.

"I'll be back." Alec began to escape the room.

Good. I didn't need him seeing any more of my vagina than necessary. Which would be none.

"Go ahead. I'll stay and help the doctor if necessary," Cassie offered.

I sat up and watched Alec give her an annoyed look then shook his head and continued to exit.

"What the hell do you think your ass is going to do? Sit down over there." I pointed to the chair away from the doctor.

Cassie gave me a "shut up" look then reluctantly moved to the chair.

"Can you get down to business, doc? I want my drugs ASAP." I kicked my legs into the stirrups.

Dr. Wet Dream laughed again then winked at Cassie. She blushed fiercely. What the hell was going on?

I no longer cared once his fingers were probing me. Closing my eyes, I forced myself to breathe deeply. Most pregnant women get used to probing fingers in their vagina. Unfortunately, I was not one of them.

"Hmm…" he said.

"What?"

"Well, it looks like you're only a few centimeters dilated. We will have to wait until you're about five centimeters to administer an epidural." He ripped off the gloves. "I will see if we can get you into a room. Looks like you've got a long road ahead of you, Ms. Bell."

"Mother fucker!" I yelled.

He blanched. Good. No more bright white smile. He turned to leave but was met with a group of people.

"We knew it was you from the mother fucker," Miranda said.

Grams pushed past everyone and sat on the side of the bed. Pulling my hand into her lap, she gave it a squeeze. "How is my girl doing?"

"Little monster is putting up a hell of a fight." I looked around at the audience that had gathered. Still no Chord. "So, what is everyone doing here?"

"Alec and Cassie texted everyone." My mother stepped next to Grams and smiled at me.

I glanced over at Cassie, who made a concerted effort to stare at her phone. She stood quickly and left without a word.

"Well, that was weird," Miranda said.

"I think we can all agree with that. So, when will you get a real room? Do we need to pull some strings?" My mother stood straighter ready to flex her celebrity muscle.

"The doctor said I should get a room soon."

"How about right now?" A nurse threw open the curtain and wheeled in a wheelchair.

"That would be fantastic." I slid off the bed and winced when I felt another pain shoot through my abdomen.

"Take your time," she said.

I waddled over to the wheelchair then sat as gently as an elephant on a cruise ship.

The nurse looked around the group. She pursed her lips then said, "All of you will have to wait here until we have Ms. Bell settled. We will let you know when you can visit."

A cacophony of voices made protests. Without addressing them, the nurse turned the wheelchair around and left everyone. I bit my lip to keep the laugh that threatened to burst through inside. We quietly moved through the emergency room area to a bank of elevators. The doors opened, letting off a doctor, and we rolled into the quiet space.

"Your family could have come," she said. I looked up at her, and she smiled down at me. "I thought you'd need a little break. Just say when and I will bring them to you."

I smiled. "Thanks but the one I'm waiting for hasn't arrived yet."

She furrowed her brow. "The baby's father hasn't arrived yet?"

"No. It's been like two hours since I texted him a snarky reply. I'm starting to get concerned the idiot took me seriously."

"I'll keep a look out for him and send him your way as soon as he steps foot in the hospital."

The elevator dinged, and we got off at the designated floor. She wheeled me to a room, and as she helped me into the bed, she gave me a sad smile.

"Are you going to be okay?"

"Yeah. You can send up the crazies."

Her eyebrows lifted in question. "Are you sure?"

"Yeah. I'd rather have their crazy drown out the thoughts that my little monster's daddy decided he didn't want us anymore." I forced my lips into a smile.

The nurse looked like she wanted to give me a hug. The look on my face must have told her that was a bad idea. Instead, she nodded then left the room.

"*You know he probably got lost or something. He is an idiot.*" Queen B piped up after being quiet for so long.

"Now you're deciding to speak up?" I mumbled.

Queen B just shrugged then began doing her nails.

46

CHORD

"How the hell did he get here?" A woman's voice floated into the darkness.

"I have no idea. His message just said downstairs they think I'm crazy. Need help asap#$&asldkfajlskd. Now, if you understand that last part you let me know." That voice sounded a lot like Alec.

"Why is he dressed like that?" the female voice asked.

"Probably something with his work. How the hell am I supposed to know? Now, are you going to help me get your cousin's baby's daddy out of this or are you going to keep asking me stupid fucking questions?"

Silence filled the darkness. "I should just let you struggle then tell Rhapsody you knew where Chord was the whole time."

Alec blew out a breath. "Just help me then you can get back to flirting with the doctor."

"Don't start, Alec. How are we getting him out of this?"

I felt a tug on my arm.

"We should probably wake him up first. Then we can figure out the restraints," Alec said.

"No problem." The voice that sounded a lot like Rhapsody's cousin, Cassie, faded away.

"Wait...wait...wait," Alec said frantically.

Ice cold water splashed onto me. I sputtered as my previously glued shut eyes were now wide open. I looked over at Alec, who grimaced and Cassie, who was grinning while holding a small ice bucket.

"What the?" I began.

"You texted me, Chord. They thought you were crazy. I can't say I really blame them with the way you're dressed."

I looked down at my soaked costume. "It...was... superhero...day." The words came out between my chattering teeth.

"Shh...we gotta try to sneak you outta here. Now, hold still while I get you out of these." Cassie began working on the restraints.

"What are you doing?" Alec asked.

"Shut up and let me work," Cassie snipped.

"Yeah," I added, unhelpful.

The restraint on my right wrist loosened, and I slid my arm out and shook out my wrist.

"Thanks."

"No problem. You'll be completely free in just a few minutes."

Alec and I watched her move from cuff to cuff. I looked over at Alec whose jaw hung open. I would have laughed if it wouldn't have alerted the orderly that funny business was going on in my room.

"Is it me or is it fucking hot that she knows her way around cuffs?" Alec murmured next to me.

"Uhm...I think you have the hots for her and whatever she does is hot to you."

Before Alec could say anything else, Cassie popped up from the last cuff. "Done."

I moved my other freed wrist and attempted to stand.

Thankfully, Alec was there to catch me. My legs wouldn't bear my weight.

"What the hell is wrong with you?" Alec asked.

"He's still messed up on whatever drugs they shot into him. I'll help you with him, but we may have to drag his ass out of here." Cassie grabbed the other side of me.

"I just need a bit of help then I'll be fine."

The two of them grunted but the three of us began a weird shuffle drag toward the door. When we heard voices coming near we froze. The door was slightly ajar. We collectively held our breaths as the two people passed by. Waiting a few more moments we let out our breaths. I leaned on Alec as Cassie peered out the door.

"Shit," Cassie said.

"What?" Alec asked.

"Don't worry about it. I'll take care of it but when you hear me giggle make a run for it, and I will meet you up in Rhapsody's room." Cassie fluffed her hair and pulled her shirt lower to expose her cleavage.

"What the hell are you doing?" Alec asked.

She glared at him then said, "What needs to be done."

When Cassie exited the room, Alec and I inched closer to the door. We could faintly hear Cassie's voice mixed with a deep voice. I could hear Alec's molars grinding the longer Cassie spoke with the man. Finally, her giggle signaled for us to move. Alec practically dragged me from the room and around the nearby corner. He stopped for just a second to look at Cassie. He didn't like what he saw if his brooding expression was any indicator.

Whatever bothered him just made him drag me faster to the elevators. He pushed the up arrow and the doors opened. Shuffling in, Alec propped me against the wall of the elevator. I was starting to get feeling back in my extremities when the doors of the elevator closed. Closing my eyes, I imagined the hell Rhapsody was going to give me with each contraction.

When I didn't feel the elevator moving, I opened my eyes and looked at Alec. He was staring at the buttons in confusion.

"What's wrong? Why isn't the elevator moving?"

"Uhm…I don't know what floor Rhapsody is on."

"What do you mean you don't know what floor she's on?" I stood a bit straighter.

"When I left her, she was still in the emergency room area."

"You mean the area we were near."

"Yep."

"Why didn't you just take me to where you last saw her?"

Alec glared at me. "Because you were in the area they put crazy people. If they thought I was busting you out I'd get arrested. I don't feel like getting arrested for my cousin who is dressed up like a superhero."

"I told you—"

"Yeah. Yeah. I know. Remember I used to live with you."

"Well, what are we going to do?"

"Uhm."

Before Alec could come up with a dumb ass idea, the elevator dinged, and the doors began to slide open. I flattened myself against the wall of the tiny metal box and hid behind Alec. When the doors completely opened, Cassie stood there grinning.

"Well, that was easy."

"Because you were easy," Alec whispered.

Cassie sucked in a breath then reached out her hand effectively slapping him. Red tinged her cheeks and a fury I'd only seen in Rhapsody shone through her cousin. "Fuck you, Alec."

Alec held his cheek. I placed my hand on his shoulder to stop him from saying something he'd regret or get kneed in the nuts for.

"Cassie, do you know if they moved Rhapsody out of the emergency room?"

She glared at Alec then looked at me. "Yes. Emmerson said they moved her to 4B."

"Great." I reached past Alec and pressed the number four.

The elevator began to move. It was surprising the thing could move at all with all the tension weighing it down. To distract myself from the unsaid argument Alec and Cassie were having, I sang "The Wheels on the Bus" in my head. In no time, the doors opened to chaos. Nurses ran around in a flurry of activity.

Two hurried by and we heard, "I can't believe they could lose a psych patient like that. This place has gone to hell."

"Oh hell," Cassie said as she pushed me against the elevator.

"What are we going to do now? You can't flirt with everyone," Alec said.

If it wasn't such a dire situation Cassie would have decked him. Thankfully, she could focus on the problem at hand. "Give me a second. Let me see how far 4B is from here. Go over there and hide. I will come back when I find her." She pointed toward the sign that said bathroom. When she exited the elevator, she looked around then waved us out.

Alec and I ran from the elevator to the bathroom. A sign on the door made my heart sink. Out of Order. Of course it was out of order. If anything went right for me leading up to my daughter's birth it would be a miracle. Alec dragged me into the next door and shoved us into a stall. It was the women's room. Great.

"The lady's room? Really, Alec?" I whispered.

"Where the hell else were we going to go? Now, shut up. I hear someone coming."

We held our breath as we listened to footsteps approach. The door swung open, and we waited. The steps grew closer. I couldn't see out the crack in the stall because Alec had shoved me behind the toilet. We didn't hear footsteps or the sound of a stall door. What in the world was the woman doing?

As that thought crossed my mind, we found out who had

entered the bathroom. Cassie kicked in the door, slamming it against Alec's face. She smiled at me and ignored Alec, whose nose was bleeding.

"Ready? I found her." Cassie held her hand out to me.

I looked at Alec sitting on the floor and moaning. "Sorry, Alec." Placing my hand in hers, I stepped over him and left with Cassie.

"Rhapsody is only a couple of doors down. I'm going to pop out of the bathroom to see if the coast is clear." She left me standing there for a moment.

Alec's moans floated over to me. A part of me felt bad but then I remembered what he said to her and that my baby was about to be born. He could fend for himself.

"Come on." Cassie grabbed ahold of my arm and dragged me down the small hall.

Luck was on our side. The hall had cleared out and quieted down. Cassie dragged me into 4B. I froze when I saw the crowd around a pissed off Rhapsody. Our eyes met, and I could have sworn I saw relief but that was quickly replaced with an anger that could melt your face off.

"Hmm...well, I guess I found the missing psych patient," a nurse said from behind me.

"Oh for fuck's sake," Rhapsody spat then yelled as a contraction hit.

47

RHAPSODY

"Told you he would have a fucked up reason." Queen B popped her gum.

"Fuck you." I gritted out between clenched teeth.

"Rhapsody! I know it's painful but no need for that language," Grams said from a nearby chair where she was knitting.

"Sorry, Grams."

"Ha. Ha. You got in trouble," Queen B taunted.

If that bitch were real, I'd throat punch her.

"Baby, how are you doing? I'm so sorry I'm late." Chord ran toward me from the door.

"Where the hell have you been?"

"It's a long story." He gave me a slow blink.

"We have time," Jimmy Ray said.

Why the fuck was that asshat still here? I get he's now Emmerson's…uhm…whatever he is and just so happens to be the baby's grandpa but that didn't mean he needed to see my vagina as it goes from a beautiful lily to bloody corn beef.

"Why are you here, Jimmy?" Miranda asked.

"I'm being supportive."

Miranda glared at him then looked at me. "If you want him to leave just let me know. I'd love to throw him out." She cracked her knuckles.

"You'd do that to your own father."

"Yes," Chord and Miranda said together.

"Why don't we give Chord and Rhapsody some time alone. I need something to drink." Grams smiled as she stood from her chair.

"We don't need to leave, Mom. I have something right here." Emmerson pulled a giant bottle of booze out of her purse.

"Leigh Anne Bell! That is not the kind of drink I am talking about. We all need some coffee. Let's go, Cassie." Grams grabbed Cassie by the arm and shot a look at everyone else.

"Hey. Why did you—" Alec's voice was muffled.

"We are leaving," Grams said as she grabbed Alec with her other hand.

Chord and I watched everyone shuffle out of the room. My nurse, whose name I'd finally learned was Bonnie, barely contained a grin as she also watched the group leave. When the last person was out the door, Bonnie looked over at Chord and me.

"I'm going to go see why that guy is bleeding from the face and make sure no one knows that a crazy person dressed as a superhero has shown up in the maternity ward. If you need me, Rhapsody, push that little button." Bonnie let herself out of the room.

Chord pulled over a chair. I watched as he flicked his cape up so he wouldn't sit on it. Good lord this man was the father of my baby.

"Yeah you could've picked better," Queen B clucked.

He cleared his throat then he stared at me. I waited for him to say something or fly through the roof with his superpowers. Either would have been better than him staring at me.

"Uhm...how are you feeling?"

I lifted my eyebrow at him. "What do you think? I'm assuming mind reading isn't your superpower."

"Yeah. Dumb question. I'm sorry I'm late. I didn't expect to be taken as a mental patient then drugged. I think I've been at the hospital for a few hours but time kind of slipped away as I was passed out."

"Well, I can't really say I'm surprised. I mean you are dressed like you're crazy. Where the hell did you get those clothes anyway? I know you didn't leave the house looking like that."

"I totally forgot it was superhero day at the library. Thankfully, Mary had some extra pieces I could scrap together. The kids would have been disappointed if I hadn't dressed up."

I couldn't help myself and I smiled, which immediately turned into a grimace as pain shot through me. Breathing in and out wasn't helping.

"Are you okay? Just breathe."

"What the fuck do you think I'm doing, Chord?" I gritted out.

He grabbed my hand in his and moved to sit on the bed with me. "Squeeze my hand. Let me help."

I squeezed his hand so hard I heard a bone crack. I fully expected him to have a hissy fit like Alec, but Chord just met my eyes. If I wasn't already in love with him, the soft look in his eyes would have melted me. Little monster didn't let me have that moment when another pain shot through me. These pains felt different.

"What's wrong? You have a strange look on your face." Chord pushed some hair off my forehead.

"Something doesn't feel right."

"I'm getting the nurse." He pushed the button next to the bed. When nothing immediately happened, he kept pushing it.

Bonnie casually walked in and pushed the button to shut it off. "Everything okay?"

I slapped my hand over Chord's mouth and said, "Something doesn't feel right."

"Okay. Let me check some things."

Bonnie began checking my vitals. It felt like she was taking her time when it was just the intense pain. She lifted the blanket, and I watched as the blood drained from her face. She placed the blanket back down and left the room.

"What's going on?" I asked Chord.

"I have no idea. I'm sure it's nothing." He gave my hand another squeeze, but the tense set of his shoulders ratcheted up my anxiety.

The handsome doctor from the emergency room walked in with his too bright smile. "How are we doing?"

Chord squinted at him then said, "What do you think, pretty boy?"

I sighed as another sharp pain made me grimace. Chord's jealousy or whatever the hell was going on wasn't something I could handle in that moment. The bright smile from the doctor was the other thing I couldn't deal with.

"Let's have a look shall we."

"Does this dick really need to be your doctor?" Chord whispered to me.

It wasn't quiet enough because Bonnie let out a snort-laugh as the doctor rolled to the end of the bed.

"Let's see what's going on down here," Dr. Smiles said with another smile. "Just take a deep breath."

I laid back trying to relax. Staring at the ceiling, I tried to ignore the pain and pressure.

"Okay. Looks like we need to do an emergency C-section." He turned away from me and whispered to the nurse.

"What's going on?" I asked Chord.

"I don't know." He stood and approached the doctor and nurse.

If I hadn't been in pain, I would have laughed. Chord stood with his hands on his hips looking like the epitome of a superhero. The worry that colored his features made my pulse spike.

"What's happening?" I called over to them.

"Tell her," he insisted.

"It looks like the baby is in a bad position and has caused some abnormal bleeding. So, for yours and the baby's safety we need to do a C-section."

The doctor's words floated through my mind. I looked over at Chord. My panic must have been evident because he rushed over to me. "It's going to be fine. I'll be right there with you."

"Okay. As long as you're there I'll feel better."

Bonnie cleared her throat. "We need to get you moving." She moved behind the bed and began pushing it.

"I'll be right in." Chord gave my hand one last squeeze before they rolled me quickly from the room.

I stared up at the lights on the ceiling as we passed. More pain shot through me, and I groaned. Faintly, I heard voices asking questions, but they got quieter and quieter as I was wheeled further down the hall.

They pushed the bed that I now realized doubled as a birthing table into an operating room. Bonnie moved to my side when the bed was stopped.

"I'm going to have to help you to the table."

Nodding, I let her grab my arm as I slid from the table. I glanced down toward my feet and saw blood had soaked my gown. How had I missed that? Nausea overtook me. Another pain shot through my body. Something was seriously wrong.

"Hang in there. Little monster will enter this world with a bang." Queen B patted my shoulder just as darkness overcame me.

48

CHORD

"Chord! What's going on?" Emmerson asked as she saw them rolling Rhapsody away.

"She's bleeding out. They need to do an emergency C-section."

"Oh my God!" she exclaimed and turned in Jimmy Ray's arms for comfort.

"I've gotta get going. They are going to let me in while they perform the C-section."

Grams patted my shoulder. "Take care of our girl."

"I will." I moved toward the nurse's station.

A young nurse looked at me and blinked. "Can I help you?"

"My girlfriend is having a C-section. I need to know where to go to join her."

Her face lit up. "Congratulations. Follow me."

We walked down the hall. She stopped to grab something then stopped in front of an open door.

"You will need to put these over...uhm...your clothes. When you're done come out here, and I will take you where you need to go."

"Thanks."

I walked into the darkened room and paused for a moment. My recent memories of getting knocked out with a shot shook me to the core. I realized it was a small bathroom and not an actual room, and I relaxed. I finally took off the mask and cape. When I began to take off the rest of the costume, I realized I didn't have other clothes to put on under the scrubs. Shrugging, I put on the scrubs then stepped out of the bathroom.

"Ready?" she asked while handing me a hair net cap thing.

Taking a deep breath, I shook my head and followed the nurse. She held up her hand, making me stop.

"I will go tell them you're ready." She disappeared behind swinging double doors.

I waited and waited. Worry started to niggle at my brain. I wasn't a doctor, but I was pretty sure I should have been in there after a few minutes. Just when I was ready to burst through those double doors the nurse came through looking worried.

"I'm sorry. It looks like you can't go in."

"What do you mean I can't go in? My girlfriend and baby are in there."

"I'm sorry. There have been complications. You will need to sit in the waiting area." She took my arm to take me to where the rest of our families had found their way.

"What's going on, Chord?" Miranda asked.

"No clue. All the nurse said was that there were complications. It sounds like there is more to it than we'd thought." I plopped into a plastic chair and held my head in my hands. "I promised Rhapsody I'd be in there."

Grams took a seat next to me and patted my leg. "Our girl is strong, Chord. So is that little one. They will be okay. Have faith."

I just nodded.

———

"The family for Rhapsody Bell?" The smiley doctor approached us.

I shot from my seat. "What's going on? We've been sitting here for hours."

He nodded and looked over my shoulder. "I think we should talk over here."

"Okay."

Following the doctor around the corner, he stopped just outside of where the family could hear us. "There were complications."

"I understand that. How is the baby? How is Rhapsody?"

His eyes got soft, and a knot formed in my stomach. "Your baby girl is healthy and has quite a set of lungs on her."

"Oh thank God." I bent at my waist and heaved in a few breaths.

"Unfortunately, that's the good news. Her mama is in a coma."

"What?"

"We don't know what happened. She lost a lot of blood but that shouldn't have been enough to force her into a coma. We are concerned it was a blood clot. She's currently in the ICU. You can see her, but we have to limit who goes in there."

"Okay. Do we know how long she will be in the coma?"

The doctor shook his head. "It could be an hour or a year or..."

"Or forever," I whispered.

"That is unfortunately true. Look on the bright side. You have that beautiful little girl." He gave my shoulder a squeeze before I walked back to the family.

They all saw my face and immediately began peppering me with questions. I answered what I could but there were more questions than I had answers. Emmerson was crying on Jimmy's shoulder. Grams was hugging Cassie while Alec comforted Miranda.

"Would you all go check on our little one in the nursery while I go see Rhapsody?"

"Of course." Emmerson gave my shoulder a squeeze.

"Thank you. I will let you know when you guys can start trickling in to see her."

I marched over to the nurse's station to get directions to the ICU. With a deep breath, I found the elevator and rode it to the one floor I wish I wasn't going to. How would I be able to survive if she doesn't wake up? She needs to see our little one. She needs to be around. Our lives were just getting started.

"Can I help you?" I looked up to see I was standing in front of another nursing station.

"Rhapsody Bell's room please."

She nodded and typed something into the computer. "She's in there." The nurse pointed to a room directly across from the station.

Beeps from other rooms made a background song that I wish I never got to experience. Walking into the dimly lit room, I wasn't sure what to expect. What I saw almost brought me to my knees. My beautiful Rhapsody was pale. The machines monitoring her vitals were the only sounds. If I hadn't seen her chest rise and fall, I would have thought she wasn't breathing.

"Oh, Rhapsody." I brought a chair closer to the bed and took her hand in mine. "This can't be happening to us. We were just starting." I kissed her hand then continued. "You have to wake up. You need to see our beautiful daughter. Granted I haven't seen her yet, but if she is even half as beautiful as you, then she's going to be a stunner. Which means when she's a teenager I'm going to have to buy a gun. No boys will be touching her."

I took a deep breath and looked at her.

"See...I'm already talking like a crazy person. I need your crazy to offset my crazy. You can't leave us to fend for ourselves. You need to wake up and tell me how fucked up I am then do whatever crazy thing you wanted to. Also, I really think something is going on with Alec and Cassie. How am I going to deal with that?"

The beeping continued to be the only noise coming from her.

Tears pooled in the corner of my eyes. "Come on, baby. You can't leave me. I really don't know if I can go on without you. My life was nothing without you in it. I didn't realize that until I was the embarrassing one pump chump the night of that wedding. We need to have our own wedding. This time filled with lots of condoms. I love that we have our little bean here, but I don't think we need to rush to give her a sibling." Tears had broken free, and I was getting choked up. "I'm going to try something from a story that Miranda was obsessed with when we were little. Maybe it will work like it did in the storybook." I stood from the seat and kissed her on the lips.

After breaking the kiss, I turned quickly away from her. Wiping away the tears, I was so focused on what I couldn't handle that I missed the uptick in the beeps.

"You know I always thought we were more Romeo and Juliet than Sleeping Beauty." Rhapsody's voice croaked.

"Rhapsody?" I spun around.

"Yeah?" She blinked, looking at me.

I went over to her and pushed the button above her head for the nurse to come in. I held her and let the tears flow. Faintly, I could hear a commotion around us. I held on to her tightly as the doctor and nurses checked all her vitals.

"You know I heard you talking to me."

I blinked at her. "You did?"

She grinned. "You acknowledge the one pump chump thing then?"

I felt heat rise. "I'm never living that down, am I?"

"You'll just have to keep making it up to me over and over and over for the rest of our lives."

I leaned forward and kissed her. "For the rest of our lives."

EPILOGUE
THREE YEARS LATER

Rhapsody

"Harmony Jane! Get away from that cake," I shouted to my rambunctious daughter.

"Mama!" she cried out then cocked out her hip in a sassy pose.

I knew exactly where Queen B went and that was into my daughter. When I woke from the shortest coma in history, I realized my crazy internal Queen B was gone. However, when I saw Harmony cock her hip out in a sassy pose for the first time I knew exactly where she'd gone.

"It's okay, Rhapsody," Chord said, kissing me on the cheek.

"She doesn't need to be in the cake before it's cut."

He cleared his throat. "Uhm…I don't think they are going to be cutting the cake any time soon."

"What do you mean?"

"Well, I heard some action going on in one of the family bathrooms. It doesn't surprise me that it's—"

"What are you two talking about?" Emmerson Lee and Jimmy Ray were standing entwined together.

"Wait…aren't you in the bathroom?"

"Uhm no. We are about to cut the cake. We wanted our little munchkin to help us." Emmerson knelt down to pick up the squealing Harmony.

Chord and I watched as our parents walked over to the cake table. The DJ announced them, and the crowd of famous people gathered around the table to see two of the most famous rock stars in history smash cake in each other's faces.

Since Harmony was born our lives had become more and more interesting. Grams decided to sell her house to downsize to an over fifty community. From what I'd seen she was quite the belle of the ball there. She even brought two beaus to her daughter's wedding.

Cassie decided to go solo or freelance or whatever she was calling it on a day ending with y. Her life has seemed to become a bit tumultuous. Something had been going on with her, but she refused to tell me or Grams.

Emmerson and Jimmy finally tied the knot. Though who knew how long it would last. One day they were on and the next they were off. I really thought they were using it as sexcuses, excuses to have crazy make-up sex. There were too many times that Chord or I walked in on them bumping uglies in places they didn't belong, like our kitchen. We revoked their key privileges after that incident.

Miranda and Alice still lived in Chord's Gramps' home at no cost. Gramps moved into the same community as Grams. And his continuous staring at her was an indication he wanted to be in line to be one of her many suitors.

Alec was busy. Well, we guessed he was. He didn't really come around anymore. Chord tried to organize some guys' day out with his old roomies but Alec bailed every time. I kept telling Chord he had a girl. Chord would shake his head then explain to me that Alec wasn't a one woman man. When I looked around at my life, I see how people can change.

Chord and I ran off to Vegas when Harmony was three

months old. It was a surprise to everyone including us. When we wandered into a chapel that offered getting married by an Ozzy Osborne look-alike we knew we had to do it. Chord surprised me with a gorgeous pear-shaped diamond ring he'd been carrying around for months. He admitted that he'd been too chicken shit to propose because he thought I'd say no. He really is an idiot sometimes.

As for me, my job was going great. I'd really grown into my position and worked very closely with Mr. Anderson. He was hinting around about promoting me to a VP, but I wasn't holding my breath. The best news I'd gotten was when I found out Daniel and Izzie were going to have baby number two. Little Isaiah was born less than a year after Harmony. I guess there was a ring of truth with pregnancy being contagious. He was the sweetest little guy. Definitely took after his mother.

Harmony's birth may have been unplanned but the happiness she brought into our lives made every pain worth it. Her presence made our Romeo and Juliet tale end with a happily ever after. Who would have thought?

"Rhapsody!" Chord yanked me out of my reverie.

"What? I was busy remembering good things."

He grabbed me by the hand and dragged me toward a closet. It sounded like there was a wild boar in it. Not to mention it was destroying everything on the shelves.

"Is that..." I began.

"Yep. It's the couple I thought were Emmerson and Jimmy. Looks like they are onto round two and quite adventurous."

I raised an eyebrow. "Don't get any ideas, Chord."

He held up his hands in surrender. "I'm not. I mean I wouldn't be against any kind of closet sex or hot tub sex or kitchen counter sex."

"Are we gonna have this conversation right now?" I sighed.

"No. No. No. I'm just saying I'm open to things."

"What are you two doing?" Grams asked with her arms linked with two very dapper men.

"Oh boy do you hear that?" Dapper man number one asked.

"What the hell is going on? It's my damn reception and there is a crowd around a damn janitor's closet." Emmerson Lee stood with her hands on her hips just as a crashing sound came from the closet.

"Oh I know what's going on. We'll have to use that later tonight." Jimmy Ray kissed Emmerson's neck.

"Gross," Chord mumbled.

"Who's in there?" Grams asked.

"No clue but—" I began just as the closet door slowly opened.

Cassie was busy pulling down her dress when she looked up to see the crowd. She froze like a deer caught in headlights. I grinned at her, but she couldn't even meet my eyes. Before I could tease her, a familiar voice came from behind her.

"Damn. I think we really fucked up that—" Alec said, shoving his shirt into his pants.

"Fuck me." Chord's mouth hung open.

In the most perfect of timing, Harmony walked past us and up to Cassie and Alec. "Aunt Cassie is funny. She makes animal noises with Uncle Alec." Harmony grinned then walked back toward Miranda.

Cassie looked around at everyone. Alec puffed out his chest and wound an arm around her. Cassie's embarrassment was too much to take. She pushed Alec back into the closet, shut the door, then ran out of the hotel.

"Well, let's just hope he used protection so we don't have another Rhapsody and Chord thing happening," Emmerson said to Jimmy. The two laughed as they walked back into the wedding reception.

It looked like the smooth life we were living was going to get exciting again.

SNEAK PEEK

If you enjoyed Chord and Rhapsody's story, I'd love you forever if you dropped a review. In the meantime, have you met Teagan and Grayson from *A Work in Progress*?

Here's a sneak peek of *A Work in Progress*

DAWN OF A NEW ME

I never dreamed that I'd be looking down the barrel of 40 years old and still be a virgin. You may be asking yourself how in the world does something like that happen. Was I kept in a dungeon most of my life? Did I live in a nunnery? Was I brought up in such a strict household that I wasn't allowed to be around boys? That would be a no for all of those. I've had boyfriends and dates but never pulled the trigger. Somehow, I've managed to meet every shitty guy out there. None of which I'd wanted to give my flower to. Though it's more like a wilting bud rather than a flower.

The flames that came off my birthday cake illuminated the singing faces of my best friends Olivia, Ember and Nomi. I am the first in our group to be only one year away from forty. As their off-key singing ended, I knew exactly what my wish would be. Blowing with all my might, I snuffed out each candle only for them to relight. The bitches that were my friends laughed like lunatics.

"Gotcha!" They yelled together.

They thought they were so funny. I pasted on a fake smile, but inside I was stabbing them with the cake knife.

"Uh Oh…Teagan has her fake smile on again," Nomi said, pulling the knife toward them.

"Chill out, Teag," Ember said next to me.

"You guys just think you're so funny. Well, you three aren't much further away from becoming crazy cat ladies than I am," I huffed.

Olivia rolled her eyes. "Oh puhlease. Here comes Tegan's pity party."

I narrowed my gaze at my supposed best friend then straightened. It was time I told them my plan for the final year of my thirties. "I've decided something."

"Here we go. What are your plans now?" Ember asked, cutting the cake and handing out slices.

"This year will be the year of Teagan. I will leave my thirties accomplishing the things I have been putting off. I will finally finish my novel. I will get in shape. I will adopt an animal that is not a cat." I stood with my shoulders back in an overly dramatic pose.

"And lose your virginity?" Olivia mumbled past the cake she'd shoveled in her mouth.

"I guess that can go on the list." I shriveled a bit with that.

"That is a must for that list. I refuse to let my best friend die a virgin," Nomi declared.

"I think you're being a bit dramatic there, Nomi. I'm not ancient and I'm not dying."

"You never know. You could walk outside to work and bang!" She pounded the table. "You're pushed into traffic by a bicyclist but manage to dodge an oncoming bus only to trip over your feet and knock yourself unconscious on a curb rolling into a puddle and drown while people watch."

"What the hell, Nomi?" I exclaimed.

"Seems feasible for you," Ember said with Olivia nodding.

I needed to find new friends.

"Anyway, this year will be a new Teagan. I refuse to let the next year pass as every other year has passed."

Ember, Olivia and Nomi stared at me. Ember lifted her glass of wine and said, "We are with you, Teag. We pledge to make sure you don't become a virgin crazy cat lady without a published book."

"I second that!" Olivia said, raising her glass.

"I third that!" Nomi raised her glass.

I rolled my eyes but smiled at the best friends a girl could have. Well, really, I could probably find better, but they've been around a while, and it's a lot of work meeting new people when you hate people. So, I raised my glass with theirs.

"Here's to taking thirty-nine by storm," I said, clinking my glass with theirs.

Teagan's ~~Get Laid~~ Bucket List
1. *Lose virginity/have mind blowing sex*
2. *Ride in a hot air balloon*
3. *Ride a mechanical bull*
4. *Go on a yacht*
5. *Go to a casino*
6. *Get a pet (not a fish, lizard or bird. Must be furry and cuddly)*
7. *Sing karaoke*
8. *Hike to a beautiful waterfall*
9. *Make-out under the stars*
10. *Do something selfless*
11. *Do an escape room*
12. *Teach a class*
13. *Run a ~~marathon~~ mile*
14. *Have cake for breakfast*
15. *Get lost on purpose*

Have sex! Have sex! Have sex! (added on an unknown date by Ember, Olivia and Nomi)

1. WINE AND DATING APPS DON'T MIX

"The glowworms of the Waitomo caves in New Zealand are some of the most beautiful creatures on planet Earth. When you look closely at them, they seem to be innocuous beings. However, they are skilled hunters. Their intricate webs trap spiders, flies and other arachnids," the British narrator explained.

I took a bite of the mint chip ice cream in my bowl as the camera panned close to the insect hanging from the cave ceiling.

"The beautiful bioluminescence is produced as a result a luciferase enzyme acting upon a small molecule of luciferin. It is used to lure in prey to the silken webs they produce. The bioluminescence isn't just found in the body of the worm." The camera panned out showing the glow worms and a pool of glowing goop below. "The large number of worms excrete the same milky substance that allows them to glow."

I looked down at my green ice cream and decided to put it aside. A banging on my front door made me pause the documentary. Whatever it was better be good. I was not in the mood for anyone to be disturbing my "Our Planet" documentary.

Opening the door, I sighed. Ember stood with her hip cocked. With the look on her face, she clearly had a plan. It was a look I'd seen many times during our college years. Every time we needed to sneak into frat parties, Ember accepted the mission, came up with a plan and smirked as the scheme went off without a hitch. She practically had her own theme song on those adventures.

"What's up, slut?" she pushed past me.

"Slut?" I shut the door behind her.

"Well, I assume you've gotten that cherry popped already because you are home on a Saturday night." She moved over to my kitchen table where she plopped a bag.

"That doesn't make sense." I watched as she unpacked the paper bag.

"It makes complete sense. Don't you remember your birthday? I mean you were pretty trashed, but I was pretty sure you were with it when we made the decision to finally get that done this year." She took a bottle of wine with her to my kitchen to retrieve my wine opener.

I ran my hand through my hair. "I remember." Of course, I remembered. I had the damn list hanging on my refrigerator taunting me every day.

"So, what have you crossed off?"

I bit my lip and turned back toward the TV.

"You haven't done a damn thing, Teagan." Ember held the list from the fridge in front of my face.

"I know." I shrugged.

"Are you even serious about this?" She asked while pouring wine into the glasses she'd also grabbed.

I watched as she poured the wine to the very top of each glass. Well, there went my evening. We were getting trashed tonight whether I wanted to or not.

"I'm serious. I just feel at a loss at how to start." Taking my wine over to the couch, I sat without spilling any. There was my miracle for the day

"I thought you'd say that. So, I came up with a plan." She whipped out her phone and began frantically scrolling as she balanced the over-filled wine glass with her other hand.

I was mesmerized watching her quickly scroll through each screen. Taking a sip of the delicious wine, I settled into the couch. Ember and I had been friends since our freshman year in high school when she moved to my school. She seemed shy, and I thought I'd make friends with her. What I didn't realize was that she was anything but shy. She was trying shy out on her new school. It didn't even last until lunch that day when she kneed a guy in his nuts for grabbing her ass in the lunch line. I knew we had to be friends after that.

Out of my three closest friends, Ember was hands down the most brash and daring. When she planned something, it always happened. Nothing got in her way. What made her really dangerous was her combination of over organization and boldness. It's what made her good at her job as a professional organizer. She had no qualms telling you how stupid your organization was before making it ten times better, all the while calling you an asshole. She was the demon spawn of Marie Kondo and Gordon Ramsey if they did a ritual with lots of blood and semen.

After a while, I got bored waiting for her to go through the meticulous files on her phone. So, I turned back toward the TV and the glow worms. They really were pretty cool with a dash of gross thanks to their poop.

"Ah Ha!" Ember raised her hand with the wine glass up, effectively spilling some on my couch.

"Should I be saying 'Eureka?'"

"Shut up, smart ass. I've got it all planned right here." She flashed her phone toward me. A dating app glowed on the screen.

"A dating app?"

"Got a better idea? Because I don't exactly see men beating

down your door or lining up in your living room to fuck you right now."

"Harsh, Ember."

She waved her hands. "I'm sorry. You know I don't mean it that way."

She was right. I knew she didn't mean for it to hurt my feelings. It didn't mean that it didn't.

"Alright. So, what is this plan?" I pressed pause on the documentary.

"First, we are putting you on this dating app. I figure the hardest part is finding the right man. If we can at least start getting you out there, then we will overcome one hurdle. The rest of it will come with those dates." She wiggled her eyebrows. She was clearly obsessed with me losing my virginity.

"Fine. Let me get some liquid courage first."

With an exaggerated sigh, I tipped the wine glass back and chugged. The wine was gone in less than a minute. It was a talent I hadn't used since our frat party days. My vision was a little fuzzy, but I saw Ember sitting there with an astonished look on her face.

"Shit. That's a lot of liquid courage. Maybe I should make slutty lush your headline."

"I don't need any barflies contacting me. We need to make this classy. Only top of the line guys." I formed words, surprisingly. My mouth felt very numb.

"No wonder you're still a virgin." Ember mumbled.

"Hey!" I said, but it came out more like a grunt.

Ember ignored me while she typed frantically on her phone. I got up feeling wobbly but quickly steadied myself then went to the kitchen to refill my wine glass. Disappointment washed over me when I couldn't find the wine bottle. *Where the hell was the wine?* It felt like I was looking for that stupid guy in the striped shirt except in wine bottle form. It wasn't in my umbrella stand by the door. It wasn't in my dishwasher. It wasn't even in my oven.

"What the hell are you doing out there?" Ember shouted at me from the couch.

"I'm trying to find the wine. Where the hell did you put it? I've looked everywhere."

"It's on the coffee table." Exasperation filled her words.

"Huh. When did you put it there? Why would you put it there?" I asked after grabbing a bag of chips.

"Just sit your ass back down on the couch." She took my glass and refilled it with a lot more wine.

"Mmm...yummy, yummy, wine. You make me feel so fine," I sang to the tune of Red, Red Wine.

Ember sighed and looked up at the TV. She furrowed her brow then asked, "What the hell is that?"

I finished half the wine in my glass again and smiled at her. "Shit."

"What?"

"It's glow worm shit. They poop that really cool stuff." I stared at the wine in my glass and continued, "I wish I had glowing poop. I bet I would get laid then."

"Oh, sweet Jesus," she grumbled.

An idea hit me. "Put in the ad that I have glowing poop. That would definitely be a cool ice breaker."

Ember sighed again. "Do you have glow-in-the-dark poop, Teagan?"

I put a finger to my lips trying to shush her, but I just succeeded in spitting on her. "They don't know that."

Ignoring Ember's muttered curses, I held my wine glass in both hands and sat cross-legged. At some point, I'd unpaused the documentary and was watching a sloth poop. It appeared this documentary loved showing animals pooping. With a shrug, I continued to listen to the sexy British accent give a play-by-play of the sloth's poop dance.

Mmm, British hottie.

"Make sure you put British men only in the ad," I said without taking my eyes off the mesmerizing poop dance.

"Sure, Teagan. Just watch your documentary while I organize your life."

"Ok," I said. Or I think I said it.

Words were hard. Oh well, I felt so good it didn't matter if my words were coherent anymore. Huh, my wine glass was empty again. Someone needed to stop drinking it. That person was a real asshole. I just needed to keep my now-refilled glass closer to me. I hugged it to my chest, effectively spilling red wine on my favorite white pajama top.

Putting the glass down, I proceeded to suck the wine from my shirt.

"God give me strength." Ember said to the ceiling.

I giggled then went back to sucking on my shirt, making a loud slurping sound.

"Hmm, good at sucking is definitely going in there." Ember said under her breath.

FOLLOW JACKIE

If you want to keep up with what is happening in my world be sure to subscribe to my newsletter at www.jackiepaxsonauthor.com.

Follow me on Facebook, Instagram, and TikTok @jackiepaxsonauthor

www.ingramcontent.com/pod-product-compliance
Lightning Source LLC
Chambersburg PA
CBHW021941120726
47992CB00001B/84